Among The Dead Part One:

Shadow of Death

Ryan Colley

***

Edited by Monique Happy Editorial Services

www.moniquehappy.com

Cover art by www.fiverr.com/oliviaprodesign

To Fiona,

I hope the nightmares stay on the page!

24.05.24

DEDICATION

This is for my mum (Michaela) who is awesome and my first reader, my sister (Blaize) who is just as obsessed with the apocalypse as me, and for my partner (Charlotte) who stuck with me through the good times and bad.

ACKNOWLEDGEMENTS

There are too many people to thank for this book, and I wish I kept better track of everyone who helped me, but here goes:

Thank you to Monique Happy, who edited my book

and accepted my British way of writing things.

Thank you to the numerous authors who offered me advice when I asked:

Shawn Chesser, Joshua Dalzelle, R.R. Haywood, Craig Martelle, John O'Brien, Frank Tayell, Mark Tufo, and Thomas Watson. All of your help was phenomenal.

Thank you to all the people who made this book possible through constructive criticism, proofreading, taking time out of their day to help me, or just listen to my nonsense.

Finally, a thank you to you, the reader.

PROLOGUE

I remember learning about something called the Cotard Delusion. The common and more exciting name for it is Walking Corpse Syndrome. Simply, it's when people believe they are dead. They believe they have died and are living in the afterlife. There was a well-known case of a man who suffered from the Cotard Delusion, and everything that happened to him just contributed as evidence to reinforce his delusion. He travelled to South Africa and believed the heat of the country was due to the fact he was in hell. Evidence surrounding the Cotard Delusion has always been a little indistinct. No one has ever been sure what to make of it. Even I thought the delusion was a ridiculous concept. With everything that happened in my life, I don't feel that way anymore.

I saw terrible and horrific acts. I committed even worse. I changed. My thoughts. My feelings. My ideology. My attitude towards life. Something that changed is my belief about the

Cotard Delusion. With everything that has happened, I feel that there is irrefutable proof that it genuinely exists. I constantly think back to that day on the coach, and how everything went from good to bad to worse. However, I realised something that causes everything else to make sense. I think on that day, so long ago, I died on that coach. It wasn't what I expected. There was no everlasting peace. I didn't see the faces of my loved ones. My life didn't flash before my eyes. It all just ... carried on. Everything that happened since is the afterlife and I'm in hell. That is clear to me. It had to be. If it wasn't true, then how would I be able to carry on living with everything I'd done?

****

The early days of the infection were *unique* to put it simply. Not because people were killing each other. As a species, we had done that ever since the first caveman bludgeoned their neighbour to death with a rock. I wouldn't even say it was unique because people were eating each other. That happened before *everything* started as well. What made it unique was that it was the fastest noticeable social change since public fear of a global terrorist attack. The news wasn't just full of reports on people attacking other people, but it was all about the level of brutality and animalistic nature of the attacks. That is what made it different. Teeth were used to rend flesh. Fingers were used as claws to maim and kill. That was before any mention of an infection, or "Daisy" as the news referred to it. I watched news reports of people trying to tear out eyes, and of family members attacking their own kin.

Dying patients attacked doctors. Doctors attacked patients in the same hospital. Yet, they weren't planned attacks or some sort of protest. Attacks were feral and bloody. Attacks happened in the night. Attacks happened in the day. In the street. In the home. In *your* home. People just weren't safe. The rich, poor, and homeless were victims. It didn't matter if you were the working class, the upper class, or anywhere in between. You just stopped going out at night. You stopped going out at all if you could help it. It was no longer classed as a domestic problem contained to homes, it was a public concern. It was insanity.

The police and government tried to find some link between the early attacks. The rumour mill believed it was a new drug that made people act crazy. The only problem with that theory was that it assumed an elderly couple in Manchester took the same drug as a homeless man in London, as well as a few school children in Liverpool. Another rumour said the cause was some sort of mental illness that caused people to act on their most primal instincts, to attack and feed. There was no logic. Research teams were just grasping at straws to find a reason behind the new epidemic.

It wasn't long before city councils called quarantine. There was a mass exodus out of cities as people returned to their respective homes and homelands. Trying to quarantine a whole city was next to impossible. Besides, it's human nature to resist authority. Well, my human nature at least. Then the military began moving. One day you could go out and there would be nothing, the next day there were military personnel everywhere. There were checkpoints set up throughout the city. The military were posted at hospitals, bus stations, the mall, and any other major institutes. The military ran everything the day they decided to turn up. I remember going into a local supermarket and I saw armed military standing around telling jokes while they handled their weapons – like it was the most casual and everyday thing in the world. Yet, we accepted it without any explanation from the government. It just happened and the citizens of Great Britain had to deal with it, and we were happy too for the most part. Conspiracy theorists went into overdrive. I imagined some of them needed a change of underwear just from the thoughts going through their heads as they connected photos on a wall with pieces of string. Some theorised that the government was rooting out the Russian sleeper agents living amongst us. Then again, those same theorists were also the sort of people you would see on a Saturday night yelling at meat in a supermarket. Most people didn't believe the theories, but they knew something was happening. I knew exactly what was happening, and I had mentally prepared my whole life for it.

Over the first few weeks of the occupation, I made my presence known to a few of the military folk, especially the ones at the local bus station. I spoke to them daily and got to know them all personally. The plan was for me to become a friendly face and, eventually, they got to know me by name too. That was the first part of my master plan.

I wanted to drag my plan out over a much longer time period than I eventually did, but something happened that meant I had to move things to a closer date. During the quarantine of the cities, I had lost contact with the love of my life, Alice, who lived a full two hundred miles away in Essex. She was the reason my secret plan had been created in the first place. The goal was to go to Essex and bring her back to Bristol, my home city, so we could live out the infection together. That was until she stopped replying to my messages. Alice and I had met at a university in Bristol. However, she was originally from Essex and, as a result, had to travel between Bristol and Essex to visit her family. Alice was back in Essex when the quarantine had kicked in, so she became stuck there. I kept track of what was happening in Essex and found that the military presence had been much more advanced compared to what I witnessed in Bristol. They were taking all sorts of initiatives to prepare Essex for the eventual apocalypse, even if they didn't know the chain of events would be of apocalyptic proportions. The preparation in Essex made sense, however, considering how close Essex is to London. Especially since the troubles started in London, or so the reports made it seem. It made sense for the nearest cities to be on alert and fully prepared for whatever headed their way. The world slowly became a horror film, and Alice never liked horror films, so that doubled my resolve to save her from a potential living nightmare. Then again, not watching horror films was probably what would keep her calm; she wouldn't even begin to think of all the horrors that existed out in the world.

I would ring Alice every day, repeatedly, until she picked up. Just to ensure that she was safe and well. That happened for a few months, and then two things happened simultaneously. The first thing was that the events in London escalated on a grand scale. What started off as a containment effort of a few *afflicted* individuals evolved into full-scale street wars. The news reports began to show the military gunning down individuals who were running at them. Bullets pounded into those individuals but they just kept going. If you looked at the footage closely, you could see it was only headshots that brought down the attackers for good. There was escalating warfare erupting on the streets of London and all that the rest of the world could do was watch. Hell, even we, the citizens of Great Britain, could only sit and watch.

Eventually, the government intervened and stopped the violent footage being played on television networks. The news stations were then given public-friendly propaganda videos that spewed the message of hope. The situation in London *was* being contained and everything *was* under control; so *we* didn't need to worry. I stopped watching when they pulled out the classic image of Winston Churchill doing the "V" for victory. That is where online resources became useful. Venturing onto the Dark Net provided completely unfiltered and uncensored access to video files for a time. That spilt over onto the internet and people began to study them to see what extra information they could garner from the footage. Imagine a group, over a million strong, studying the same videos and all the various conclusions they came to. Let's just say, the collective people of the internet got a hell of a lot more right than the fine members of Parliament.

The second thing to happen was the mass evacuation of London. When events took a turn for the worse, the military began evacuating people by the coachload at random. Coincidently, the "random" coachloads were the wealthy. It was good to see that even when the end was near, money still had a hold on people. Next, the coachloads of people were taken to evacuee camps all over England; one of which was in Bristol. On days that the coaches arrived, I would go to the bus station and watch. It was oddly satisfying to see hundreds of the upper class in their Armani suits sharing makeshift housing with one portable toilet between all of them. I felt an odd sense of justice.

I continued preparing for what was to come, and the online world played a major part in it. In a week I had learned how to field strip and reassemble some of the basic military guns as well as their proper maintenance; visually anyway. I used tutorials to learn how to drive; in theory. I learned how to hotwire a vehicle, change a tyre, and when your vehicle was beyond saving. I also spent every spare moment I had honing my body to perfection. I lost my excess weight that had accumulated from a lazy student lifestyle and soon had a reasonably toned body, something most people would kill to have. I learned first aid basics and read as many books on survival as I could. I needed to know everything, just in case I found myself in any dire situation. I even learned how to open a can of food without a can opener or knife, which I thought was fairly impressive. All of those skills, while seemingly useless, could very well save my life.

My family consisted of my mother and sister, Tracey and Kelsey, respectively. My mother was a kind, caring, and overweight lady who desperately tried to lose said weight; she was pretty good at it too. My sister was a cow. Not a literal cow but a figurative one; she was so annoying. I suppose that is what siblings do though. She was the sort of girl who cared more about her looks than most other things. She would refuse to take out the rubbish without makeup on just in case someone saw her. They both had their quirks and their ways to annoy me, but they were family and I would miss them. My father, although dead to me, was still alive and not a *nice* man. For years I wished the status of the former would change.

I was kind of a misfit in terms of appearance when compared to the rest of my family. I was taller than all of them, which wasn't hard when you're six foot two. I had dirty blond hair which, if left to grow too long, ended up looking like Lego hair; kind of one texture and just placed on top of my head. It wasn't a good look. When asked how I would describe myself, personality wise, I often went back to a quote a college teacher had used to describe what I was like. It was after class and two teachers and I were sat around chatting.

The teacher, who had never had me as a student, asked my regular teacher, "So what is Sam like as a student?"

My teacher looked between me and his colleague before answering, "It's like having a genius sat in the class, albeit an evil genius."

He was joking of course. Sure I was intelligent, but no more than most. Still, that description had always stuck with me and I used it. Mainly because it was funny and I felt as though I was a funny guy. I never said I was a humble person …

CHAPTER 1

"Alice, I don't know how many times I've called you. I know you're probably busy, but it is crucial you get back to me as soon as you can. I'll chat to you later. I love you," I said as I left yet another voicemail.

The situation in London had already been bad, but it had gone from bad to hellhole. There were rumours that the infection spread beyond London, although the media heavily censored any news which would contribute to the nation's decreasing morale. Regarding the infection, it was determined by the government that anyone who got bit or scratched by an infected individual would later die and then reanimate as infected themselves. Although the government never used the words "die" or "reanimate," everyone knew what they actually meant. Most people in the Western world had watched a zombie movie and, even if they didn't want to admit it, knew what was really happening. About the time the infection had spread out of London, if you believed the rumours, Alice had missed three days' worth of calls. A system I had set up to keep track of her wellbeing. With no contact and the infection spreading, I naturally expected the worst. I hadn't expressed my concerns to my family. I knew they would just give me false hope with empty words. They would just tell me to leave her be. They needed me to keep a level head because, in all our

11

hypothetical scenarios concerning the end of the world, I did most of the planning. I was a key player in the survival of my family should the infection spread to Bristol, which is why what I did was so selfish and disloyal. The Judas act I committed? I left Bristol.

****

Over the few days after I had lost contact with Alice, I wrote out every scenario for survival I could think of. By the time I had finished, I had a printed document ready to give to my family. It was every thought I had ever had about an infection like the one which spread through England: a zombie outbreak. It was around one hundred and thirty pages, double-sided, with diagrams; I had even bound it with a spiral spine and laminated covers. If I was going to do something, I wanted to do it right, and with some awesome presentation. I hadn't even put that much care into my university work! I had packed a bag of basic survival tools in case I came across harsh conditions. I even purchased a combat knife and wristwatch from the nearest military surplus store; a pricey item which I hoped I wouldn't need. I also managed to find a pair of military-grade boots in the same store. They took ages to wear in properly but once they had, it was like wrapping my feet in clouds they were so comfortable. I packed a sleeping bag, a torch with batteries, and a few other bits and pieces. My next move was to leave in the middle of the day. It would seem less suspicious than if I left in the middle of the night. It was also a lot less cliché. With my heart full of self-anger for what I was about to do, and an edge of excitement at the prospect of something different, I told my family I was "going out for a walk." They said "bye" and "see you soon," not expecting me to leave for good. They barely gave me a glance as I began to leave. I hesitated at the boundary between the inside of my home and the outside of the world. I stared at my family. It was how I would remember them: my mum in the kitchen preparing food, and my sister with her horrible noise she called music upstairs. I took a deep breath and swallowed the lump in my throat. I left them the survival document, jokingly named "The Tao of Sam" by the telephone so they would see it next time it rang. I also left a letter which explained my intentions, even if it felt like an excuse for my betrayal. I scooped up my bag of supplies and left. Had I not trained my body over the months, the large rucksack would have seemed heavy, but now it felt more of a minor inconvenience than a burden. I walked quickly, drawing as little attention to myself as possible. I avoided neighbours and friends when I saw them and continued onwards to the bus station. Not that they would have suspected anything anyway. I wore jeans, my military boots, a t-shirt and a hooded jumper. Just comfy clothes which I could move in. I momentarily doubted my choice of underwear and considered going back to change, but I knew that was just procrastination to delay the inevitable. If I went back, I knew I would never leave again.

I began to feel sick, and I almost vomited once and nearly turned back twice. But, perhaps unluckily for me, my resolve was steady. I approached the military guard post at the bus station.

"Hey Sam, haven't seen you in a few days!" one of the guards said, a husky man named David. He was one of the men I had spoken to most and seemed the friendliest. I could have almost considered him a friend if I hadn't been using him to achieve my plan. He was slightly shorter than me, with shaved brown hair. He normally wore glasses but used contact lenses when he could get away with it.

"Hey man," I replied. I opened my mouth to say more but closed it nervously. He stared at me, confused by my nervous disposition, and that's when he spotted my bag.

"Going on holiday, lad?" He laughed. I laughed too. Nervousness and not mirth was the cause.

"Not exactly," I replied uneasily. I looked him in the eye before continuing, "I need a favour, one bigger than you have probably ever done for anyone."

David took a partial and uncertain step back, but the military in him came to the forefront and he straightened up.

"What is it?" he asked cautiously. His thoughts didn't even come close to what I would ask.

"I need you to let me on one of the coaches back into London," I replied quickly and in one breath. Even though the streets of London were a constant warzone, people were still being evacuated little by little. The bus stations were major hubs of activity as people tried to leave. The plan was simple: catch a ride into London, and then get one of the evacuation coaches to Essex – a near perfect plan.

"You know I can't do that, lad," he replied sternly, his role of guard overruling his friendship with a stranger.

"Why not?" I protested. I had prepared my argument word for word, knowing it was my only chance to get through, "At this point, they're only taking people out of London because of how bad it is. The only reason they're not letting people back in is because no one is that kind of stupid. Unfortunately, I am that kind of stupid."

"Why, lad?" he said softly, "Nothing is worth going there for."

I shrugged and asked, "So, is that a yes?"

David cursed, a little at me, and a little at the situation. He then looked me straight in the eyes and said what I had been hoping to hear, "Okay, but dammit … you realise I'm signing your death warrant?"

"No, you're not," I replied, smiling. "You're just letting some idiot do what he needs to do."

David smiled at this and led me through the guard post constructed of chain-link fencing. He waved someone over to carry on at his post while he showed me the way.

"Won't they say anything?" I asked when I saw a soldier staring at me.

"They will, later, but at the moment they don't care enough either way. There are bigger things going on than some kid wandering through," David replied matter-of-factly, like he knew a lot more than he was letting on. He cast a glance at his watch and sped up his pace. "The next coach leaves in five, so we have to be quick about it."

"Thanks for this, man," I replied. "You don't realise how much you've helped me."

"Hey lad, if you want to chase after a woman, who am I to stop you?" David said with a smile.

I turned to him and asked, "What makes you think this is about a woman?"

"Everything stupid done by any man has been done because of a woman. Fact," David laughed, although he was completely serious in his sexist belief.

"Fair enough, nice guess," I shrugged, and added with a grin, "you're right."

A few minutes passed before David replied. He looked at me sadly. He was so sure I would die.

"You do realise that whoever she is, she isn't worth it?"

he asked quietly.

I smiled at him before saying in a barely audible whisper, "Alice is."

We walked the rest of the way in silence. What was once a familiar bus station for me was no longer recognisable. It was a makeshift military outpost. Where sleepy travellers normally would wait for buses which rarely turned up on time, there were now armed men walking around; some with purpose but most were bored. As we got closer to the coach, nervousness choked me. I was leaving everything and everyone I ever knew behind for, what most would consider, a journey of a madman. If I was a superstitious man, I would have thought that the tightness was the hangman's noose around my throat getting tighter with each step, but that was a ridiculous thought. I swallowed away the lump, the thoughts of seeing Alice melting it slightly.

We approached the coach. The driver sat tensely at the wheel, waiting for his time to leave. He had learned that when the military wanted him to leave at a certain time, they meant that second and not a minute or so later. I certainly hoped they were paying him more than just overtime. David knocked on the doors, and the driver opened them immediately.

"Here's a passenger, no questions," David said sternly to the man, displaying an authority I hadn't seen from him before. I stepped onto the coach and turned to David.

"Goodbye man, you've been a good friend," I said and smiled. He looked at me sadly, and then looked around him to make sure no one watched as he did the unexpected. He withdrew his handgun. I recognised it as a Browning 9mm. I had many years of video games and a great memory to thank for that knowledge. It was the standard issue of the British military, although there was talk of changing it at some point. Would they ever get around to changing it with the current state of the world?

"It's dangerous, especially when going alone, so take this," David said and handed me the gun. I stared at it dumbly. The black metal tool was heavy and cold in my clammy hands. David continued, "It has thirteen shots. Make sure they count."

I nodded, temporarily unable to speak. He then searched his pocket and withdrew a single round. He put it in my pocket before adding, "And that one is for you, in case *you* need it."

"Thank you," I whispered quietly to him. The gun weighed as heavily in my hands as it did in my mind. Although I would need every bullet he had given me, I knew the significance of that last round; a thought which I couldn't bear to think about.

"Be safe and get going," David replied, placing a hand on my shoulder. He then nodded at the driver: the symbol to leave. The driver nodded in return and started up the coach. I continued to stare at David as we pulled away, and he did the same in return. When he was out of sight, I sighed heavily and slumped into a seat about midway up the coach. I felt mentally drained and my adventure had only just begun. I so badly wanted to sleep, but adrenaline pulsed through my blood, almost in anticipation for what was to come. I closed my eyes, thoughts of my family I had so eagerly left behind dancing through my head. *I needed this; I needed to get away and do what I was doing.* A few tears rolled down my face but I wiped them away quickly, almost so I wouldn't catch myself crying. I looked around the empty coach, just the driver and me, and I drifted off slowly to sleep. The simple exertions of the day had caught up with me.

CHAPTER 2

I hadn't been asleep long. I could tell by both the lack of change in scenery outside and the wristwatch I wore. I had woken with a sense of unease, like when you walk into a dark room and can sense someone is hiding in the dark waiting to scare you. I opened my eyes and looked around, momentarily forgetting I was on a coach and why I was there to begin with, but those memories came back to me in a flash. I sat up straight and stretched. I looked around and found the source of my unease. The driver of the coach stared at me in his mirror. Not a casual look, but a full-on stare. My eyes met his in the mirror and yet he still didn't look away.

"Was I out for long?" I asked him, knowing the answer but desperate to get his gaze off of me.

"Not at all, about twelve minutes," he replied. It was creepy enough to know he was watching me sleep, but even creepier that he knew to a precise degree how long for. A wave of goosebumps washed up my arms and raised the hair on my neck.

"Ah," I exclaimed, unsure of how I should act. Was he okay with the fact I had caught him staring? Or did he simply not care either way? A second shiver ran through me, but I shook it off. I tried a different approach and asked him a question.

"Made this journey often then?"

"Oh, about seven times. Fourteen if we're counting there and back," the driver answered, "Seen all manner of things."

"Like?" I asked, curiosity piqued.

"Seen a man almost beat another to death right at the back there," he replied matter-of-factly and gestured to the rear of the coach from over his shoulder.

"Do you know why?" I asked in surprise.

"Rival bankers, both very high up, or some nonsense. Been in competition for years. One made a remark about a stain on the other's suit and he flipped out and started pounding him. Took the escort aiming a gun at him to stop him," the driver answered. I couldn't tell if he was serious as he delivered the story so nonchalantly. I didn't entirely want to know either way. People doing what people did wasn't exactly new. I would watch the news if I wanted to hear anything like that. Instead, I focused on another aspect of his story.

"What did you mean, 'escort'?" I questioned. His eyes were back on the road, and I began to suspect he was just weird as opposed to menacing. I imagined his journeys got lonely, and the sense of unease began to disperse.

"Well, in the early days of the evacuation, each coach had a soldier onboard. More so to keep peace and watch for the infection," the driver replied, while he drove us along the empty roads. "As time went on and the infection got worse, they stopped putting one on the coach. Probably because they would rather the forces were somewhere else, I suppose. They also became much more selective as to who they let on to begin with. Got a sniffle or some blood on you? Access denied."

"Did you ever see any of the *infected*?" I asked, surprised at his openness to discuss it. Most people tried to avoid the subject.

"One or two I thinks," he answered thoughtfully, casting a glance at me in the rear-view mirror. "On my way out of London, seen some army shooting at people. Think they were infected."

There were a few moments of thoughtful silence. I broke it with a very straightforward, yet widely debated question: "What do you think is really going on?"

The driver let out a bark of laughter before he replied. "Seriously? They're zombies! Short and simple," he said with a smirk. I smiled. At least someone in all the madness agreed with me and used the "zed" word. I relaxed back down into my seat, the gun still on the seat next to me. It was strange to have a gun within touching distance, let alone having the expectation of using it. That was one thing video games hadn't prepared me for.

We drove in silence for the next hour, neither of us wanted to talk but both deep in thought. We didn't pass a single car along the way, nor a single person, living or *infected.* Eventually the coach began to slow, pulling me out of my contemplative state. Surely we weren't there already? I walked to the front of the coach to see why we were rolling to a stop. London was nowhere in sight, but in the middle of the lanes was a car. It had flipped over, and glass was smashed all across the road. A barrier between both sides of the road was heavily damaged, obviously from where the car had hit it. The most disturbing part was the blood. There was blood smeared across the car and glass; it looked like someone had crawled out of the window. However, the trail didn't stop there. There was a trail all the way across the road, which disappeared down into the grassy embankment.

"What're we gonna do?" I asked the driver, staring at the bloodied car.

"We can't go round it, too much debris. The glass would be fine, but the metal … we can't risk it with the tyres," he replied uneasily. He looked at me with a nervous smile. He expected me to get out and move it! I sighed and began walking towards my seat to get the gun – *my* gun. Adrenaline began to pump through my blood as I prepared myself for the unknown, and that was when I heard a thump. It was loud and very close. The whole coach shuddered with the noise. I turned to look at the driver, doubting my sanity for a moment. He craned his neck to try and find the source. He had also heard it. Suddenly, there was another thump, followed by another. It came from the outside of the coach, on the right side. There were a few more thumps which shook the whole coach. I edged over to the window to see the source of the noise. What I saw caused me to freeze in disbelief. Running out of the line of trees, not very far away, were thirty or so people. Yet, I could see they weren't quite *people*. They weren't close enough to see "the whites of their eyes" but, even from the coach, it was clear something was wrong. Some were covered in blood and others had parts missing. Some had splinters of bone hanging out of the ragged flesh where an arm, or another body part, used to be. Some were dressed in ripped clothes, others in suits, some wore nothing at all. There were four at the base of the coach pushing against it as if it wasn't even there. As the seconds passed, the other infected from the woods got closer.

I finally managed to free my mouth from shock-induced silence and shout, "Reverse!"

The driver, wrenched from his shock as well, didn't wait for me to ask again and began to reverse … but it was too late at that point. There was a resounding thump and metal crumpling as thirty or more bodies of the infected collided with the coach. It shook the entire vehicle and threw me to the floor. There was a groaning and creaking of metal being stressed beyond the breaking point. I thought I must have hit my head when I fell because, when I looked up, I saw the floor was shifting and leaning sideways. I tried to stand up but began to fall again. It wasn't my head that caused the coach to shift … the sheer amount of weight pushing against the coach had begun to tip it over! I wanted to strap myself down with a seatbelt, but there wasn't time. I braced myself between the seats, ready for what was about to happen. The coach went from being vertical to diagonal, to horizontal in less than three seconds. There was a deafening crash as it hit the concrete. I was thrown along the length of the coach, head over heels. I remember glass exploding upwards, and metal crumpling inwards. I slammed into something but had no idea what. Whatever it was, I hit it hard and I hit it fast. I blacked out …

TAO OF SAM – HYGIENE: THE BASICS

It isn't the most important thing, but how you wear your hair may be very important to your survival. Long hair gets tangled up. It can get caught on things. It can get grabbed by the undead. You don't want long hair. That goes double for Kelsey. Hair down to your backside just won't do! You need short hair. It will give you an extra edge over others.

The other advantage is in the long run. Long hair takes effort to maintain. When it is dirty, it is uncomfortable and you can get lice. Short hair is easier. If things go as badly as I expect they will, water will be in short supply. Eventually, the infrastructure will probably collapse. Many types of illness will run rampant. Short hair means less chance becoming infested or sick.

There may be a psychological aspect also. When dealing with other survivors, shaved heads may be intimidating. You want others to fear you. Life without confrontation is impossible, but at least you can prevent some of it.

Secondly is general hygiene. Yes, you should wash. It will keep illness and disease at bay. But only wash as minimally as you need to. Do not waste resources. Especially you, Mum. You do NOT need to wash twice a day. Get over it. A basic wash every other day will suffice. Antibacterial gel may be useful just for hands. Washing has to be done if you get covered in gore. We don't know how the infection works yet. Adjust your behaviour when you do.

CHAPTER 3

Ears ringing, brain screaming. Agony. Where was I? I tried to lift myself up, but pain shot through my head. I fell again. The pain wasn't just my head. My entire body protested. I pushed myself to my feet again, prepared for the pain the second time. The shattered glass cut into my hands as I used them to regain balance. I gritted my teeth and heaved myself up. My hands might have burned, but everything else hurt worse. As the ringing subsided, I realised it wasn't my brain screaming. I could *hear* screaming. I had been thrown between two seats and ended up lying on the broken glass in a crumpled mess. I pulled myself out the gap, balancing on the sides of the seats. I could see the driver thrashing in his seat and realised he was the source of the screams. I ignored my pain and began to climb forward slowly over the sides of the seats. As I got closer, I saw the reason for his screams. The glass was cracked and the infected reached through a small hole they had created. They reached through with their entire arms but could only try to claw at him as their shoulders prevented them from reaching further. They didn't have the cognitive ability to tell them they needed a bigger hole, or to break the glass even more.

"Help!" he screamed, as he saw me approach in the mirror. "I'm stuck! I think my arm is broken!"

"Relax!" I called to him wearily, scanning the coach for

my bag and gun. My bag was at the front of the coach, but there was no sign of the gun. I crawled further along the seats and made my way to him until I stood on what used to be the door. The driver dangled above me in his seat. My appearance had caused excitement among the infected. They began pushing against the glass more aggressively, as if they couldn't even see the glass was there. That wasn't what concerned me though. The more they pushed, the more cracks grew. I grabbed up my bag. I looked up at the driver, who only stayed where he was due to the seatbelt. I could see he was a lot worse than he had said. His arm was broken for sure, and his ribs were crushed in places where the steering column had slammed into him. His head was also bleeding. Very badly. The infected hands were inches from his face, yet still out of reach as he pushed himself against the seat to gain some more distance. The stench was unbelievable. It was unimaginable even. As bad as you imagined rotten flesh to be, multiply that by ten and you still aren't anywhere near the intensity that flooded into the coach.

I unhooked his seatbelt, which caused him to crumple into a screaming pile as all his weight was forced onto the steering column.

"I'm so sorry!" I said to him, wincing at his agony. I tried to adjust him, but it was just met with more screams. I didn't know how to try to move him. Every time I tried, he screamed. Worse than that: as each second passed, the glass came closer to breaking. I heard the glass crinkle as the cracks spread further. I had to react and not think it through. I grabbed his good arm and hooked it around me, ignoring his protests and screams. It was for his own good. I pulled and moved him until he was free of his seat. I'm certain he passed out once or twice in the process. I looked at the obstacle course of seats ahead of me. I knew I had no chance of getting out with him. The front was no good after all. I needed backup. I placed him down.

"Please don't leave me!" the driver begged. "Please! Please don't leave me! Please!"

"I'm not," I said, crouching to look him in the eye. "If we're going to get out, I need to find my gun."

He nodded with desperation in his eyes. I climbed over the seats, looking between each for the gun. I heard the glass giving way as I spotted the gun. I jumped to it and scooped it up. As I spun around to face the front, I saw the glass collapse as the infected poured in. They swarmed onto the driver, whose screams emanated around me before being cut short. I had a brief flicker of thought as I realised I didn't even know the dead man's name. I felt bile rise in my throat but swallowed it down. When the infected were done with the driver, they turned to me. There was no hesitation before they advanced. They were fast but clumsy. Their movement and timing was off, as if it wasn't natural to them. They moved forward slowly. They fell and stumbled as they tried to climb over the seats. They snarled. They moaned. They reached for me hungrily. I clambered over the seats, heading towards the back window. I jumped each seat, imagining each as a hurdle. I slammed into the back window, but nothing happened. The infected approached still and I was stuck! It was then I noticed an emergency hammer. I grabbed it and, despite the situation, I took some glee in hitting the window with the hammer. I expected the glass to fall to pieces, the way I had always pictured it would, but it just cracked. The infected got closer. I slammed myself into the glass, feeling it bulge outwards. I took a deep breath and slammed into it again. The glass finally gave way and I escaped the deathly grasp of the infected! I wasn't safe though. I tumbled out into the road. My body ached, both from being thrown about and from the adrenaline. I picked myself up and began running. Not towards the woods, but towards the embankment. I dived down it, tumbling through the grass. In front of me, there was a grassy expanse with a farmhouse in the distance. That was my target. I ran. My legs and thighs burned. It felt as though acid pumped through me. I risked a glance over my shoulder and saw that nothing chased me. I slowed to a jog and then stopped, confused. Some of the infected shuffled around by the coach, while others sprinted down the road. None of them looked at me. I quickly dropped to the ground and hid in the long grass. My brain raced. Why hadn't they followed me? I thought about their behaviour. I hated jumping to conclusions but … the only logical reason was that they had a one-track mind. Once I was out of sight, I was out of mind; hence them just wandering about without aim. Whereas the others who carried on running must have done so simply because they didn't remember the reason they had started to begin with. I knew one thing though: The longer I waited, the more spread out they would become and more likely to notice me. I had to move. I crawled through the grass slowly, heading towards the farmhouse. I didn't know what I would do once I got there, but I could plan in safety. I kept going, checking over my shoulder every couple of minutes. Most of the infected had vanished from view, but that didn't mean they weren't around. Occasionally, I found streaks of blood in the grass. I readied my gun, just in case. Something bloody had been through there, and the upturned car told me what. I took a deep breath and continued my laborious crawl.

I eventually arrived at the house, uninterrupted by any nasties hiding in the grass. I noticed more blood wiped across the wooden decking and across the door, which had been left ajar. I almost turned back. Maybe there was somewhere else I could hide? Typically, as with every horror movie, that's when the rain started to fall. Huge gobs of water splashed down and, before long, it was a torrential downpour. The decision had been made for me by some cruel and twisted God. Gun in hand, I pushed the door open and stepped inside.

CHAPTER 4

The house was dark, which was expected with a storm outside and the curtains were drawn. I could make out stuff in the dim light that crept around the edges of the curtains. It was the opposite of a stereotypical farmhouse. Everything was top of the range and new, as if someone wanted to keep up with the times. I could hear talking in the next room but recognised it as staged television chatter as opposed to actual conversation. I closed the door gently behind me, the broken lock stopping it from being shut fully, and moved further into the house. I was in the hallway, stairs leading up to my left and a door further down the hallway on the right leading to, I assumed, the front room. That's where the bloody trail led. The floor was laminated, so the blood was slick and slippery. It still looked fresh. I crept towards the door, my gun levelled in front of me, the weight heavy and unfamiliar. If there were any of the infected in the house, I had to deal with them first. I could feel bile burning the back of my throat. I felt my heart rate increase and the exhaustion left my body as I felt re-energised. Everything felt hypersensitive, as though I was floating. *Adrenaline.* I walked through the partially open door, and everything in the room hit me at once.

A horrendous stench. I instantly knew it was the smell of the infected. I still didn't know how to describe it. Dog scat boiled for a week in cat urine added with God knows what else? The bile which had been hovering in my throat ejected itself all over the once-blue carpet. The sound which bored through the room was a horrible grinding noise, like a dog chewing on a bone. How horribly close I was. What I saw could automatically outweigh all my other senses. Apart from the fresh vomit on the blue carpet, the room was fairly basic. There was a television which was stuck on some sort of chat show. In front of the television was a single armchair. At the risk of sounding sexist, it was the house of a single man: no fancy and pointless ornaments, but everything there existed out of necessity. In the chair was a body. It was an older man, probably middle-aged. In one hand was an empty bottle of vodka, in the other was a shotgun. The man was clearly dead, not just because of the sickly pallor of his skin, or the way his body hung limply. It wasn't even that almost the entirety of his head was missing and just a bloody stump remained. The spent shotgun shell on the floor was all the evidence I needed for what had happened. What truly gave away that he was dead wasn't the fact that the mangled infected woman on the floor pulled strips of flesh from the man's legs, which was followed by her mechanically shoving the flesh into her mouth and chewing it hungrily. It was the fact he didn't scream or try to move that gave it away. The female corpse, which is what it was and nothing more, made me realise these were no longer "infected" people. They were undead. The undead woman was, without a doubt, the car crash victim. She no longer had any legs; only bloody and mashed stumps remained of where they had once been. One of her arms was missing, and half of her face was torn away. Still, driven by hunger, she had managed to drag herself until she found something to eat. The undead woman was so busy feasting on the man, she hadn't even noticed me. I lifted my handgun and aimed at her head. I breathed deeply and tried to steady my hand, which shook wildly. I tried not to think about what I was about to do. She used to be a person after all. I always used to laugh at people in films who wouldn't kill the monster of someone they once knew. I was in that situation, except I couldn't pull the trigger myself, and I didn't even know the person. I closed my eyes and squeezed the trigger. The concentrated explosion of the bullet that left the gun was deafening and left my ears ringing. No amount of video games or movies could have prepared me for it. I opened my eyes to see the damage and saw my shot had gone wide. The undead woman *now* had taken notice of me. She discarded the flesh of the dead man for fresher game and began to crawl towards me with surprising speed for something with so few limbs. I levelled my gun again and stepped backwards slowly as I did so, trying to keep my distance from the crawler. The back of my leg hit something, but my body just kept going. I landed on my backside, legs tangled with a footstool. I had thrown my gun to one side when I fell, and no longer had a weapon. I began to crawl backwards, and the crawler gained on me. I kept going back until I hit a wall. I couldn't go any further. Panic took over. I felt sick. I just kept looking around wildly for a way out. In the corner next to me was an umbrella stand. In it were three umbrellas and a wooden handle. The wooden handle looked familiar deep in the recesses of my brain. I grabbed it and pulled it out. To my luck, and for whatever reason he had it, the owner of the house had kept an axe in the umbrella stand. I gripped it tightly and pushed myself up against the wall until I stood fully upright. The crawler was less than four feet away.

"Listen," I started desperately. "If there is any humanity left in you, you will stop and leave now."

There was no obvious recognition as the once human crawled towards me. I lifted the axe high above my head, gripping it tightly between both hands. The woman was a foot away from me, and she reached desperately up for me. You could almost forget she was trying to kill me with the sadness in her eyes.

"I'm so sorry," I whispered with an odd sense of calmness as I slammed the axe into her head. Television had clearly given me the wrong impression of human anatomy, as I expected it to be a lot frailer than it actually was. Although the strike slowed her, it didn't stop her. She carried on coming at me, so I wrenched the axe free, leaving a gory gash through which I could see the splinters of bone and the pinkish grey of the brain. Bloody arches of flesh clung from axe to skull. I slammed the axe down again, aiming for the same spot. It hit home. The axe crashed through the already damaged skull. The woman slumped to the floor dead … finally dead … again.

I stood over her tensely for a few minutes, expecting her to move again. She didn't. I sighed, dropped the axe, and slumped to the floor. I put my hand over my eyes and tears began to flow. I didn't know whether it was from the exhaustion, the homesickness, or the killing of a once human life, but the tears wouldn't stop. I could feel hysterical laughter looming beneath the surface. My mind felt fit to crack and I didn't know how to respond. Between the hysterical laughs and sobs, I heard a sudden creak and everything immediately stopped for me. I grabbed the axe and jumped to my feet in preparation for combat. I was tense, but that was broken when I saw something I never expected: a cat.

"Meow?" it said, cocking its head to one side and looking at me.

I don't know why, but I asked, "Are you hungry, buddy?"

The cat mewed again and brushed up against my leg, purring.

"Ok, let's find you some food," I said, smiling, face salty from tears. I opened the closest door and saw it was the kitchen. I walked in and looked through the cupboards for a bowl and food. I eventually found both. I filled the bowl and left it on the floor.

"That should get you by," I said again, smiling as the cat ate. "I'm just going to check the rest of the house."

I picked up the gun and axe, making a point not to look at any of the death and destruction around me. I crept up the stairs, surprisingly without a single one creaking. I found nothing in any of the rooms. However, my earlier suspicions about it being a man's house was confirmed; the toilet seat was left up. The bed was king-sized and there were lots of books in an office. Every man's home is his castle! I looked out of a gap between the curtains and saw nightfall had pretty much closed in, the darkness made worse by the storm. I couldn't see any movement outside but could feel the undead out there.

I turned and looked at the room. I didn't like being in someone else's room, but it would have to do for the night. I moved over to the bed and stripped the bedding before changing it for new. Call me crazy, but I couldn't sleep in someone's unwashed bedding, even if I had just brutally caved in a person's skull. I pushed that thought from my head. I closed the door just as the cat darted into the room.

"Didn't want to be alone either, eh?" I said to the cat. It mewed in reply. I shut the door completely and, as an extra measure, pushed the wardrobe in front of it. I sighed and climbed into my temporary bed still clothed, in case I needed a quick escape. I laid down and closed my eyes, stroking the cat for comfort.

"What the hell have I done?" I said aloud, before more tears came, before falling into a fitful sleep.

TAO OF SAM – WEAPONS: THE BASICS

Let's keep this simple.

Handheld weapons are your weapon of choice; something light which can crush or cut through the skull. Anything which isn't ranged. No guns or other devices. You want something up close and personal; a non-projectile weapon! You want to be able to destroy the brain, but you want to do it as quietly as possible. Heavy weapons like sledgehammers will slow you down before you get anywhere. Think axes and machetes.

Guns are useful, but avoid them. They are loud and need reloading. They will be a hindrance. They are time-consuming in terms of maintenance and finding ammunition. However, they make an impression on the living; another group you need to guard yourself against.

Homemade weapons will be your way forward. You can mix and match things, like a knife taped to a snooker cue. This will give you enough range to keep distance and dispatch the undead. Just use your imagination!

A combination of silence and range will save you. Remember, blades and such don't need reloading!

CHAPTER 5

I was pulled from a restless sleep by a strange buzzing sound. I opened my eyes. They were wet. I'd been crying in my sleep. What was the buzzing? It was continuous and close. It took a moment as the grogginess of almost-sleep fell away for me to realise it was my phone vibrating: a phone call. I reached for, and fumbled with, it. I looked at the screen. I didn't answer. It was my mother calling, as well as fifty-five other missed calls from various family members. Mother. Sister. Grandad. I continued to stare at the phone, as if I'd never seen one before, and waited until the call went to voicemail. I looked away in shame. I physically couldn't answer it. I considered sending them a text but, in my head, I still thought of my journey as a short trip. A quick there and back again. It would have been so easy to send a message or ring. I don't know why I didn't. I crawled out of bed and plugged my phone in to charge it, making another call to Alice as I did so. *Answer the phone. Please answer the phone.* It went to voicemail. I put my phone down and hoped for a callback. Nothing. I sighed and ran my hand through my hair; a coping mechanism for stress. I looked around the room as the light from my phone disappeared. The room was essentially pitch-black. No light at all, even from the window. I crept over to the curtains, stepping ever so quietly, and peeled them back just enough to look through. There was very little light outside; the only light came from the street lamps and distant twilight sky. The abandoned coach was illuminated like a beacon. I could see some of the undead, the majority of which still shuffled around and didn't stray too far from the coach. A few had wandered into the field. One was even in the immediate vicinity of the house. I watched it for a few moments as it walked without direction. It didn't even seem aware of the house. My eyes slowly adjusted to the almost darkness. I turned from the curtain and let them close again. I could see the cat sleeping peacefully on the bed. I knew I couldn't go back to sleep at that point, no matter how tired I was. My brain was wide awake and ready for action. I crept around the bedroom as silently as I could and prepared to leave. I didn't plan to leave immediately, but it kept my thoughts away from the horror scene downstairs. I couldn't handle it currently; it could wait until the sun was higher in the sky. Instead, I sat silently on the edge of the bed and replayed the events of the previous twenty-four hours, with censorship on certain parts which I didn't feel quite ready to face yet. I doubted I ever would be able to. I breathed quietly and listened to the sounds of the house. Somewhere along the line, I fell asleep …

I awoke with a jolt as my head fell backwards. I became fully awake in that instant. Light poured around the edges of the curtains. I had slept through the rest of the night. The cat was sat by the cupboard, ready to leave. I, not intending to be the cat's slave, collected my belongings first before moving the cupboard and opening the door. The cat darted out and downstairs without hesitation, uncaring of the bodies that lay below. I, on the other hand, went to the bathroom and washed, as I had done every day of my life for as long as I could remember. What can I say? Old habits die hard. My gun never left my side. A new habit. Once I was done, I proceeded to look through the top floor of the house. I found, and stole, a few odd bits: medication, including antibiotics, and the potential makings of a first aid kit. I also found a reel of duct tape. I almost cast it to one side when I had a sudden idea, a moment of survival genius. I wrapped a few lengths of it around my wrists, ankles, and midsection; basically where any clothing was exceptionally baggy. The logic that there was less chance for the clothing to get snagged on things or, in a worst-case scenario, grabbed by the undead. I gave myself a quick look over in a mirror. I looked like a homeless man. I tucked the rest of the duct tape into my bag. With a deep breath, I walked downstairs.

I could already smell the putrid stink of the unnaturalness which happened the day before. The deep breath filled my lungs with the stench. I ejected the contents of my almost empty stomach. In an attempt to filter some of the smell out, I covered my mouth and nose with a flannel I'd picked up. I continued downwards, axe in hand and poised, ready to attack. The cat was waiting to go into the living room and, I assumed, the kitchen for food. I opened the living room door slowly, half-expecting the dead to be undead again. They weren't. The horrific smell permeated the flannel and my eyes began to water. The room was full of flies; mostly on the corpses. I waded through the flying pests and made my way into the kitchen. I wished I had some sort of netting to cover my face. I was looking for anything useful to take. The most I found was a can opener. I opened the remaining cans of cat food and dumped them all in a bowl. After I left, there wouldn't be anyone to feed the cat. The cat was of no use to me, but it was the little things which mattered, after all. I opened the back door, which was also in the kitchen, and pushed it open carefully. I looked outside, slowly putting my head through the gap. There was an open field behind the house, with no sign of any undead. If I was going to leave, it needed to be soon. I looked back at the cat, which was happily eating out of its bowl.

"Look," I began to the cat, "no one is going to look after you anymore. The world is yours now."

I gestured to the world outside of the door. The cat ignored me. I pulled out my phone and opened the map application. My current location wasn't far from Reading, but closer to Slough. From there I could follow the rail line straight into London while avoiding any main roads and, in turn, the undead. I had no idea how far the infection had escalated, but it was undeniably no longer contained to London as the news suggested. Before I left, I took one last look out of the front window; even more undead wandered the field. The back door was definitely my only exit.

Once I knew the direction I was heading, I strapped my bag and shook it a few times to make sure it made minimal noise when moved. When I was happy with it, I tucked the gun into my waistband, gripped the axe tightly, and walked outside. I planned to head for the tree line and follow it; the cover of nature would hide me from the undead. I edged along the side of the house, wanting to take a quick look around the corner to see if I would be in sight of any undead when I made my move. I slowly put my head around the corner of the house and let out an audible shriek. I was face to *very* rotten face. Being that close, you couldn't help but take in details. The skin had become slack and hung away from the bone structure beneath. The skin, where it had not been torn to reveal the gory sinew, was yellowed and blackening, in various stages of decay. There were flies crawling in and out of its mouth. The worst part, even worse than the heavy stench in my throat and nose, were the eyes. I never really appreciated the meaning behind the phrase that "eyes are the windows to the soul" until that moment. Living eyes are surprisingly bright, even if you don't notice it. Looking at a zombie, into its eyes … there was no way to describe it other than the light was just gone. No one was home. My momentary panic subsided and I brought my axe up high above me and then slammed it down onto the zombie's head. The infected dropped to the ground in one hit. I had learned from my previous mistake. I quickly stepped back from the body, just in case there was still movement left in it. There were videos of snakes attacking its killer once it entered its death throes. I didn't want to see if the undead had a similar mechanism. I stared at the body and realised that was a big mistake. I started noticing details about the zombie. The infected *man*.

The man had been in some sort of office job in his life. He wore a suit which was tattered, bloody, and dirty. On one foot was a shoe almost completely worn through; a once shiny shoe now scuffed and holey in places. On the other foot was nothing. At some point, the poor infected man had lost a shoe and carried on walking. The result wasn't pretty. What had once been a foot was now mostly just a stump. Huge chunks were missing, and what was left was worn bloody. How he ever remained upright, I'd never know. Looking at his face, he would have been considered handsome in life. Probably had a wife and kids. That was half-confirmed by the wedding band on his finger. I tried to imagine what his life would have been like; the ideal image of a nuclear family with the white picket fence came to mind. I felt sorrow for the life that once was, and guilt for the once life I had taken. I pushed those thoughts from my mind and buried them under cold logic. I couldn't humanise the monsters which roamed an unknown portion of

England. I gritted my teeth and wiped the axe clean on the clothing of the man. The *undead* man. The zombie. I snuck another glance around the side of the building and saw that none of the undead had noticed the commotion which had just taken place. Perfect. I ran for the tree line and kept out of sight of the remaining undead. I kept throwing glances over my shoulder, but nothing followed.

At the tree line, I made my way in a metre or so deeper. Far enough to keep out of sight of any undead but close enough for me to keep an eye on the landscape. I rechecked my phone, looking at the compass. I reoriented myself and began to head east. I had my axe poised in the air, ready to strike. The undead weren't going to get the jump on me again. My pistol had the safety on. I wasn't using it unless I really had to. I had limited bullets, lack of real gun training, and the noise of the shot would probably attract the undead. That brought a cascade of thoughts about the undead and what category they fell into.

I'd seen a lot of zombie films, read a lot of zombie books, and played even more zombie video games, so I was aware of the general conventions and tropes that the undead followed. *My* undead were definitely not the slow, shambling kind of the older, traditional films. They could be fast when they needed to, as I had seen during the coach incident. I'd already established their mindset: a one-track system. They would probably forget about you if you stayed hidden long enough, but were just as likely to pursue you forever even if they didn't remember why. That was just a suspicion. I hadn't faced enough undead to confirm it, thankfully. I had to confirm how much they could manoeuvre. Could they open doors? Climb ladders? Did they know to tear down barricades? Hell, looking at some media about the undead, could they use weapons or tools? Those were all questions I needed to be answered if I was going to survive in the new world. There was also the issue of "special" undead. A lot of modern media about the undead had evolved them beyond the mindless hunger that they were. Frequently you would see a mutated zombie with unique abilities, strengths, or cognitive function, making it a better hunter of the living. Even undead animals sometimes appeared. If those did exist, I felt as though humanity's lifeline would grow a lot shorter at a very exponential rate. A depressing thought. I really hoped that wasn't the case. The idea of undead dogs was bad enough, let alone "special" undead. I shuddered. The only hope I had was that London, according to the media, had survived over a year in an undead war. If the undead were aided by "special" or animal infected, then I believed London would have fallen a lot quicker. *What about special animal undead?* That made a visible shiver run up my spine. Being alone with my own thoughts caused them to wander to the dark recesses of my overly vivid mind. *What if one was hunting me?* I looked around quickly at that thought. Ground level was clear. I smiled. I carried on walking. *What if they're lurking behind the trees ready for me to pass?* I had already established that they couldn't plan and think. *No, you just assumed.* I was becoming annoyed with myself. *If there are undead animals, they could be in the trees waiting for you.*

"Don't be stupid," I said aloud, laughing nervously. "Talk about—"

CRACK.

I was cut off by branches snapping. My initial thought was to look up in the trees. I had started getting to myself. I'd probably imagined—

CRACK.

Definitely hadn't imagined. I stopped moving and crouched a little. I didn't know why. Instinct? I began circling on the spot, axe ready again. I had inadvertently let it drop as I walked. A single zombie stumbled out of the deeper trees. It tripped on the undergrowth and tree roots. I smiled, despite the deep fear. It wasn't stalking me. It just wandered, looking for food. It was even more lost than I. I scolded myself for this thought.

They. Were. *Not.* People.

It took a few moments for it to notice me. When it did, it became visibly more excited. Its jaws started gnashing as it hurriedly came towards me. It didn't start running, however. It raised its hands in front of itself, grasping at the air. Perhaps in preparation to grab me? I wasn't going to be in that situation to find out. I began to flank sideways. The zombie began to turn to follow me. It was surprisingly slow at it and couldn't coordinate. I charged forward, the stench of death filling my nostrils as I struck with my axe. It sank deep into the temple. The zombie went momentarily stiff, and then limp, before collapsing to the ground. I stared at its face, a morbid curiosity coming over me. Its face was split horizontally, a permanent death snarl on it. It stared at me hungrily, and angrily, but also with accusation.

It said, *"You did this to me. You killed me. You took my half-life from me."*

I began to feel sick. I bent down and rolled the corpse over to keep its stare off of me. The smell, which I had somehow ignored, made me retch. Luckily, there wasn't anything in my stomach to be ejected. I stood up, still feeling a little green around the gills, and carried on walking. If I'd looked back, I would have seen the corpse still stared at me, equally as lifeless as before. Nothing was going to remove the accusation on its face. That look burned itself into my memory. I carried on walking. Onwards to London.

CHAPTER 6

I had slain a few more zombies when night had started to fall. I became surprisingly good at it too. Whether that skill was good or bad, I didn't know; I was just thankful for it. However, I noticed that no matter how many undead I faced, I never got used to the smell. Every time the ghastly stench hit the back of my tongue and burned its way into my nostrils, I swear I could still smell it hours later. Maybe my sense of smell would never be the same again? Maybe the stink just lingered in the air no matter where I was? I didn't know. My stomach started to growl halfway through the day. Constant adrenaline had kept my hunger mostly at bay but, eventually, my biological needs overcame the chemical effects on my body. I would have carried on without food if I could due to fear of bringing it back up at my next conflict with the undead. Fear of attracting the undead with the noises from my stomach outweighed that. I was certain my stomach growled the words "feed me" at one point. I took off my rucksack and grabbed one of the pre-packed energy bars from it. I marvelled at how I'd packed that less than forty-eight hours ago; it felt more like weeks. I ate the bar as fast as I could and carried on walking. I licked the bits out of my teeth in disgust while thinking of a bacon sandwich. It was *almost* something, I suppose. I began to think back to the farmhouse and cursed myself. With everything going on, I'd forgot to empty the fridge. The stench of the dead kept the thoughts of food a million miles away. I would trudge on with only energy bars to keep me going. *Great!*

One thing that truly surprised me was my stamina. I had walked almost an entire day without tiring while carrying out strenuous activity, such as re-killing the undead. I kept touching my toned stomach and smiling. As of six months prior, I was a lazy male living a student lifestyle that had to take breaks after walking upstairs. Six months later, I was walking all day and fighting to survive. I would never have survived if I still had my previous physique. I could run an exercise course which could rival any dieting program. Throw a bunch of flabby survivors into a ring with the undead, tell them to survive, and watch the pounds drop off them. Hell, I could even get a television show out of it. I smiled at that thought, then I realised how messed up that was. Was I already cracking? Surely it couldn't happen that fast? I pushed those thoughts down. I always pushed my darker thoughts to one side. I didn't need either of those … I had always had dark thoughts before the dead walked, horrible thoughts which even scared me sometimes. Everyone did though, right? But then again … it was a little funny. I let out a little laugh. Yeah, definitely cracking … I needed to sleep. I rubbed my palms into my eyes, causing flashes of light to run through the darkness. I always did it as a child. It was like a free firework show. I felt exhausted. I got out my phone again, thanking whatever God there was for smartphones. I noticed the charge was low, cursing whatever God there was for smartphones. I clicked past the one hundred and seven missed calls from my family, ignoring them entirely, and opened the map. There was only a single building nearby: a bus depot. That was where I needed to go. A ten-minute walk on flat ground, but a thirty-minute one through these trees. I was just thankful it wasn't near any main roads. That would hopefully mean there were less, if any, undead. I checked the surrounding areas of the trees. It was little hilly so I couldn't see far, but there didn't appear to be any *unfriendlies* in the area. I left the tree line where I had spent my entire day. Darkness was falling quickly. I hated the short days and long nights of winter. It hadn't set in just yet, but signs of winter's arrival were definitely there. The changing leaves, the frost in the morning … my grandfather had taught me about those things, the signs to look out for. I wondered how he was doing. He was a bit of a survival nut; he was all about self-sufficiency.

I made my way quickly across the uneven landscape. Adrenaline flowed through me, as it had almost all day. I had to keep that in check, otherwise my body was going to give up on me, whether through a heart attack or exhaustion. I had my phone in one hand with the map displayed, fighting against the one-per cent battery charge and hoping it would hold out. My axe, as was the norm, was in my other hand, ready to be coated in blood.

I made my way over the last hill just as my phone died. I cursed. I knew the bus depot was nearby but had no idea where. In the hilly landscape, it could be easily missed. However, whatever luck there was in the world was with me at that moment. As I came to the top of the next hill, I saw a building at the bottom of it. It was on flat concrete foundations. One road in and out, obviously leading to the main road for the access of buses.

As I approached the bus depot, night had almost fallen entirely. I focused intently on my place of rest for that night. By the looks of it, the bus depot was no longer in use. Not just because the undead roamed the land. It clearly hadn't been used in years. It was an old building; mostly small, square panes of glass that made up a larger window. However, those frames were now empty. Most were smashed, and the few which remained were broken in some form or another. Graffiti was scrawled across the old-fashioned red brickwork, and not the artistic kind either. It was a black scrawl of someone tagging their name, not the creative political satire I had often seen in my city. It could have passed as a drug den if not for the "middle of nowhere" location. I approached the chain-link fence which once stood around the building to protect it from vandals. It laid crumpled and rusted. I imagined the worms crawling around in the mud beneath it and shuddered. I couldn't help it. I could put down the undead without a second thought, but I couldn't get over a lifetime fear of worms. Human nature is a funny thing. I stepped over the fence. If anyone had asked me why I would have told them it was so I didn't make any noise but, in reality, it was to avoid the imagined worms.

I walked across the concrete, my eyes rapidly adjusting to the descending darkness. The state of the building was what the world would begin to look like if the infection got out of control. The world would look like an abandoned building, no longer of any use and reclaimed by the planet. That was if the government couldn't stop the infection, which I had no doubt they would. Everyone had seen a zombie film. They knew how to handle that sort of thing … didn't they? Then again, London had already fallen, depending on whom you listened to. Evidence of the undead I had seen outside of London suggested it had. What was to stop it from spreading even further? That sort of thing only happened in horror films. People surely weren't that stupid? I thought of all the times there was an earthquake or forest fire. The government and people cared about it initially, but they would move right back into the same area and be equally surprised when it happened again a few years down the line. Maybe the government was stupid after all.

The bus depot was open plan, merely a shelter for the buses. There wasn't a door on the front, just raised shutters and the dark within. As I stared into it, my breath caught in my throat. I think there is an inherent fear built into humans when it comes to the darkness. Not necessarily because of the dark, but because of what could be lurking in there. I continued forward, my hand instinctively tightening around the axe. CRUNCH. I stopped moving and took a defensive stance. Nothing. Another step forward. CRUNCH … I must have been tired. It took me a full three minutes of unmoving silence to realise the noise came from me standing on broken glass. I shook my head and carried on noisily. When I was near the edge of the darkness swirling around the inside of the bus shelter, I took out my flashlight. It was a compact little thing, able to fit in the palm of my hand. I shone the powerful bluish light into it; I expected hundreds of undead to be lurking within. No undead. There were some broken-up pieces of cars and buses, but no people or undead. To the back was a door; I suspected an office. There was a small window in the door. I walked over to it, avoiding the metal panels and larger pieces of broken glass. I noticed there was a dirty, possibly wet, sofa to one side. The supports had obviously broken at some point and it laid on the ground. There were few crushed beer cans and empty food packets next to the sofa.

"Weird place for a sofa," I thought aloud with a puzzled smile. I carried on to the window and peered in with the assistance of my flashlight. There was almost nothing in there, just a desk and filing cabinet. I went in. There was the smell of stale air, a nice change from the rotting flesh of the dead. There was a surprising lack of dust for an abandoned room. I was pleased to see there was a lock on the door too, which I twisted. I saw there was a plug socket on the wall, which I promptly plugged my phone into. I waited for a few moments before realising that the power had probably been switched off long ago and that's why my phone didn't respond. Hoping for a miracle. I unbuckled my sleeping bag and laid it out beneath the desk, which was up against the wall next to the door. If anyone, or anything, looked in they wouldn't see me. Also, at first glance, if anything came in I wouldn't be seen either; giving me chance to react first. I put my combat knife, axe, and gun next to my temporary bed. Just in case. I kicked off my boots and climbed into the sleeping bag, using my rucksack as a pillow. The floor was hard, the room smelled and it was cold, but beggars couldn't be choosers. That room was my home for the night. Normally I would have earphones in when sleeping in an unfamiliar place. Usually, an "unfamiliar place" constituted a friend's house, not an old bus depot in the middle of nowhere with the potential to be eaten alive. I needed to stay alert so, for the night, I would sleep in the finest discomfort available. And, despite it all, I fell asleep immediately.

CHAPTER 7

Most of my life, I had dreams about zombies. I would be running from the undead and trying my utmost to survive. That was probably a result of consuming anything zombie related. With it finally happening, I say "finally" because most people wish for an apocalypse at some point in their life, I didn't want it. What I did want, however, was to be free of *it* all and finally some peace. What does that say about people anyway? Wanting an apocalypse? I think people have many reasons for wanting one. I, on one hand, wanted the freedom from life. I wouldn't have to worry about my education anymore. A degree or two in psychology would be worthless in the new world. I wouldn't have to find a job and would be free from the need for money. I would finally be free of the problems which seemed to plague my family … it would be bliss. The world was full of horrors, even close to home, so what difference did the undead make? Others wanted an apocalypse for different reasons. Some wanted to be free of social norms. Some to lead a simple life. You would live just for that day. You wouldn't worry about paying the tax bill or earning enough money to afford food the next month. A freedom from responsibilities and freedom from a mediocre life. A freedom where I could do whatever I wanted. A world where anyone could be the hero. Maybe the hero could try to find a cure? Or maybe he could save the girl he loves and everything would be okay again? It was a beautiful idea. Unfortunately, the world isn't like the Hollywood, romanticised version of events. Life is cruel and unkind. New stresses that would replace the old. The fear of death would be a constant. Every. Single. Day.

I had always dreamed about zombies. Except for that night in the bus depot. I didn't dream of the family I had abandoned. I didn't dream of the responsibilities I had left behind. I didn't dream of the girl I was chasing. I didn't even dream of the unspeakable horror spreading throughout the once *Great* Britain. I dreamed of the school I hadn't been to for over ten years. The dream was nonsense, but I was thankful for it. I knew all wasn't right in the world outside of my dreamscape, but a distraction from the last time I was truly happy was welcomed.

Eventually, the voice of my mother floated over.

"It's my day off," I mumbled in return and rolled over. It was too late though. I was awake. *Why was I in a sleeping bag?* I looked down at myself, confused. I could hear male laughter. Then I heard the sound of glass crunching. I rose groggily, saw the desk above, and remembered everything. My hand flew to my combat knife and gun. The footsteps and laughter got closer. They were alive, but that didn't mean they were friendly. I clutched the knife and curled under the table further, bringing my belongings with me. I wanted to remain out of sight but be ready for knee-stabbing action. I heard the handle turn several times.

"Joey, you lock this yesterday?" a man shouted.

"Musta," the man called Joey giggled. The first man started fiddling with the lock. I heard the sound of metal sliding on metal as he made short work of the door and opened it slowly. He stepped in, silhouetted by the light behind him. He had a screwdriver in his hand, possibly what he used to open the door. He walked into the small room and opened the filing cabinet. He retrieved four cans of beer. I could see he was large, possibly a bodybuilder. I couldn't beat him in a fair fight, especially if he had a friend. Amazingly, he left the room without even glancing at me. I could hear the sound of glass breaking as he walked back over it, the crack and hiss of an opened can, as well as the slurping as he drank thirstily. He had left the door ajar, meaning any movement from me could possibly be seen or heard. I was trapped until they left. I heard a lot of laughing and not much talking. The laughter of the high and drunk. A recognisable sound for someone from a generation of substance abuse. There was a long silence before an interesting conversation began.

"How'd you think it started?" Joey inquired out of the blue.

"Space rocks," the bodybuilder-guy replied matter-of-factly. "Probably the one which came down in Russia a while back."

"I heard it was infected monkeys," Joey replied conspiratorially.

"That was a movie," the big guy laughed.

"Oh yeah. Jay, I feel really stupid right now," Joey answered with some shame in his voice. Jay laughed. This resulted in them both laughing for much longer than the comment warranted. That told me there were only two of them: Jay and Joey. If there were more, they would have at least spoken at that point. I slipped on my boots and rolled up my sleeping bag, reattaching it to my rucksack. I tucked my gun into my waistband. I needed a holster, or something, because it felt ridiculous. I realised I was wasting precious time waiting for the drunken stoners to leave. I had a vague sense of a plan, which relied on a pretty big bluff. I tucked my knife back into the sheath, scooped up my axe, and strode out of the office.

I saw that the two men, more teenagers, were sat on the old sofa and drinking their beer. That explained the empty cans scattered about the place. I walked confidently and began heading through the depot with the intention of leaving. It was an ambitious plan, but far from simple.

"Who's that?" I heard Joey say, puzzled.

"Hell if I know, mate," Jay said intensely. He stared at me as I passed through. He pushed himself to his feet unsteadily. He voiced his curiosity about me with the vocabulary of a potato. "Who you, mate?"

I carried on walking and hoped my silence would get me out of there.

"Christ sake, bro," Joey called. I wasn't sure whom he was talking to.

"Oi, mate," Jay practically screamed at me from less than ten feet away. "You gonna answer or what?"

Why couldn't it be easy? Why couldn't *anything* be easy? I sighed and turned to him. "I'm on my way out, just leave it."

"Like bloody hell am I gonna leave it," Jay shouted angrily. He took my answer as a threat. "This is our place, mate."

"And I'm leaving," I replied and carried on walking. I shook my head in frustration.

"No. You aren't," Jay replied, a lot calmer than he had been, but that didn't hide the malice in his voice. I turned to him and saw a hammer in his hand. It was nothing special, probably picked up from a DIY store or a scrap heap. My body tensed and I felt my heart rate increase as my body prepared for conflict. He saw me staring at the hammer and he smiled. He obviously felt as though he was in full control of the situation. "I've killed people, you know."

His statement was simple, yet also cold and calculating. He hoped it would have an impact and unsteady me.

I replied coolly with a lie, "So have I."

It was now him who was taken aback. Whether it was the alcohol or drugs which was the cause, I saw the paranoia pass over his face as he realised that I may have the upper hand.

He shrugged this off and said with an uneasy smile, "That don't matter anymore. We ain't stupid. We know what's happening too, so one more death don't matter."

"He means you," Joey said with a giggle, just to clarify what was evidently clear. They were both unhinged and ready to act on that madness at any moment. I was certain that was the case before the drugs and the undead. Those factors probably only exacerbated things. Jay stared at Joey, clearly annoyed by his intrusion, but that soon disappeared. He looked back to me, hammer pointed towards me as if he could strike me down from where he was. There was a long silence as we stared at and sized each other up. Jay, who thought he was the winner, finally spoke. "We're taking your stuff."

Jay began walking towards me, covering half the distance in a few seconds as he strode confidently. It was at this moment I laughed and decided to retrieve the handgun wedged into my waistband. That was my ace in the hole.

"Really?" I laughed, waving the gun at him in an almost comedic fashion. "Just try it!"

Jay flinched and took a step back. Joey screamed and rolled onto his stomach as he covered his face with his hands, as if that would stop any bullets fired. Jay retreated slowly, making his way back to the sofa.

"We didn't mean no harm, mate," Jay said weakly, forcing a smile. His features softened but were nervous.

"Course you didn't," I said, sounding gullible with my features also softening. They hardened again as I said, "Just like you didn't mean to threaten me."

"It was just about survival," Jay said even more weakly.

"Whatever, man. This right here could just as easily be about survival for me!" I snapped. I then had an idea. I shouted at him, "Sit down!"

He did.

"Now slide your hammer over to me," I demanded forcefully.

He stared briefly at the hammer still in his hand, crazy thoughts passing through his head before he slid it over. I walked the few steps towards the hammer, handgun trained on Jay and Joey at all times. I stood on the head of the hammer and crouched slightly, just enough to wrap my hand around the wooden handle of the hammer. I pulled the handle up towards me until it splintered and snapped.

"The hell!" Jay replied as both a question and a statement, anger suddenly filling him again. "What am I meant to do now?"

"Survive," I snarled. I scooped up the head of the hammer and put it into my pocket. I threw him the broken wooden handle and turned to walk out.

"You're a real douche," Jay shouted at me as I walked away.

"And still the one with the gun!" I shouted without turning around. I held the gun up to emphasise my point, just in case he tried to follow.

When I was out of sight of the bus depot, I started to run. Although I had acted coolly in front of Jay and Joey, I was shaking inside. Fear had gripped me while we faced off; I doubt I could have maintained composure without the gun. My hand shook wildly. Fighting the undead was bad, but at least they were predictable. People, they were the scary ones. They were unpredictable. When I was on top of the hill, lungs burning and heart thumping, I turned to look at the depot below. I just had to check they hadn't got any more crazy ideas and followed. They hadn't. I took the head of the hammer out of my pocket and dropped it in the grass. I looked at the landscape around me. It was still a hilly landscape, but it slowly flattened into farmland. The road continued into the distance on my left, which meant I was heading in the right direction. The lack of cars was disturbing. Numerous times I had made that trip by coach, and there had always been traffic. It was also a relief. Fewer cars meant fewer people, and fewer people meant even fewer undead; something I definitely didn't mind. I was annoyed at the lack of phone and, in turn, map. I knew the general direction I needed to go. I didn't know the distance, but then my eyes fell on the road and I thought of the obvious; a road had signs. I jogged to the roadside, staying low when I could. The closest sign read that my destination was fifty miles away. Not only did I have to walk it, but I also needed to walk across the uneven land of the hills, which would slow me down. Also, I didn't like the idea of long hikes. I'd keep going in one direction until I hit my destination. Since I was aiming for a large town, I couldn't miss it. My train of thought was cut short by an angry and hungry growl. It was my stomach.

If it could speak, it probably would have said something like, "*Hey, put something in me NOW!*"

Doing a quick mental inventory of all the food I had, I realised I still had some energy bars. I was sick of energy bars … and I had only had one in my entire life. They tasted like someone had already digested them. I also had water with me, which I needed to ration. For someone who tended to plan for everything, I had really underestimated what I would need. However, I tried not to consider "what ifs." That wasn't the way things unfolded. Lingering on "what ifs" could drive a man mad in his time of need. So, I opened an energy bar and ate it gingerly. I took a few swigs of water to remove the dryness from my mouth. I took a quick breather, rubbing the corners of my eyes until all the crispiness of sleep was gone. At any other time in my life, I wouldn't be caught dead without having a shower or brushing my teeth. I was off the chain! I laughed at my own joke, quite shamefully too. Another reason I needed Alice back in my life. I'm sure she would laugh at my jokes. She would probably scold me about how bad it was and crack a smile when she thought I wasn't looking. That was motivation to keep going. I tightened the straps on my bag and pushed forward, images of my Alice floating through my head.

While hard marching, I remembered the first time I met Alice. We were both at university. We had turned up to an after-hours psychological lecture about the effects of stress-induced psychosis. I was alone. She approached me during the break and asked for my number. Not in a dating kind of way. We were both looking for a friend and nothing more. The next day she texted me about meeting up. Not the most romantic story in the world, but that is what it was. That is how we began talking. After that, our conversations became daily, almost hourly at the rate I texted her. Then a year later, I made my move. I'd fallen madly in love. She never admitted it, but she had been trying to make a move on me for over a year. We went on a few dates. She was my best friend and the love of my life all in one. It was fantastic. Thinking of old memories, especially the good ones, passed the time quickly. I remembered the time I had written a story for her as a present. What was it about? Zombies, of course. I wrote her a love story about zombies. I shook my head, a small smile creeping over my lips. Oh, the way things turn out.

I jogged most of the day, only stopping to empty my bladder over a fence. I was surprised to see animals in some of the fields, when there clearly hadn't been any farm activity for weeks; hedgerows and grass were overgrown. I thought about why the animals were there. I could understand why the farmer had left them. It would be difficult to transport them all. But *why* were they still alive? They had food and water, but why hadn't the undead attacked them? Perhaps they hadn't passed that way yet or, the option I was hoping for, the undead didn't attack animals. That would explain the cat still being alive in the farmhouse. That would also support my theory that animals couldn't be infected, which would make my life a lot easier.

I always imagined the undead being hard to deal with but, as I walked, I reflected on how easy it was to do just that. The hardest part was the smell, but that could easily be overcome in the moment. I had only dealt with a limited amount of undead singularly, and they hadn't been that fast or smart. Surely a group wouldn't be any harder? As long as you can split them up and focus on one at a time, it shouldn't be that hard. Could it?

CHAPTER 8

Maidenhead. I looked at it from a distance. I laid in the grass on a hill, keeping low. I watched through binoculars. It looked like any town: quaint and grey. On my route, it was before Slough. What was different about that town were the plumes of smoke that rose from it. There were cars trying to leave; many abandoned. It looked like the cliché movie scene where cars were backed up as far as the eye could see. It was chaos. I watched people climb out their cars and run as the undead descended upon the small pockets of the living. Some people were trapped in their cars as the undead slammed against the doors until they finally breached. People were pulled from their vehicles and torn apart indiscriminately. Women and children, young and infirm. It didn't matter to the undead. I only looked away when I saw a baby torn apart like it was a poorly made doll. There were military amongst the crowd fighting the undead tooth and claw. They put up a brave fight, and it was truly awe-inspiring to watch. Those were the sort of men who would bring back the world from the dead. The soldiers took down twenty to thirty undead each. It was an impressive feat to watch. Eventually, the soldiers began to fall one by one as they faced insurmountable odds. They were overrun, almost drowned, in the undead. Death came to them all. Either while they reloaded their weapons, or when one was backed up against a car and couldn't move any further.

Another ran when he was out of ammo but collided with a woman who had just climbed out of her car. The undead swarmed onto them both and tore them apart in seconds. Not much later, what was left of them rose from the dead and moved on to kill others. It didn't matter how hard or how well they fought; there were only so many of them and a seemingly endless amount of undead. I hadn't planned to head through the town anyway, but I had even more reason not to. If the outer town was overrun from undead leaving it, then what sort of state was the heart of the town in? Almost to reinforce the point, there were loud explosions in the distance, followed by even more smoke rising upwards. As far as I was concerned, Maidenhead was lost. I had a horrible realisation at that moment. The next part of my journey was going to be a lot worse than anything I'd seen. I swallowed, trying to shift the lump in my throat. I headed away from the town. I wasn't dumb enough to think I could make it through the chaos. The plan was to head around Maidenhead, hopefully avoiding most of the undead by giving it a wide berth. I wasn't stupid enough to not be afraid but, at the same time, I could handle that fear. It was the sort of fear that kept you alive. I could deal with the guilt of leaving home, and the unknown of being on the road. I could even face the undead without so much as a blink. However, I had a new fear creeping through me, something which I had a brief encounter with before: the desperate living. Cities and towns were falling. Desperate people would begin to be a common sight and a regular threat. Perhaps more so than the undead. People could think and be cruel when they needed to be, and they would hurt people when their own survival was on the line. I had to be wary.

What should have been a couple of hours of jogging to Slough took most of the day. My journey consisted of crouching and wading through the grass slowly, ducking out of sight at the slightest sound or sight of movement. I took to hiding in woodland as much as I could. I never realised there was so much of it in England. At one point I saw a family of three passing amongst the trees: a mother, father, and young daughter. They looked weary and bloody. I almost called to them, but then I saw the madness in the father's eyes. He stumbled along, wide-eyed. He had a double-barrelled shotgun which he kept twisting from side to side fearfully. If he wasn't careful, he was going to discharge it into one of his family members. The mother looked like she had already given up. She had the thousand-yard stare which was so common in war stories. The daughter was bleeding profusely from her arm. It was very apparent it was a bite. Her family, in the madness of leaving their home, had failed to even do something about the wound. She would bleed out soon. I pressed against a tree and watched them pass. The father, who looked at everything, didn't see anything. He looked around wildly. He made eye contact with me twice but didn't even realise. They carried on through the woods, destined to die soon. They were already lost souls in the world. Although I wouldn't admit it, I knew that I was also a lost soul. The line from Dante's Inferno came to mind:

"When I had journeyed half of our life's way,

I found myself within a shadowed forest,

For I had lost the path that does not stray."

Or, as I had always heavily paraphrased, "Halfway through life, I had lost my way." I had always thought it meant being physically lost in the world. It was only now I realised that it referred to being spiritually lost as well. I watched the family disappear further into the woods, for *they* had lost the path that does not stray. A few moments later, I saw a horde of fifteen or so undead tear through the woods also. They headed in the same direction as the family. A few moments later, I heard a scream, two shotgun blasts, followed by more screams. I listened, heart in my throat, to their death cries. Then they suddenly stopped. I decided it was time to move. It was a very long time before I thought about that family again; not while awake anyway. They would occasionally creep up in my dreams … in my nightmares. I would push them deep down upon waking. I knew I could have helped them, maybe even saved them. I knew I should have. At the same time, I knew my quest to save my Alice was more important. To me, anyway. I didn't believe in an afterlife, but that was probably a good thing. At that time, the scales didn't weigh in my favour. I sighed, wearily, and left the woodland.

Not long later, I was faced with another issue.

"If only you meat sacks could understand me," I laughed nervously. Two zombies converged on me. One was relatively faster than the other and was closing in. The other was a shambler. It had difficulty even moving, let alone attacking me. The runner quickly overtook the other and headed straight towards me. I waited for the last second before diving to one side. I fell to the ground clumsily, and so did the zombie. It turned around and started to crawl towards me without even trying to get up. It scrambled over itself to get to me. I sat up, axe in hand, as the undead grabbed my foot. He tried to pull me towards him, and I tried to pull myself away. I started kicking it in the head with my other foot. It wasn't even remotely fazed by it. Eventually, it managed to pull itself closer towards me. It opened its mouth, bloody strings of flesh between its teeth stretching as its maw opened ever wider, and bit down hard on my foot. I screamed, waiting for the searing pain. It didn't come. I looked down at my foot, fearful of what I would see. If I wasn't in such a life-threatening scenario, it would have been almost funny to watch. The walking abomination, a threat to all mankind, was trying without success to chew its way through my leather boot. It's what I imagined a toothless woman trying to eat a steak would look like. *What the hell was wrong with me?* I slammed my foot one more time into the undead face. Some of the flesh slid away from the skull with the force. Half of its face hung loosely below its chin. It momentarily relented before it doubled its efforts. I dived forward and slammed my axe into its face, killing the zombie in one hit. I tried to wrench my axe free. I heard wood splinter as I pulled the wooden handle away from the zombie's skull. The axe head was still embedded in the zombie. I stared at the splintered handle in my hand. *What the hell would I do?* I quickly spun around as I remembered the slower zombie. It wasn't far away from me, but I could probably have done a couple of backflips in the time it would take to reach me. I didn't do said backflips though, but strode towards it instead. I held the axe handle the same way you would hold a knife. With one swift and hard pump, I shoved the splintered handle into the zombie's eye socket, deep enough until I felt it strike the back of the skull. I have no idea how much flesh, muscle, and membrane it must have torn through to make that journey. The zombie fell to the ground unmoving as the natural order was restored. I looked at the two undead corpses; both young males. The only real difference was the levels of decomposition. The shambler was much more decomposed than the runner. *Maybe that was what made the difference?* The more decomposed they were, the slower they were? That would be something of interest to investigate.

It certainly gave hope for the future. Maybe the undead would eventually just rot themselves to death? Who knew? Time would tell. However, there was still the question of what I could use for a weapon. I still had my combat knife and gun, both useful and ineffective in their own ways. It was then I had a moment of genius, or madness depending on how you look at it. I removed the axe handle from the undead brain. Black-grey brain matter dropped off the end. My face instinctively screwed up in disgust. I wiped it on the undead man's clothes to remove most of the gore. I rummaged through my bag, looking for something I was sure I had packed. Eventually, I found a small reel of duct tape which I had picked up in the farmhouse. I also unsheathed my combat knife and lined up the handle of the knife with the length of wood that remained of the axe handle. I wrapped duct tape around it until they were fitted tightly together. What I had in my hand was a very crude, very simple, spear. It wasn't much, but it was longer than the knife by itself. That extra distance would mean a lot when facing the undead. I smiled a little. I couldn't help being a little smug with my customised weapon. I slipped it into my belt loop and carried on running. Slough would soon be in sight.

CHAPTER 9

On the outskirts of Slough, I found my target: the train tracks. My plan was very simple: follow said tracks. They went through the town and out of the other side and straight into London. I had to keep my mind focussed on each destination. At that moment Essex and Alice seemed so far away. By focussing on each stop ahead of me, it felt like a small success when I reached it, which meant I got even closer with each destination I crossed off. By following the train tracks, I would be able to skip nearly the entirety of Slough. Sure, I would have to actually go through the town, but it meant I could avoid the streets, the people and the undead. The trains had been shut off long ago, due to the quarantine, so the tracks would mostly be clear. It was insane, but I lived in an insane world.

At the edge of the town, I found the tracks. There was a military blockade there; *was* being the keyword. There were piles of sandbags arranged in a defensive manner, although it looked they were more interested in keeping people in the town rather than out. The sandbags were splattered with blood and there were two bodies: one military, one previously undead. The zombie's body was puckered with bullet holes. The military woman had a torn neck, which explained the gore in the mouth of the zombie, and a bullet hole in the top of her head. In her hand was a handgun with an expended shell next

67

to it. The woman had clearly been bitten. She probably took out the zombie afterwards, and then shot herself. If I had checked the roof of her mouth, I was sure I would find an entry wound. This woman was a hero in my books! She may have taken her own life, but she put herself out the equation. A brave woman in her own right. That told me one thing: the military treated the infection as transferable by bite. Why else would she take her own life? Not only were the undead infected, but it also probably meant they were carriers. A bite equalled death. *Classic zombie trope.* I leaned forward and took the handgun from the dead soldier. I felt dirty doing it, but she didn't need it anymore; I did. I was still wary about getting so close to the dead soldier, even though I knew she was dead-dead. A new instinct developing? I checked the soldier's pockets for anything of use. Nothing. With that addition, I had two guns tucked into my waistband. I was building quite an arsenal.

I followed the train tracks, spear-knife in hand. I didn't see another being, living or dead. As I got further into the town, I could smell smoke, a horrible smell as the poisons filled the air from items which should never be burnt. There was also something else burning which made me feel sick to my stomach: the smell of burning flesh. It was an easily recognisable smell, because I had smelled it once before. A lot less ominous than it sounded. It was actually a fairly civilised event. As part of work experience, I had been allowed to stand in an operating theatre while a spinal operation took place. Part of the surgery involved searing some flesh. The smell, even through a surgical mask, was horrific. It was what I imagined bad meat being barbecued on tyres smelt like, and even that wasn't quite right. Nonetheless, I recognised the smell.

Throughout Slough, I heard the screams of the remaining survivors as they come into contact with the undead. There was also the staccato of machine gun fire as soldiers put up resistance against the undead. It was truly total war for that town in Berkshire. I flinched at every loud noise, constantly twisting left and right. If I didn't end up with Post-Traumatic Stress Disorder after it all, I didn't know what would do it … and then it was over. I was out the other side and on my way to London. I travelled undisturbed through Slough and put that place behind me. Night had fallen and I was exhausted. The stench of death was a constant. Whether that was because of the wind, or because there were undead nearby, I didn't know. I didn't want to know.

While walking, I realised something about the world. Without any unnatural light, it was a very dark place. I couldn't see ten feet in front of my face. Luckily, that meant the world was dark for the undead too. Nothing attacked me. I didn't even encounter anything. All I did was follow the train tracks. The further I travelled, the more I noticed the ground rising up around me. I was getting lower and lower into the ground. The London Underground. I would be there soon, under the source of all the chaos. All I would have to do then was get to the coach station and I would be travelling to Essex safe and sound. I smiled at that. I would be there soon. Part one of my mission completed!

CHAPTER 10

I eventually reached a tunnel entrance. There was a strong wind blowing through it, which sent a chill through me. It was a cold draught, bringing the smell of death, decay, and smoke. I took a deep breath and immediately regretted it. While I had previously been in London, I was thankful for the breeze. The underground got stuffy in the summer, and any bit of air was appreciated. Now it only brought fear. It also brought uncertainty. The trains had stopped, so why was there the shifting of air? That only happened when trains moved through the tunnels, didn't it? Something wasn't right. The tunnel was even darker than the outside world, and that didn't help that feeling either. I chose not to turn on a flashlight as I went through the tunnel; anything could see my approach. I didn't want to give any enemy that advantage. I kept one hand on the wall at all times to help guide me through. I knew eventually I would reach a way out. Another terrifying factor was that the tunnel carried noises extremely well; especially gunfire. A sound I had never heard in real life before the dead walked became an hourly occurrence. It made my hair stand on end. That was nothing compared to the sounds that followed. Unsteady shuffling, followed by moans. I pressed myself against the wall and froze. My stomach dropped and I felt sick. The smell of death grew stronger by the second. The undead were in the tunnel. I just wanted to disappear. I couldn't use my gun. I could miss and alert them to my presence, or the bullets could ricochet and hit me. All I could do was wait.

The shuffling grew louder, the undead a mere few feet away. They would be on me at any moment! I could feel panic crushing my chest with each passing second. I was going to die! I *was* going to die. *I was going to–* And that's when I felt them. The undead shuffled by me. I felt the very air around me chill and a small shiver ran up my spine. I wanted to run. Every fibre of my being told me to just *run*! That feeling grew tenfold when one brushed up against me. It felt more like a shove. I didn't make a sound. I stopped an escaping gasp before it could make a sound. I waited. One zombie started to snarl, as if agitated. That seemed to cause a few others to also snarl, as if they were communicating with each other. Could they sense something wasn't right? They continued onwards. Each noise made by the undead expelled heavy and horrific-smelling gases. Vomit crept up my throat, which I forced myself to swallow down. Another zombie bumped into me but ignored the obstruction and carried on without hesitation. I felt its cold, clammy skin slide away from me as it continued. I waited until their moans were out of earshot before I even began to catch my breath in the putrid and stale air. I managed a smile. Although terrifying, I had learned something: the primary hunting technique of the undead was sight and sound, not sense of smell. Also, the more I thought about it, I didn't believe the undead communicated with each other. They just reacted to audio cues. I couldn't work out how many undead had passed me, and the sound may have been amplified by the tunnel, but I would say that the number was up in the fifties. London was disgorging undead into the rest of England at a very rapid rate. It was no wonder the infection had spread so rapidly in the space of time it did. About eight point three million potential walking abominations existed in London.

I continued my journey onwards, and a few more undead passed me. They didn't know I was there, and I didn't bother with them. I could see the light at the end of the tunnel. Not a metaphorical, spiritual light; an actual light. It was a station. As I neared the station, the shouts and screams grew louder. I broke into a light jog. I was so close to the end of my journey. I was *so* desperate to have it over and done with. I reached the underground station and was bathed in the bright overhead lights. I looked at the chaos. The screams. The blood. The stench. The fire. The smoke. The death.

I had finally reached hell.

CHAPTER 11

In secondary school, the head teacher thought it would be a great idea to buy, and fill, fish tanks with tropical fish. He didn't do any research and simply bought whatever looked nice; a mistake on his part. To begin with, the school didn't need any fish. Being between the ages of thirteen and seventeen, the students didn't give a damn about some colourful fish. That wasn't the biggest mistake, however. Midway through the school day, I noticed the fish were darting around abnormally, so I went over to investigate. At first, it looked like the fish were chasing each other. On closer inspection, I realised that I was witnessing fish-on-fish cannibalism. One fish kept "hitting" into others, pulling pieces of scaly flesh off. It kept doing it until the other fish stopped moving. It then picked pieces off the remains. I watched the entire ordeal unfold with a morbid fascination. There was something cool and macabre about it at the same time. Those images had always stuck with me, as tiny and irrelevant as they were, across the years. It was something which had disturbed me. Maybe it was the moral wrongness of something eating a member of its own species? What I saw that day in the London Underground was so much worse than anything I could have imagined, yet it dragged up old memories of that fish tank. It was an unthinkable horror. A horror I wished I would just forget. Yet, it had seared its way into my core. I would never be the same after seeing it. Words would never justify the intensity and darkness of the experience. Living it was on a whole new level to what words could tell.

What I saw was horrific. The scene was illuminated by the emergency lighting of the London Underground. The power must have gone at some point. There was a cacophony of noise. I heard screams of the living, who would soon lose that title. I could hear gunfire of surviving military, as they fought until their last breath. I heard the feral moans of the undead, as they tore into the living. Chaos didn't even come close to describing it. There was a train on the tracks. It hadn't fully docked and remained half in the station, but it looked like it had been abandoned. The driver had probably been made to exit it, leaving the train where it stood.

I crept along quietly, disguised by shadows, the train tracks bathed in darkness. There was a gap between train and tunnel exit, where I had just come from, which would allow me to climb into the station. I almost did, but stopped when a soldier was thrown to the floor, his finger still on the trigger of his gun, firing as he fell. Bullets slammed into the ceiling of the underground station. Dust and debris rained down where the bullets impacted. That didn't slow the undead as they piled on top of him. I was just two feet away from him, hidden in the darkness, but I saw everything. The undead scrambled over each other to get at him. They sank their rotten fingers, some just splinters of exposed bones, into the soft flesh of his stomach. And neck. And legs. Anything they could grab hold of. The soldier squirmed and screamed, still squeezing the trigger of his gun, which just clicked due to the now empty magazine. That didn't stop him. He managed to flip onto his stomach, and his intestines and other unrecognisable innards fell to the floor as he attempted to crawl away. The undead scooped his entrails up and started shovelling what offal they found hungrily into their mouths. The bodily fluids and blood ran down their face and between their fingers. Unfazed by this, they chewed slowly and deliberately. Their faces almost looked orgasmic as they ate. The soldier still tried to crawl away into the darkness. I stared at him, unable to move. His eyes met mine.

"Kill ... kill me," he mouthed, before he disappeared from sight as the undead grabbed him around his ankles and dragged him further away. He didn't scream once, not even when his throat was finally torn out. I only hoped that he would soon die and leave our Earth.

I couldn't go up onto the station floor. If I went onto it, I wouldn't leave alive. I still needed to exit though, and through the slaughterhouse seemed to be my only way. While I contemplated my next move, the screams got quieter. I looked around. The undead outnumbered the living at least ten to one. The screams weren't getting quieter because the living were winning, but because there were less of them. There were still more screams than any person should ever hear. It was only then that I noticed the emergency door on the back end of the train. I dropped to the ground and took off my rucksack. I fumbled with it in the darkness until I found what I was looking for: a flashlight. I pulled the handle and the emergency door swung open to reveal the equally dark inside of the train. There was a terrible stench in there, worse than the undead but still close to it. I climbed up the single step and into the train. I shut the door behind me; not completely, just in case I needed to leave. Caged in with the stink made my eyes water and I retched violently. I covered my nose and played with my flashlight, eventually flicking the switch and lighting the darkness. It was blindingly bright. With some more careful fumbling, I lowered the brightness. What I saw was almost worse than the destruction I had seen outside. There were corpses everywhere. Not lined up neatly, or one here or there. The floor was carpeted with the dead, bodies on bodies, as if they had just fallen where they stood. I reached for my spear-knife combination, terrified that they were about to get up. Then I saw the shells. Spread throughout the carriage, on and between the bodies, were hundreds of brass bullet shells. I leaned down to looked at one of the bodies. It was a young woman, beautiful while alive, but not anymore. Her body had almost been torn apart, not by the undead, but by gunfire. Her body was peppered with bullet holes. There was one in her forehead as well. I checked another body. An old man, same situation. I checked another, and another, and another. All the bodies were the same: riddled with bullets and then a single shot to the forehead. They had been gunned down and then finished off to make sure they wouldn't rise from the dead. It was the work of the military. Perhaps some armchair general giving orders? Or, even worse, because they had to? The situation was getting out of hand. What was meant to be confined to London had spread further afield, which I had witnessed first-hand, and now London was beyond overrun. It was no longer a quarantine effort on the military's part, but an extermination.

I stared out of the train window and watched the madness unfold. The undead had almost won the skirmish, although the victory would be meaningless to them. There were no more living in the station, just dead and undead. The last resistance came from a couple of men who had picked up the soldiers' weapons. They gunned down any undead who got close to the stairs, and they were almost successful too. I even thought they had a chance of winning and silently cheered for them, especially when actual military walked down the stairs to join them. That turned out not to be the case. They did pull out their guns and took aim, but their targets were the living as much as the undead. They opened fire from almost point blank range and tore the survivors apart. They continued downwards, firing at the undead as they moved. I ducked in case they looked my way. I risked a quick glance through the window and saw the men setting up several *packages* on the walls around the stairs. The soldiers left, leaving the mysterious items behind. I squinted to get a better look. It only took a moment and then it hit me what the packages were.

They say you can't learn anything from video games, which I often disagreed with. I had learned all sorts: trivia, laws of velocity and acceleration, how to rule Hell with only sweet, sweet heavy metal. I had played a lot of video games over the years, especially ones with guns. I always considered it a training simulator, as I had learned how to reload over a hundred different guns ranging from the Second World War to modern-day conflicts. It wasn't a perfect teaching tool, but I considered myself a small expert on the subject. I had also learned how to recognise some explosives; specifically how to plant and detonate them. It was all at the most basic level, of course. One which often came up was C4 explosives. To use a very basic and layman understanding: C4 is a type of explosive which consists of several chemicals set in a modelling-clay-like brick. It cannot be detonated with heat, gunshots, or fire. What does cause it to explode is a detonator set into it, which is remotely controlled. C4 can often be used in demolition, or death and destruction. It could even be fixed to walls when needed …

My eyes went wide the moment I realised that it was C4 lining the walls. I didn't know what to do. I couldn't run to the steps in case the C4 was detonated. Even if I did make it in time, I would probably be gunned down by the military. Either way, I lost in that scenario. I paced back and forth, unsure of what to do next. *I couldn't die here.* Suddenly, my time for planning dropped to zero. I didn't have time to think. The detonator had been pressed and there was the expected explosion. I felt the explosion before I saw it. There was a huge shockwave as the world around me rocked. My bones felt like they were made of glass and had been shattered. There was a sudden flash of blinding white light and I was thrown through the train carriage. If I had time to think, I would have realised the oddity of that happening twice in one week. But I didn't have time to think as my world went black.

CHAPTER 12

I awoke. Head ringing. Smoke and dust filled my lungs. I tasted blood. I coughed. I opened my eyes. Darkness surrounded me. I began to panic. Had the explosion blinded me? Had glass been blown into my face? What was I going to do? I would never find Alice blind! Tears began to well in the corners of my eyes … I felt for them tenderly with my fingers. They were still in my head and, as far as I could tell, intact. That meant that the explosion had probably knocked out the emergency lighting, and my vision was fine. I sat up and spluttered out dust and blood. My body ached all over and sharp pain riveted throughout. I patted myself down, looking for major injuries and painful open wounds. I winced when touching my ribs. Shards of glass had peppered me in the blast. I touched my skin and felt the sharp edges of glass. I was relieved. It meant that the glass wasn't deep. I began to pick it out, bit by bit. I clenched my teeth and winced as I removed each piece. I focussed on the pain; pain meant I was alive and able to fight. The skin around my ribs bled, but it wasn't a heavy flow. I took a deep breath as I stood up and coughed. I could taste and feel the grit in my mouth. I carried on wheezing and coughing; the sharp taste of iron. I kept coughing, momentarily fearing that I had punctured a lung, but it soon subsided as did the pain in my chest. I pushed myself onto a train seat. Before the undead, I would have had difficulty getting a seat on the London Underground. Now I had my choice of the whole carriage, if I didn't mind bodily fluids on the seats. Then again, bodily fluids on the seats wasn't anything new.

My eyes slowly adjusted to the almost utter darkness. However, I could see a dim light from beneath a body. I walked forward, trying to avoid stepping on the dead. I failed miserably as I tripped and stumbled every couple of steps. Eventually, I reached the dim source of light and rolled the body over. I found my torch, which must have been cast across the carriage during the blast. I picked it up and shone it around the carriage. The bodies had been tossed about during the explosion also, making the scene even more gruesome than before. I noticed my hand shook wildly, and no matter how much I tried to steady it, it wouldn't listen, as if the blast had served the link between my body and brain. I used the flashlight to look around me. Parts of the carriage had been crumpled and twisted, the glass had been blasted away, and parts of the walkway had collapsed. Regardless of the destruction, the carriage had protected me from certain death. In a way, that poor soldier's death had saved my life. Dust swirled in the air still, so thick it almost blocked out the light. There was debris scattered throughout the station, as well as on the bodies that died there. Among the dead, I could see a few guns which had been dropped. I crept over to the door midway down the carriage and forced them open. They had buckled slightly, which made it difficult to pry them apart. I pushed with my body and forced it open, wincing at the sound of metal on metal as they ground open uneasily. It caused the dust in the air to swirl around my face. I quickly covered my mouth and nose with my sleeve, using it as a filter. I continued slowly out of the carriage, wary that there may still be undead amongst the bodies. With the torch in one hand and the other covering my face, I would have very little time to defend myself. I worked my way towards the guns on the ground. I stepped over the dead, believing that at any moment one would rise and bite me. I had watched far too many films.

I reached the bodies closest to the blast, where the guns were. They were in a horrible state. Parts missing and scattered. Gore spilt out from the wounds and spread across the dusty floor. You could tell which bodies had been undead or just dead when the explosion had gone off by the spread of the blood: bright red blood for the living, and dark brown congealed sludge for the undead. I tried to ignore it and went for one of the guns. The gifts of the dead. It was next to a soldier, head caved in by some debris. No way he was rising as a zombie. I should have felt terrible about looting the dead, but my need was greater than theirs. I'm sure that whatever God there was would forgive me for that transgression; perhaps not my other crimes, but definitely that one. I put down my torch, casting long shadows of the corpses, and grabbed one of the guns. The man still clutched it in a death grasp. I closed my eyes, took a deep breath, and removed my hand from my mouth. I reached down and twisted the gun out of the dead man's hold. It was the standard issue SA80; an assault rifle. It had a short barrel, and the magazine sat behind the handle and trigger. It had a unique feel. I could feel the dust coating my lips and all I could think about was how useful a third hand would be in that moment. I picked up my torch and inspected the gun. The barrel and forefront of the gun were crippled; it was slightly twisted to one side. It was useless. If I ever tried to fire a shot it would probably explode in my hands. I slid the intact magazine out, complete with a few rounds, and put it in my pocket. It would come in useful if I found a working gun. I re-covered my mouth and inspected the rest of the guns by torchlight. They were also crumpled and crushed, plus the way the dead clutched their guns was enough to move me on. I would find a working gun later. It could wait. As for my escape … The stairway wasn't an option. It had collapsed. Neither was the tunnel by which I had entered. The only choice was to continue down the tunnel and hope I made it to the next station. *Hope I made it.* Is that what it had come to, hoping I would survive? Is that how I was thinking? It was only a matter of semantics, but it must have subconsciously come from somewhere. I pushed my thoughts downwards. I was sure I would snap and break down if I didn't.

I peered down the tunnel, illuminating it with my flashlight. I couldn't see anything but, then again, the tunnel had a bend in it. Anything beyond that point was invisible to me. I forced open the emergency door of the train, the clang echoing through the silent tunnels. I waited for a moment to see if any undead came running to the new noises. Without the gunfire and screaming, the tunnels were eerily quiet. Hauntingly quiet. *Stop it!* My imagination was running away with itself. I took a deep breath through my sleeve and clicked off my torch. I would rather be in the darkness where the undead couldn't see me. I would at least be on an equal ground with them. Besides, my sense of smell would alert me to them better than theirs would to me. I jumped down into the dark of the train tracks. I walked over to the wall and let it guide me as I had done before. *If it ain't broke, don't fix it.* I walked through the tunnel. A strong breeze blew through it. I closed my eyes whenever I felt the wind and let the cool breeze wash over me. I needed it. I felt hot and sticky and the breeze was perfect. I inhaled deeply. The air was clean. Clean of dirt and dust. Clean of the smell of death. That probably meant the tunnel was free of undead … for the time being anyway. That was a small victory. It was a shame I couldn't walk all the way through the tunnels and be free of the hell which was London. Unfortunately, I needed to make it to the coach station and catch an evacuation ride to Essex. I would be free; well, not in the literal sense but spiritually. I was almost there. All the effort and my journey would finally be over.

"*Well, what then?*" my inner voice said almost mockingly. "*What will you do from there?*"

"*I haven't really thought that far ahead,*" another voice within me retorted. "*I'll probably return home to Bristol with Alice and her family.*"

"*She probably won't want to. She's safe there with her family,*" the voice replied logically.

"*But I need her,*" the voice on my side replied urgently.

"*Well isn't that selfish of you!*" the first voice sneered with self-loathing.

"*I could protect her!*" my voice mentally shouted in return. However, there was no reply. After all, it was only my inner monologue arguing to validate my journey. It didn't need to reply because I already knew the answer. I was being selfish. Sure, I was trying to save her, but it was more so for me. It may have been a planned journey, but it was a journey of impulse. *A journey of escape.* Selfishness. A word after my own heart it appeared, and I completely agreed.

So that begged the question of what I would do when I reached Essex and, in turn, Alice. If everything was fine in Essex, I would find out the situation in Bristol. If all was fine, and even if it wasn't, I would contact my family. I would have to find out their position and how they were holding up. If they weren't doing well, I would return for them. I would make the journey again and bring them to the safe haven I would, hopefully, create in Essex. On the other hand, if Essex was overrun and Bristol was fine, I would drag Alice and her family all the way back to Bristol and its safety. It would take some convincing, but I was sure they would see I was right. The journey wouldn't be over, not even close, when I reached Alice, but it would be a start. In my head, reaching Alice had developed the mystical qualities of safety and survival. That is how it had to stay. Otherwise, what would be the point of it all?

Occasionally, my mind would wander to the fringes of the darkness I had pushed down. It touched, ever so slightly, on the fears and worries I tried to keep hidden, even from myself. Consciously I had yet to deal with the idea that Alice and her family had died. I tried not to think about the idea that Bristol had fallen, or that my family may have died with it. I couldn't mentally, physically, emotionally, or spiritually deal with it. I would crumble. I would have no more reason to exist. What would be the point of survival? It simply couldn't bear thinking about. I would cross that bridge when I came to it; although I knew it was a bridge I would never be able to come back from once I had. Until then, I would carry on. Fighting and surviving.

TAO OF SAM – CLOTHES: THE BASICS

Just like your hair, you need tight-fitting clothes. Loose clothes can get grabbed by the undead. It can also get caught on things. That will get you killed. The looser parts of your clothes can be made so that it hugs your body.

At the same time, clothes which are too tight will hinder you. Jeans will restrict your movement too much. You won't be able to climb walls or fences if you're restricted.

You can probably find a way to protect yourself through clothing. Something which is thick so that it can't be bitten through. The human jaw is not that strong. You will have to make compromises. Protective clothes will be somewhat restrictive. Make a few adjustments to make it less restricting.

Basically, you're going to sacrifice a degree of comfort, mobility or protection with whatever type of clothes you wear.

CHAPTER 13

I approached the next station slowly; the glow of the emergency lighting illuminated the last few metres for me. I didn't encounter any undead along the way. I stepped into the station while crouched. There weren't any undead there either. However, there were plenty of the dead around. The scene resembled the previous station, with the difference being that the soldiers had clearly lost the battle that time. There was gore strewn across the floor and up the walls. Pieces of people were everywhere. The destruction had made its way onto the train tracks as well. I couldn't get over the expense of life; especially how viciously it was taken. The corpse closest to me was stripped of all flesh, and anything else the undead considered worth consuming. The man's, or possibly woman's, ribcage was completely exposed, albeit slick with chunky and bloody scraps. That corpse wasn't the only one like it either. Every corpse had been utterly destroyed. There wasn't enough left to rise as undead. The undead had obviously moved onwards to better pickings and left the station, leaving it as the mass grave that it was. Towards the stairway were the bodies of soldiers. They were picked clean just as much as the rest of the bodies. The only thing setting them apart were the scraps of military fatigues, dog tags, and guns. I jogged over, eyes wildly taking in everything at once, and grabbed up one of the undamaged guns; the same model as the crippled ones I had found previously. I checked the basics, pulled the clip out and reinserted it. The gun appeared to be in working order. There was no scope to it. I would have to rely on the iron sight on top if I wanted to aim. I put the strap over my head and secured it to my body. I felt more confident with an assault rifle at my side, even if I didn't know how to use it. I checked the rest of the soldiers, finding various magazines for the gun; more than I could carry. I was a little disappointed to find a complete lack of attachments for the gun. I didn't expect to find an under barrel grenade launcher, but a bayonet would have been nice! I was probably better equipped than the soldiers had been. If all the soldiers had been that under-equipped, it was no wonder London was falling. I began walking up the stairs when I noticed a satchel discarded to one side. Curiosity had me, so I opened it to inspect the contents and found several packages of C4; the detonator included. I almost left it where it was. I even considered disposing of it after all the trouble it had caused me. Then I had a moment of clarity. As much as I was angry at the soldiers for killing innocent people, and annoyed at them for destroying the stairway and leaving me for dead, I realised what they were doing was right. They needed to stop the undead leaving London if the rest of the UK was to be protected. Admittedly the infection had already spread beyond its boundaries, but why not try stopping it further? *Anything* would help. I picked up the bag of C4, taking the detonator in my other hand. I was going to carry on what the soldiers died doing, with just a slight difference. I strode with purpose towards the tunnel entrance with gritted teeth.

I placed the last charge on the wall. The small tunnel had about six individual C4 explosives along it. I wasn't taking any chances. I was sure it was overkill but, at the same time, I was a little bit excited. Not many people could say they had detonated C4, and at such a quantity. I retreated to the staircase and braced myself against the wall. I held the detonator, took a deep breath, and clicked it, hoping I had done it all correctly. There was an earth-shattering blast and I was thrown off my feet as the ground rocked. I could hear crashing and crumbling as the tunnel collapsed under its own weight with only the persuasion from the explosives. I risked a look to admire my handiwork. The air thick with dust was enough of a confirmation that it had worked. That would be enough to stop the undead leaving the city via the underground; at that section anyway. I let the amusement linger momentarily on my face before turning towards the staircase. I discarded the detonator and took out my makeshift spear-knife and handgun. Depending on what I saw above ground would decide whether I used the SA80 or not. I took a deep breath and walked up the stairs. My footfalls got heavier and heavier with each step. Exhaustion was beginning to take its toll.

The closer I got to the surface, the louder the sound of gunfire became. It was a continuous sound, a constant staccato of shots overlaid with that of other shots. There wasn't a single break in the noise. There would occasionally be a burst of louder shots in the background as a heavier weapon was fired. The higher I climbed, the more the sound felt as though it was reaching a crescendo, yet it didn't end. At surface level, the chaos was unbelievable. Normally the roads would have been busy anyway, but it was even worse than "normal" London. Cars were turned upside down. Smoke poured out of some and there was fire in others. Some were compacted into each other from collisions in the panic. There were one or two vehicles even through shop windows. I was certain I saw tread marks from a tank too. There was one thing almost the same with every vehicle though: they had been abandoned, doors left open. Almost every alarm available sounded: car alarms, shop alarms, house alarms, and fire alarms. Somewhere in the distance was an air raid siren. There weren't any screams or shouts of survivors. I guess there were so few left at that point. However, there was the constant moan and guttural snarls of the undead. Those undead were a lot more active than those encountered previously. That could be due to the more abundant supply of food. There was automatic gunfire nearby, concentrated and careful. Possibly a military defensive position. I could head there for safety! I looked at the nearby undead, none of which looked at me, so I kept low and ran for the nearest car. I crouched behind the backend of it. I waited a few seconds and ran for the next car. Smoke was so thick in the air in places that it obscured my view of anything beyond it. One of the back doors was open, and I dived in. I laid face up on the backseat and breathed heavily. Exhaustion wore me down, and even the shortest distance had become an effort; my reserves of stamina were almost non-existent. I sat up and looked out the back window. A couple of undead headed in my direction. I didn't know if it was because of the noise I had made or because that was the direction they were going anyway. Needless to say, I would be in trouble if they saw me. It wasn't just them I would alert but any nearby undead, and London had a lot of them. I ducked back down, almost completely on my back. I spread my legs into a V-shape and steadied my handgun, aiming between them and out the door, ready for the undead to pass. My hands shook, and it felt like an eternity waiting the few minutes I did. Eventually, the two zombies shambled past, their movements jerky and uncoordinated. Admittedly, I smelled the pair before I saw them. As bad as the stench of death was, it worked as a good indicator of their arrival. They both moved past the door, oblivious to my presence. I sighed and relaxed slightly. I rolled onto my front and looked out of the window opposite the door I had entered. My next stop was through a shattered shop window where I would plan my next move. I opened the other door slowly to avoid any noise. I proceeded to crawl out of the car head first. I'd focussed so much on being quiet that I didn't notice the single undead female lying on the ground outside. It was half-trapped under the car that I was in, which had clearly run it over. I had barely stuck my head out when its one free hand flew to my face. It grabbed my hair, which was just an inch or so long. Since it couldn't lift itself to me, it tried to pull me down to it. I opened my mouth to shout out in pain but stopped myself. I couldn't risk any noise. The undead woman snarled into my face, teeth bared and gnashing hungrily. I quickly brought my hand, which held my spear-knife, up and stabbed the zombie in the face. It was an awkward angle, but I managed to get the blade in all the way into the creature's flesh, through its skull, and up to the handle. The zombie slumped down, dead again, and its arm relaxed. Unfortunately, its hand didn't. It remained tangled in my hair, fingers tightly grasped. I tried to pull away but it wouldn't give. I awkwardly tried to pry its fingers apart but they had frozen in place. I had to cut my hair … I didn't want to do what I needed to do, but I had to do it if I was going to get away. If I waited any longer then more zombies may arrive, and that meant they could spot me. I pulled my spear-knife from the zombie's head, thick globs of fleshy *goo* dripping from the blade. I pulled it up disdainfully and pressed it against my hair. I pulled my hair taut and began to cut. I could feel the undead juices running through my scalp, sliding through my hair and eventually dripping off my forehead. The inside smelled worse than the outside and I began to heave. I emptied my almost empty stomach; mostly stomach acid came up. It tasted disgusting and splattered against the undead face. The sight of zombie and my vomit was grotesque and, if I'd had more to sick up, I would have.

I eventually managed to cut my hair free of the death grasp and made a dash for the broken shop window as fast as I could. I pretty much dived through the window and landed on shards of broken glass. Luckily, none of it cut into me. I grabbed up the first piece of material I could find: a pack of cloths on a shelf. I tore them open and began to mop the gunk off of my head. I threw the cloth to one side, not even acknowledging what was on it, and used another. I got up and began to take in my surroundings. It was a locally owned convenience store, which sold all sorts of stuff. I wandered the shop. Most of the stock had been looted or destroyed. I saw a couple of bottles of water at the back of one of the shelves which I took and drank greedily. After inhaling dust and vomiting up my stomach's contents, I felt like I hadn't had a drink for weeks. I threw both empty bottles to one side. I spun on the spot, looking for anything else of help, and found a stand full of tourist maps of London. I opened one up on the counter. It was a very basic map, with most of the attractions and underground entrances marked. I didn't plan on visiting the Natural History Museum that day. I found where I was, with great difficulty, and where I needed to be. It wasn't far, and I could take an almost direct route there, if the roads were free of the undead, anyway. I memorised the route and a few alternative ones also, just in case. Things hadn't been going my way, so I needed to be prepared. I got ready to leave, gun and spear-knife prepped to go, when I heard voices. I ducked against the wall to listen.

"I heard shots up this way!" I heard a woman say. She sounded out of breath like she had been jogging.

"You can hear shots everywhere!" a deep male voice replied. He seemed extremely calm for the situation.

"I know what I heard," she snapped. She had stopped right outside the window. I heard a gunshot and the voices fell silent for a moment. The woman then continued in a hushed, rushed tone, "We will have to move on before more zeds arrive. We will be safe once we get to where the shots came from."

"I'm pretty sure shots probably means it isn't safe," I heard the man retort as they began to walk away. I followed the two people from inside the safety of the shop. They chatted about inane rubbish. Suddenly they were cut short.

"Stop where you are!" a strong female voice yelled.

"I told you we would be fine!" the first woman laughed. I watched from the broken shop window. The newcomer was a tall white woman in military fatigues. She had a gun pointed at the two civilians.

"Drop the weapons!" the military woman shouted again. They did as they were told, although the male seemed more reluctant to do so.

"We're not bit, don't wo–" the woman began but was cut short as several rounds from the military woman's gun tore through the civilian.

"What the hel–" the man began before he was gunned down too. I covered my mouth to stop myself shouting out. The military woman then walked over to the two bodies she had just gunned down, mere feet from me, and shot them both in the head with single shots.

"It was just a couple of civvies," the woman said harshly, speaking into a radio. "I dealt with them."

There was some talking from the radio, and the woman moved onwards. That completely ruled out going to the military for help. Or any other human if that is what the world had come too. I felt completely sickened by what I had witnessed. It reinforced what I had seen in the subway. The military were killing everyone they saw. Living or dead. If it moved, they would shoot it. I briefly stuck my head out the window. There were no undead or soldiers in sight. Local undead would probably try to follow the source of the noise. I had to move before they closed in. I ran across the road and down the street. I kept close to the walls of the high street. I was less likely to be spotted that way.

I made it about one block from my destination and the gunfire had gotten louder. It was like I was heading to the epicentre of the undead war. It was about to get a lot more dangerous, and I doubted my spear-knife would be enough anymore. I had my handgun, but that still didn't feel quite right. I pulled out my assault rifle and switched it from multi-shot fire to single shot. I readied it, and it felt a lot better in my hands. It was heavy but comforting. There was a lone zombie wandering about along the roadside. It hadn't seen me. I lined up my shot, stared down the sight of the gun, and let off a shot. It felt powerful and it was deafening. I felt a little overcome with the power in my hands. The shot came close to the zombie but didn't hit it. The recoil, which I had expected, still almost threw the gun out of my hands. The butt of the gun slammed back into my shoulder. The force would no doubt leave a bruise. The undead female began to look around, instantly on edge and ready to attack. I fired another shot; that one hit it in the shoulder. Although we both had a shoulder injury, hers was a lot worse. Bloody gore exploded from the wound where the bullet had struck. It left a nasty hole. It saw me and began running, its face twisted into a snarl. I let off another shot. It hit her dead in the head, "dead" being the keyword. The shot threw the zombie off its feet and to the ground, disintegrating part of its head as the bullet passed through. I was sure the shots would attract others; it didn't matter if they were living or undead because both were equally threatening. However, I felt a lot more prepared to handle them. I knew it was foolish overconfidence. After all, it took three shots to take out one target! I shouldered the weapon and packed away my spear-knife. I felt less and less like a scared youth and more and more like a warrior as the hours passed.

CHAPTER 14

In my head, I was going to stride up to the coach station, armed to the teeth and ready for war. I would gain access to a coach, through means I hadn't yet figured out, and my journey would then be over. I would be on my way to Essex and I would see Alice. Everything would be fine. Everything would be over. That was how I had built it up in my head. I felt like a hero at the end of my quest, ready to receive a reward for my trials. Unfortunately, life has a way of screwing you and your plans over.

Part of my plan did go ahead as I imagined. I did stride up to the coach station, armed to the teeth and ready for war. Only after I dodged my way through endless amounts of the undead, and corpses they left, was that possible. There were hundreds of them swarming the streets, as if they were drawn to the station. It was only my able-bodied coordination that kept me alive in the horde of undead. There were also a few survivors still running around with no direction. Some were leaving the coach station, some were running back in, all unsure of what to do. None of them lived long in the sea of undead. I, on the other hand, was so determined to get on the coach that I ignored all of it. I didn't have time to concern myself with the fates of others. I ran through the coach station entrance, adrenaline pounding through me. I shot at any undead which got too close to me, or any which were obstructing my path. Many of my shots went wild, but a lot hit and re-killed the undead. I dodged and weaved between the undead before they could react. I ran through the open gates and into the bay where the coaches normally waited for the passengers. It was a wide-open space which could normally accommodate five or six coaches side by side, as well as the people to fill them. They were normally in an orderly fashion, where the painted lines and metal signs were obeyed by all … but not in that moment. A coach burned, unleashing plumes of black smoke that filled the condensed space. Two were tipped over onto their side, with undead dragging people out, like food out of a can. One coach tried to leave; the windows on it were smashed and people leaned out, shooting guns. There also seemed to be people shooting at others on the coach also. It didn't get far and crashed into a wall. People tried to leave the crippled vehicle but didn't make it far. There were so many undead in the station that any survivors of the coach were barely getting to their feet when they were set upon by undead. There was a third coach on its side, which people looked as though they were making a last stand on. Soldiers and non-military survivors alike stood side by side on top of the vehicle. Anyone who could hold a gun was fighting to the end. Anyone without a weapon still carried on fighting with their fists. In the end, regardless of orders or motivations, they were going to die together. That much was obvious, they were going to die. Yet they fought. That final act gave me a little hope for the future of man. A zombie ran towards me, which I quickly took out. I wasn't worried about the noise I made anymore. What was one more drop in the ocean? The coach station was lost. I had to retreat and rethink my next move. Except … I couldn't retreat because of the hundreds of undead that were running into the station behind me, dragging down any survivors they came across. I couldn't advance either, because of the wall of undead in front of me. I was trapped! Then I saw it, almost by chance: a door on the far side with the illuminated sign "Quarantine" above it. So I ran for it. I ducked, dodged and dived between all the undead. I could have been a rugby player in another life. I slammed into the closed door. Undead were closing in on me at high speed. I quickly pushed at the door. It didn't budge. The undead were closing the distance. I realised the door read "Pull" next to the small handle, so that's what I did. I fell into the room. I quickly twisted my body on the spot and saw undead almost through the door. I grabbed the edge of the door and slammed it as fast as I could. I leaned against the door, wheezing from the exertion. There was a reverberating thud, and then another, and another as multiple undead bodies slammed into the door to try and get to me, unperturbed by the sudden obstacle. I twisted the small metal lock, which wouldn't hold anyone any more than the actual door would. The thudding and pounding grew louder and louder. I pulled a heavy, metal work table up against the door; the first thing I saw. Confident that it would keep the undead out, I put my back against a wall and slid to the floor. I breathed heavily and ran my hand through my hair, looking around the room properly for the first time. It was very … white. It was a clinical room of some kind. White walls. White floor. Bright, white light. There were cabinets all along the walls, and an almost dentist-like chair in the middle. The arms of this chair had restraints, however. Posters covered the walls. Colourful posters which were almost calming. I had a shiver run down my spine and my hair stood on end. Not because there were undead behind me, separated by a few inches of door, but because I was in a hospital setting. Some things you are conditioned to hate no matter the situation. I *hated* hospitals so much; people died in hospital. I doubted the room had always been the clinic-styled room it was then. Perhaps it was some staff or storeroom which had been refitted for the outbreak? Nonetheless, it looked very out of place.

The thuds on the door eventually grew quieter until, eventually, there wasn't any at all. The undead finally lost interest or forgot about me. They probably moved on to easier pickings. I waited until I was certain there wouldn't be any more attempts at entry before I stood up and walked around the room. There was a small, orange biohazard bin to one side of the room, which was filled with used syringes; another instinctual phobia of mine. For someone who is phobic of any medical settings, an aversion to blood, and a slight disdain of social situations, I wasn't doing too badly! There was a small metal fridge, which I opened, only to find blood packs. I was AB, so any of them would work for me should I need it. I grimaced at that and quickly shut the fridge. In the cupboards was everything one needed to make a decent first aid kit, which I proceeded to take. No one was using them, and I was needy. I took bandages, antibiotics, and bottles of painkillers. They were bound to all come in handy at some point. It was even to the point where my rucksack was becoming too full. Who would have thought there would be so much lying around during the almost-end of the world? Taking a closer look at the posters, I saw they were about how to quarantine the infection and, surprisingly, about prevention and vaccination against it. Vaccination? That was news to me. As far as I was concerned, there was no vaccination. Why wasn't the government promoting it? I continued my examination of the room. There was a vending machine in the corner, full of delicious treats. I was a little disappointed because I didn't have any money on me. On the other side of the room was another door, which also read "Quarantine." I approached it. There was a colourful, almost cartoonish, poster on it. It was a simple poster of what to expect. It showed people being taken down the corridor through the door, receiving an injection and, in the last panel, a man with thumbs up showing everything was "OK." If I could get my hands on a vaccination, life would be a lot easier. My mouth began to salivate at the idea of being protected against the infection. I opened the door and walked inside. The corridor was just as clinical as the previous room. All white: floor, walls and ceiling. At the end was a large metal door. It looked new and recently installed. The corridor smelled odd, like burnt toast, but worse. I had smelled it a couple of times before … I could smell petrol too. *Something wasn't right.* Next to the door were several buttons and a dial. I had no idea what it was for. I approached the door, wrapped my hand around the huge metal handle, and pulled it open.

Inside was an incredibly horrible stench, and the source was evident. There were burnt, black husks on the floor. There were heaps of *something* dotted all over the room. They were oddly human-shaped, like someone lying in the foetal position. I bent over to look at one closely, trying to figure out what it was. A strange noise emanated from the husks. It started off as an odd cracking and creaking noise, combined with the sound of tearing paper. Then the black mass began to move. Pieces tore away as the parts began to pull away from the rest of it. It was like a macabre cocoon hatching. Long, thin appendages broke away and unfolded as it began to reach towards me. It pulled a dome-like object up. There were no features on it whatsoever except for two dark hollows towards the top and one gaping hole at the bottom. It was then I realised that the "black husks" had been people. The "dome" was just a blackened sphere which was its head. The dark hollows were empty, black sockets which clearly used to be eyes. The gaping hole was a lipless mouth. The creature opened its "mouth" further, exposing blackened stumps of teeth; there was no tongue. A noise came from its mouth. It wasn't the snarl of the undead I was used to, but a ghastly whisper of air leaving its body. It began to reach for me slowly, its black, paper-thin skin tearing and falling apart. Flakes fell to the floor. I stood up, disgusted by what I saw. It started to pull itself towards me, legs expanding in the process. There was a gory mess on the floor where it had been. Without a second's hesitation, I stomped on the creature's head. Its skull concaved with very little force. My boot was covered in the blackened gore. Within a couple of seconds, the other blackened masses began to move. I stepped out of the room and slammed the heavy door shut with no plans to ever enter again. I walked out of the corridor as well. If I had waited around any longer, I'm sure I would have heard blackened claws scratching at the door.

I stumbled back into the first room I had entered and slumped down in the chair. I felt ill and had a cold sweat. I would never know *officially* what had gone on in that room, but I could assume. The government had probably tried to quarantine those whom they thought were infected, especially at areas where evacuations would take place. When that didn't work, there was an offer of a "vaccination," which people accepted. Maybe the government started off with good intentions of trying to cure the infection. Maybe they started taking blood to try and figure it out, but there wasn't a cure. So they invented the "Quarantine" room. Patients would be taken in there to be "vaccinated," except in reality they would be taken to an execution chamber where they were incinerated. People were lured in and killed. I couldn't be sure that was the case, but the evidence at hand suggested it. When the government pulled out of the area, they just left things as they were. The government had fallen so far. They hadn't even bothered to clean up the bodies they had left. Did all the bodies ended up as blackened undead? Did the government realise that when they removed others? If they hadn't, there could be blackened corpses wandering the land, instilling fear wherever they went. I had enough. I suddenly realised how tired I felt. All the missed sleep and bodily exertion had caught up with me. I needed to sleep so badly, and it felt like my body would give into it at any moment. I couldn't sleep just then, however. I dragged myself up and over to the filing cabinets in the corner. I moved them one by one and stacked them in front of the door and on the table. If the undead wanted to get through the door, it wouldn't stop them, but it would certainly slow them down. I went through my rucksack to retrieve my sleeping bag and some food. I was so hungry and so tired. You couldn't survive on energy bars. I looked at the vending machine again. It was a shame I didn't have any money. Then again, I *was* hungry, and there wasn't anyone around … I approached the vending machine to commit a crime which I'd never get caught for. I caught my reflection in the glass. I had a little look of glee in my eyes. I let the mirth spread to my lips and had a full grin in seconds. With that, I lifted my foot and put my heel through the glass, exposing the delicious snacks within. Suddenly, a small tinny alarm began to sound. I panicked. There was pounding on the door again as the undead heard the commotion. I reached behind the back of the machine and yanked the plug from the wall. The alarm died as soon as the power was cut. The pounding continued. The undead had been alerted to my presence in the room and were suddenly very interested in me again. I felt like a *very* rich old guy at a bikini model convention.

"I feel so used right now," I said, more so to myself, with a weak nervous laugh. *One step closer to the edge of insanity*. The pounding continued, equally unperturbed by my comment. I ignored the sound and took a lot of the lovely and colourful snacks from the vending machine: chocolate bars, crisps, and *more* chocolate bars. I was going to have a feast which diabetics would envy. I started back to my chair with my snacks but, almost as a second thought, collected my phone charger as well. I plugged in my phone where the vending machine had been. Within a few minutes, my phone lit up as it turned on. I expected a lot of missed calls, but there weren't many. There were texts though. I checked the time of the last one. It had only been a day earlier from my mother and read:

"Help"

That was all it said. There were no missed calls after that point. Had the infection reached Bristol? Was that why there were no more messages? Maybe they had just given up waiting for me? I didn't know. Any of those scenarios just meant that I had to persevere and move forward. I hadn't come so far to turn back! I curled up in the chair and dragged my sleeping bag over me like a blanket. I placed my assault rifle next to me with the safety on. It was facing the door, as was the chair. I curled my finger around the trigger. I was ready for the undead if, or when, they broke down the door. I had snacks resting on my chest ready to eat as I got comfy in the chair. I listened to the noises around me. There was still thudding on the door. There was also still a lot of noise outside. The screams had been replaced by occasional shouts. The weaker of the survivors had obviously died and only the strong lived. I imagined it was only soldiers, maybe a few survivors with guns, left. There was an occasional burst of gunfire. Maybe the survivors had built up a good defence? Or maybe there weren't many of them left? I rubbed my eyes and went to blink, but didn't open them again. I had fallen into a deep and peaceful sleep, regardless of the death and destruction around me. I was safe in a room. I was the warm centre of survival.

TAO OF SAM – WATER: THE BASICS

Eventually, the water is going to be switched off. In the early days, find ways to store as much water as possible. Also, you should hoard a lot of bottled water. Keep it safe and protected. Ration it.

Remember, you can boil water to purify it. Perhaps invest in some purification capsules.

Find a way to catch rainwater. Maybe build a well. Find a way to harvest dew or something.

Remember, you can survive, on average, for three days without water.

If worst comes to worst, fizzy drinks will probably be in great supply. Something is better than nothing!

Just find and store water.

CHAPTER 15

I awoke. Not jolted awake by the undead tearing through the door. Or by gunfire tearing its way through me. I just woke up. I had slept dreamlessly and quietly. It took me a few moments to realise that almost all noise outside had ceased. There was no more pounding on the door. No more gunfire. No more shouting. That could either be a good sign or a bad one; I felt the latter was more likely. Either way, I doubted my presence would be a warm welcome by whomever, or whatever, was out there. I sat up, spilling all the snacks onto the floor. I yawned. Was it day or night outside? Seeing the food reminded me of how hungry I was and, almost in agreement, my stomach grumbled loudly. It almost sounded like it was eating itself. I pulled open a bag of crisps and ate them hungrily, followed by another and then a chocolate bar. I stood up and stretched, bones clicking and popping as I did so. It felt so good! I strolled over to the vending machine, admiring my vandalism. I reached through the broken glass and into the machine and pulled out a bottle of unbranded cola. I took several huge gulps and belched loudly. I loved the sugary-caffeine rush it provided, although I would have preferred a branded drink. I took a smaller sip and was hit with a horrible realisation. At some point in the near future, fizzy drinks and sweet snacks would be a rare commodity. Once the factories shut down, and the looters had taken what there was, there wouldn't be any more made. Never again. I savoured the last few mouthfuls of cola as if it was my last. I did take a few bottles and put them into my bag. I also took a bottle of water. I knew that I should probably have taken the water over the cola but, at the same time, I could find water almost anywhere; cola not so much. After packing, I did something which disgusted me but couldn't be helped. I relieved my bowels in the corner whilst squatting over the bin, using tissues from the cupboard to clean up my mess. What can I say? Every adventurer has to answer the call of nature sometime, and it is *never* pretty.

I double checked I was ready to go and walked over to the door. I shifted everything I had placed in front of the door. I wrapped my fingers around the handle. My hand lingered there for a few moments. I was unwilling to leave the safety of the room. I closed my eyes and took a deep breath. I thumbed off the safety on my assault rifle; it was still on single shot. I levelled the gun at waist height and pushed open the door slowly. It only moved a couple of inches before meeting resistance. I almost stuck my head through the gap to see why, but cold, dead fingers slowly wrapped around the edge of the door. They began to tug at the door but ended up pulling themselves towards the door. Then a face pushed through the gap, pale eyes staring. The undead creature, with half its neck missing, darted towards me and snarled angrily. I had forgotten how bad the stench of the undead was and almost stumbled back to get away from it. Luckily, it was a case of mind over body and I halted my retreat. I quickly pulled the door shut. The door almost hit home and shut, but the undead fingers halted that. The sharp edge of the metal door cut through the soft, dead flesh of the zombie until it hit bone. Unfortunately, the door wasn't sharp enough to sever them. Instead, I had to struggle in a tug of war for the door. The zombie hungrily tried to pull it open, and I desperately tried to close it. Every time I almost had it, I hit the bone of the fingers. I let my assault rifle drop; it swung on the strap and hung in the air, but it freed up my other hand to assist me. I used my spare hand to pull the handgun out of my waistband and aimed it point blank at the fingers. I tensed my arm, ready for the recoil, closed my eyes and scrunched up my face in anticipation of the shot. I pulled the trigger. I felt the pull on the door give way and finally close. There was an intense ringing in my ears from the shot and I felt entirely disorientated from it. My head spun and I almost lost my balance. I wasn't in a rush to do that again any time soon! I opened my eyes and squinted at the door. I saw a large hole in the door from where the bullet connected and passed through. I stared at the hole. There was a long silence before an almighty hammering begun. I couldn't see through the door, but I knew there were a lot more undead there than previously. There must have been a huge number of them trying to get through. That did answer one question, however; the living had lost the battle at the coach station and only the undead remained.

Normally I would have waited out the assault, but time wasn't an option. Time was of the essence when it came to Alice, an issue for future-Sam. Present-Sam had a more pressing issue. The door had started to bulge inwards. The sheer force of the undead pressing and pounding on the door was causing it to give way. There was a fold developing in the metal, starting at the bullet hole and spreading outwards. The undead would break through, and it would be my fault. I caused the weakness in the door which would lead to my demise. I didn't have much time before the door collapsed and I was trapped. I paced back and forth, unsure of what to do. I ran my hand nervously through my sweaty hair as I tried to formulate my next move. Thinking wasn't doing me any good. I needed action! With that, I bolted into motion. I moved more objects to the door, although I doubted it would hold the undead at all. I just wanted to slow them down. I had one more option: move into the death chamber with its thick metal door. The only problem was that I would just be trapped further in the building with even less chance of escape. I shuddered at the thought of the blackened undead. *Why were they so psychologically terrify*ing? That idea was better than nothing. I opened the door leading into the corridor and was hit with the tinge of burnt flesh. I almost stepped through but then I noticed there was a small gap between the door and the wall when opened. The gears of my mind turned as ideas formed. I jogged down the corridor to the death chamber and swung that door open. The horrible burnt smell hit me again, but I ignored it. I pulled out my spear-knife and stabbed all the charred undead. Flakes of ashen flesh crumbled away, finishing them off for good. I then left the door open and retreated to the first door. I proceeded to squeeze behind it and into the corner where I was snug between the wall and door. I pulled the door closer to me; it completely removed me from sight. I held my breath, and I waited and listened. I could hear the sound of tearing metal as the door crumpled and came off its hinges. I imagined the undead tumbling over each other to get at me. I heard the undead run through the room, knocking over and breaking stuff as they went, completely uncaring and unaware as they did so. They carried on down the corridor and eventually into the death chamber. The undead kept on pouring through the room and into the corridor. I couldn't see anything, but I heard everything! I waited until I couldn't hear any more pounding of feet before slamming the heavy door shut. I only snatched a quick glance into the corridor and saw that the entirety of it was filled with the newly trapped undead. There had to be at least one hundred of them in there. Undead pounded on the door trying to get back out to me, but to no avail. They were *never* getting through that door. I waited with my assault rifle aimed at the door, but no undead wandered through. I considered leaving as soon as possible but realised I couldn't leave the undead trapped like that. Not because I felt sympathetic for them, but because anyone could wander in and open the door, letting a tidal wave of undead out onto them and the world. I needed to warn future travellers about them. I quickly opened all the cupboards and drawers, looking for a marker of some kind. Nothing. Instead, I ran over to the cupboard and took out some latex medical gloves. I opened the fridge and took out one blood pack. I cut it open and spilt it onto the floor. Such a disgusting task. I tried to imagine it was paint. That didn't work. I rubbed my gloved hands in it until they were soaked in blood. I walked up to the door and smeared the blood over the cool metal. When I had finished, there were two words:

"UNDEAD INSIDE"

That would be sufficient … hopefully. If it wasn't, I hoped the puddle of blood at the foot of the door would be. I tore off the gloves, making sure I didn't get any of the mystery blood on me. And I left.

Outside, there were only a couple of zombies. I quickly dispatched them with shots from my assault rifle. Most shots missed, often leaving a bloody and gory tear through the neck, or blowing apart shoulder blades. I did notice, however, that I was getting noticeably more accurate with each shot. The final one went down on the first attempt.

I looked around at the destruction which used to be Victoria Coach Station. The floor was essentially a carpet of the dead. Nearly every inch was covered by bloody corpses. A lot had bullet wounds in their heads and were riddled with bullets. A lot were pale with jagged chunks missing from various parts of their body. I stepped uneasily over them as I tried to leave, aware that any could still be undead. The entire glass front of the station walls had been shattered and fire raged within. Given a day or so, Victoria Coach Station would probably no longer be standing, or gutted beyond recognition. I looked over to where survivors had made a last stand on top of the coach. They had put up one hell of a fight and would probably be considered pretty amazing if it was a movie. It wasn't, however. It was a brutal reality. Dead were piled around the coach, creating an uneven stairway up to the coach where the survivors had stood. The sheer amount they had killed probably led to their own downfall as they had created a way for the undead to climb up to them. There were no bodies on top, just blood and weapons. I wasn't making an attempt to claim them. I didn't want to climb the hill of the dead to get to them. Instead, I moved on.

I walked out of the coach station onto the main road. There was a surprising lack of undead. No runners, mind you, just a couple of walkers shambling about. Some just stood there, lurking. Lurkers, Walkers, Shamblers, and Runners. My undead vocabulary grew. Although there wasn't any difference between the undead, it described their behaviour. I walked by a Lurker, assault rifle aimed at it. It made a swipe for me but didn't make any further attempt to get me. It was the laziest zombie I'd seen. I carried on walking, stepping between the dead on the ground, careful not to get too close in case it was a zombie patiently waiting, although I doubted they were that smart to plan a trap. The further I got from the station, the fewer cars there were. It didn't make sense, especially as the road was a main way out of the city. I continued onwards and just followed the road. I hid from most of the undead behind cars, or just waited for them to pass. I didn't think the undead could feel, but they looked the same way soldiers looked: the "thousand-yard" stare, like they had seen the most terrible things. I really needed to stop humanising the walking monsters. Even though I avoided most of the undead, I had to dispatch the occasional zombie, using my spear-knife where I could. I avoided guns entirely. I didn't want to attract more undead, especially in such a populated city where thousands more potentially waited.

As I walked down the roads of London, electronic billboards watched me from overhead. When I first went to London and saw them, I was amazed. I had always thought electronic billboards were just in futuristic films; to find out they actually existed was amazing. Those same signs now loomed over the city like huge tombstones. The image of a woman smiling with door-sized teeth, which showed off her "movie star smile" she had so say gained from the toothpaste on the same image, was now eerie. The enormous face now looked down on the death, destruction, and gore with an almost monstrous grin. There were a few splashes of blood on it which added to its macabre. Is that all which would remain of London? What would the future people of Earth think when they found it in many years to come? How long would those signs display their adverts while the world fell apart? It would be a testament to our time as a species on the planet. It wasn't much to be proud of. I moved on and ignored the changing images around me. Adverts were amiss in the new world.

Eventually, I found the reason why there were so few cars leaving the city: a military roadblock. It wasn't just a roadblock to check on people in vehicles. It was set up to prevent people from leaving or entering the city. There were sandbags, metal walls, and a stationary machine gun set up. Behind the roadblock, I could see a couple of structures. They weren't quite buildings; definitely shelter of some kind. It was more of a small fort than a blockade. No one was getting through it, dead or alive; that phrase was too literal for my liking. It looked like the soldiers lived at the roadblock at all times. I carefully approached. I expected someone to appear and gun me down, although the scene I saw suggested it was much more likely that I would be chased down and eaten. There were a lot of bodies and a lot of shells, but nothing moved. I took a deep breath and climbed over the sandbags and into the blockade. It was the same in the blockade as outside: a lot of blood and a lot of shells. I noticed there was a distinct lack of bodies, however. That confused me momentarily until realisation hit. The lack of bodies probably meant that the soldiers had been killed and, eventually, rose as undead before moving onwards to kill others. Attack. Kill. Reanimate. Repeat. The way of the undead. Even though there was a lack of movement, I still had to be careful. There wasn't much room to manoeuvre and if one of the undead decided to step out and attack, I wouldn't have time to react. I had to move slowly through the blockade.

As I got closer, I realised that the structures that confused me before were actually tents, albeit stronger and better than anything I had seen. They stood almost eight feet tall and more than ten feet wide. I moved the flaps aside on each one I passed to look inside. Most were filled with bunks and footlockers at the end of each bed. I checked each footlocker on the first couple of tents I passed, but stopped looking after the twelfth locker. I realised they were filled with personal mementoes and nothing of use. However, I stopped looking, not just because there was *nothing* useful, but because it felt morally wrong to rifle through a dead soldier's personal life. I carried on, only looking in each tent as opposed to a thorough search. There was almost nothing of use in the entire blockade. Weapons and medicines were gone. Probably looted. Food seemed almost absent, except some military packaged food called MREs (meals ready to eat). I picked a few up and rammed them into my bulging rucksack. It was almost at bursting point, but it was all necessary. I had heard and read a lot about how bad MREs were, often compared to old mud, but I didn't care. Food was food, something which may become a rare commodity.

I carried on through the blockade and out the other side. I didn't encounter another being the entire time. It was almost a dull experience. However, outside the blockade, I saw something amazing. What I saw was a godsend and, possibly, the second most exciting thing in my life. The first most had been the time I went to see the first Pokémon movie in the cinema. I had wanted to see it for months before it was even out, but my mum had told me we didn't have enough money. One day, my mum took me out for a drive and pulled up to the cinema. I didn't understand why we were there. Looking back, it was obvious. My mum bought us tickets to see it. I was so excited I nearly threw up. What I saw outside the blockade was nowhere near as exciting as that but, in the current situation, it was pretty damn amazing. It was a simple military Jeep which had been abandoned on the road. The Jeep was military green and it had a mounted General Purpose Machine Gun on the back. It had a closed cabin and was, what I imagined to be, reasonably bulletproof. I didn't recognise it, as it wasn't the standard military Range Rover; it looked more like an American military Humvee. I wasn't complaining, however. I always thought their Humvees were superior to our Range Rovers by a long shot. Perhaps the British Army had changed their design with the undead threat? It would be the perfect vehicle for travelling to Essex. What wasn't perfect was that the door was open and there was blood on the floor, as if someone had been dragged out and killed. There wasn't a body, which meant no keys. However, I remembered a random titbit of information I had heard years prior. Apparently, military vehicles didn't have a key for the ignition; that was to avoid loss of keys during a combat situation, or the keys being a hindrance of any kind. I jogged over to the open vehicle and checked the steering column. No keyhole. Brilliant! I climbed into the vehicle, checking it for other occupants as I did so. I wouldn't fall foul of the horror film cliché where the driver is killed at a key moment, simply because they didn't check the backseat. Nothing lurked in the vehicle. I chucked my rucksack and guns onto the passenger seat. I slammed the door and turned the keyless ignition. The engine started up without hesitation. I put my foot down and pulled away. I smiled. Things were finally getting better. Nothing more could go wrong! I had made it through hell and out the other side. Or so I thought … Had I known that London was only the beginning, I would have turned back on that day.

TAO OF SAM – SURVIVORS: THE BASICS

Other survivors are going to be more of a threat than the undead eventually. Living people are smart and vicious. They will threaten you for everything you own and then kill you for it anyway. Do *not* trust the living. Our family is its own unit and we take care of our own. If they aren't blood, they can't be trusted. Defend your home. It is your fortress. Do *not* make deals. Be careful who you do trust. The people who you knew before the outbreak won't be same people after it. The world is a bad place. Trust your instincts.

Remember, people lie and kill when there is law and order. They become monsters without it.

CHAPTER 16

The Jeep drove amazingly smooth. It handled almost perfectly and responded to the slightest adjustments. I suppose if the vehicle was designed for off-road travel in a warzone, then a well-maintained tarmac road should be even better. I cruised along happily. There wasn't a single other person in sight. I doubted another human had ever been able to drive out of London without seeing another car. Every time I caught a coach out of London, the traffic was terrible. I'd spend more time leaving London than I did on the rest of my journey. The unadventurous drive was exactly what I wanted after what I'd seen. All I needed was some music and I could almost imagine it as a road trip.

I cruised along slowly, unconsciously sticking to the speed limit. I realised that and pushed my foot down on the accelerator. The speedometer climbed another ten miles per hour. I watched my surroundings fly by; I could easily get used to it. I wound down the window and felt a cool breeze blow through the cabin. I noticed there was a radio with a transmitter connected to it. I flicked it on, almost as second nature, hoping to hear other voices. It was a lonely drive. Nothing but static. I flicked through the wavebands. Nothing on any of the channels. No military chatter. No music. No crazy religious leader preaching about the end of days …

creepy. I never liked the radio, but no radio was worse than any of the modern rubbish that … actually, no radio was probably better than some of the noise they called music.

There were very few undead on the road. The ones I saw just wandered aimlessly. As I passed, they tried to run towards me but quickly disappeared in the rear-view mirror as I sped onwards. They couldn't catch me, and I enjoyed having the speed to not have to worry about them. The further out of London I got, I started to notice abandoned cars. There were an odd few which had swerved to a stop, signified by black tyre marks on the road. Others looked as though they had simply run out of fuel and the driver had abandoned it; doors had been left open with no sign of a struggle. I had to slow and go around the odd car. I would begin to build up speed again, and then there would be another car on the opposite side of the road, and further ahead would be the same. It felt intentional, like someone had tried to make a speed trap to slow people down. I even thought that I saw someone sitting in one of the cars. I felt paranoid and sleep-deprived. I dodged slowly between them. Everything blurred together. I almost didn't see it, but as I swerved around one of the cars, an undead man in his birthday suit stepped out in front of me. He had probably moved to investigate the noise with a hungry curiosity. Before I knew it, I hit him. I slammed my foot on the brake. The vehicle slowed, but the momentum kept it moving forward. The collision didn't go unnoticed as the metal grill slammed into the zombie. The jolt shook through the car. The Jeep kept going for a few more seconds and the brakes screeched. There was no doubt the man was undead. I could tell that by the blackened gore on the front of the vehicle; not the fresh red blood of the living. I waited a few seconds as I breathed heavily. I decided to keep going. I was fine, albeit shook up.

Nothing prepared me for hitting something. There was no point waiting around though. It was just a zombie. I changed gear and put my foot on the accelerator. The Jeep moved forward, slowly at first, but picked up speed again. There was a grinding and a crunch as the wheels passed over the bones of the zombie. I learned my lesson and drove even slower than before to avoid any nasty surprises. I checked my rear-view mirror and could see the gory smear on the road where I had hit the zombie. I readjusted the mirror so I didn't have to look at the mess anymore – otherwise, I would have seen it crawl away, even with its shattered and splintered shin bones.

I drove for another mile before I noticed the vehicle didn't feel quite right. There was an odd noise and the vehicle pulled to one side. When I was confident there weren't any undead nearby, I slowed down and stopped. I jumped out but left the vehicle running, just in case I needed to make a speedy escape. I walked around the vehicle, inspecting each tyre to figure out what was wrong. I realised what it was when I checked the front right tyre. It was flat. The cause? About six inches of shin bone lodged through the tyre at an angle. The wheel couldn't be repaired; even if I got the glistening red shard of white out. I gave another look around for any zombies. Still none in sight. I checked the Jeep for tools and a spare tyre, all of which I found. I set my SA80 on the ground next to the busted tyre and put the car jack under the vehicle. I quickly turned it until it was high enough off the ground. I got to work undoing the bolts, surprised at how exhausting the task was. It was just so tedious! The tyre eventually came free. I lifted it off and let it fall to the ground. It thudded heavily and rolled a foot or so away before falling onto its side. The noise almost masked the sound of approaching footsteps. It took a few precious seconds for my ears to register it. I quickly grabbed my rifle and looked under the Jeep for the source of the noise. There were feet at the passenger door, just standing there. I heard the pull of the handle as well as the snap back into place when it failed to open. Luckily the locks had been set. The feet started to walk round to the driver's side of the vehicle; my side. The feet moved with purpose, not the uneasy shuffle of the undead. Could it be a survivor? My heart leapt at the thought of seeing someone else. My heart just as quickly sank when I thought of the brutality the hands of the living had caused in London. I was probably in just as much in danger either way. I got into a crouch, assault rifle aimed at where the person's head ought to be when they came around the front of the vehicle. I saw him before he saw me.

"I suggest you go away, mate," I replied, my face turned into a snarl. The man's eyes widened at the sight of the barrel. He stared down the gun, and sweat began to form on his forehead. He was a tall man, taller than me. He was bald; shaven. His arms bulged in his t-shirt, and his legs were the same in his jeans. He was very muscular. He could tear me in half with one arm. The expression on his face, on the other hand, said he wouldn't. He looked afraid.

"I don't want any trouble, guy," he said gently, almost apologetically. He held his hands above his head; one hand had a tyre iron in it.

"Drop the weapon," I demanded. I motioned with my gun for the action I wanted.

"With all due respect," the man said, obviously finding some courage, "you have the gun. You're in charge. I'm not a threat. I just want to defend myself from any hostiles. You would easily win this, so there shouldn't be a problem with me keeping it."

He was one smooth talker. I was half-convinced to let

him keep it. My survival instinct kicked in and I reinforced my point with the gun. Someone that strong could do a lot of damage with *just* a tyre iron. The guy sighed and crouched slowly, putting it on the ground.

"What do you want?" I asked, gun still pointed at him.

"Just a ride," the man replied calmly. Now that he knew what the situation was, he seemed like he was more in control of himself.

"And you didn't see me get out of it? You didn't think it was someone else's?" I snapped, angry that someone would leave another for dead.

"No. I didn't," he replied. "I literally just came from that way."

He pointed in the direction he had come. I found it hard to believe. At the same time, he had made no direct threat towards me.

"What did you do in life?" I asked suddenly.

"Huh?" he asked, clearly confused by my question.

"Your job!" I replied impatiently. "What profession did you have before all this happened?

"Did have?" he replied sceptically, before replying properly, "Police officer. I'm a police officer. Still am, in fact."

"Prove it," I replied. I had no idea why I asked him to do that. I don't even know why I asked what his profession was to begin with. Maybe to justify what I wanted to do next. He reached for his pocket but stopped when he saw my hand tighten on the gun.

"I'm just getting my badge," he replied calmly. I nodded for him to carry on. He reached into his pocket and slowly pulled out a black wallet. He tossed it to me, and I caught it. I flipped it open and saw his ID and badge. He wasn't lying. His name was James Morrison; not *that* James Morrison. Even though the world had been flipped on its head, I felt as though I could still trust an officer of the law. Some childhood thought perhaps? I threw his badge back to him and lowered my gun slightly.

"Where are you heading?" I asked, a little softer than I had been previously.

"Scotland," he replied confidently. "No infection up there. You?"

"Essex," I replied without explanation.

"Why Essex?" the man replied with an edge of concern. He lowered his arms now. "I thought it fell days ago?"

"What?!" I asked in alarm. "They were still transporting people there. The news said …"

"You can't believe the news, guy. They're lying," he replied, then added with confusion, "It was you military types who told the Con-stab that."

"Military types?" I replied equally, if not more, confused. I looked down at myself. Military-grade boots, guns, and driving a military vehicle. I could see how he made the mistake. "Not military, James."

"You act like one," he laughed. He suddenly lunged forward with hand outstretched. I aimed my gun at his chest, fear driving me. His eyes widened again and he started saying loudly, "Whoa, whoa, whoa. Just gonna shake your hand. We're still a civilised species after all." He leaned forward again, slowly this time, hand outstretched. My finger hovered over the trigger as I reached out with my other hand. We shook our hands, gentlemen at the end of the world.

"I'm James Morrison. Official introduction over with," he laughed, gripping my hand tightly, "And you are?"

"Sam. Sam Lincoln-Ward," I replied, releasing his hand.

"Posh name," he remarked with a smile.

"Not so posh person," I said, smiling back. The smile lingered on my face, even though I needed to say something which wasn't so nice. "Look, I can take you as far as Essex. It may be out your way a little bit, but you will be far enough from London that it might be safer."

"That would be brilliant," James replied, interrupting me as a huge smile spread across his face.

"But!" I said loudly to reinforce my point. "There will be some rules. Firstly, I still don't trust you entirely."

"The way of the world now." He nodded in agreement.

"Secondly, I need you to tell me everything you know about Essex and a few other things," I said slowly. I wanted to make the point clear. I *needed* to know every little detail.

"Will do what I can," he smiled. He seemed genuine and more than happy to help. He reached for his tyre iron.

"Thirdly, I want you to leave all weapons in the back of the Jeep," I quickly said before he could retrieve it. He began to protest, but I added, "I will do the same. We can think of it as a show of trust."

He didn't look happy about it but agreed anyway. He put his weapons in the back of the Jeep, as did I. My assault rifle and handgun anyway, he didn't need to know about my spear-knife. I wasn't stupid enough to trust him. I returned to the wheel, struggling to put the new one on. James stood there and stared at me while I struggled. I dropped the heavy tyre and kicked it angrily.

"Piece of junk," I spat in frustration. James stepped forward; clearly uneasy about being around me. That was fine, I felt the same.

"Never changed a tyre before?" he asked cautiously.

I shook my head. "Only in theory."

"Let me show you," he said, looking at the tyre iron in my

hand and smiling. He had been using one as a weapon. I had used it as a tool. He held his hand out for it, and I passed it uneasily. My hand shifted slightly, ready to grab my spear-knife if I needed to. He took the tool and bent down to work on the tyre. He talked me through it, and I watched, taking every little detail in. I had just read descriptions online; actually watching it done made a lot more sense. Within minutes, the new tyre was on and the bolts were in place. We were ready to roll. He handed me back the tyre iron; a gesture of trust and reassurance. I took it and smiled. Things could turn out alright.

As we both climbed into the car, I said to him, almost as a last ditch effort, "Just don't make me regret trusting you."

"You and me both," Officer James Morrison laughed, slamming his door. I pushed my foot down on the accelerator and we were off.

CHAPTER 17

We travelled in silence for the first part of the journey. Neither of us spoke. We had nothing to talk about. We were together out of convenience more than anything else. Sure he had information for me, but we had a long journey ahead. Why would I want to waste that one chance of conversation so early on? James leaned forward and switch the radio on, looking for something to break the silence. He found only static. He adjusted the frequency and left it on.

"The military use this frequency for emergency broadcasts," he explained before he put his head back and closed his eyes. He was really trusting. Something which would get him killed. For a fleeting moment, I considered stabbing him in the neck to teach him a lesson about the new world. Then the thought was gone. What the hell was wrong with me? Where the hell had that came from? I looked at the reflection of myself in the car mirror. Looking back at me was the familiar, albeit tired, face. It probably was the exhaustion. Hopefully.

After a few more minutes of silence, with James asleep and myself deep in thought, it was broken. There was a voice, but the source wasn't either of us. It was the radio crackling to life. James opened his eyes with instant awareness of where he was. Even in my own bed, I would often wake with confusion;

James was the opposite. Both our eyes darted to each other and then the radio. There was shouting in the background of wherever the broadcast was coming from. We both shared an excited look. After a few moments of static and background noise, a voice came through the speakers.

"This is Major Byron calling for a full retreat of London. It is lost," the voice said urgently, full of sorrow. There was gunfire in the background, followed by screams. "All military forces have approximately ten minutes to exit London. Get the hell out of there."

More background conversation.

"I am disregarding my orders by warning you," he stated, and then added more quietly, for the people with him, "I am going down with the city."

There was an outcry in the background and a few protests of those closest to the major. He silenced them with a shout.

"If you don't leave London, you will die," the major continued. "I have received a message from the Brass that Operation: Guy Fawkes has been initiated."

That was clearly a message for the armed forces only. What the hell was "Operation: Guy Fawkes"?

"The Prime Minister is dead. Finally, consider this confirmation of the disbanding of the British Army and any loyal organised military force. I have no one left to report to. This is it. Whoever is left out there, good luck," the major said, signing off for the last time. There were a few moments of silence as gunfire continued in the background. The radio had been left on and the major added, perhaps to the men around him and those listening in, "It has been an honour serving with each and every one of you."

There were more screams, and snarls of the undead, closer to the transmitter that time. There was heavy gunfire, a loud and sudden gunshot, followed by a heavy thud. No more human voices came over that radio again. There were only the snarls of the undead, and the crunch of bones for another minute before I finally switched it off. We didn't need to hear it. We looked at each other uneasily. It wasn't pleasant hearing the final moments of a man's life, even more so when they were ended in such a brutal manner. What hit home harder, however, was the fact that London had officially fallen. It had finally happened. There had been fighting for months to stem the tide of undead. I knew the news gave us propaganda, but I still believed we had a chance of winning. The city had actually fallen. *The city which defied the odds.* Now it belonged to the undead. It was impossible to get my head around. Actual confirmation that it was a lost cause was just so … terrifying. London: previous population, eight point three million … current *living* population: *unknown.* A secondary blow came when I realised there would be no more military fighting for "Queen and Country." The military were potential enemies.

That was the day order fell apart. That's how it started; the beginning of the end. The rest of the world would follow London.

That was it, the apocalypse.

CHAPTER 18

Minutes passed and neither of us spoke. We drove along slowly. We were both adjusting to the information we had just heard. So many unanswered questions. How did it finally come to it? Who gave the final orders? Why had the military disbanded? One question that would be answered in mere minutes was, "What was Operation: Guy Fawkes"? We continued driving for approximately ten minutes when we heard an intense rumbling. It reverberated through the vehicle and in my bones. It felt as though the ground was splitting apart to swallow me whole. At least that would relieve me of the horror I was living in. I brought the Jeep to a standstill, staring around me and then up at the sky. Several black objects in the distance sped towards me and passed overhead. They were military jets. They almost went by unseen. I opened the door and climbed out. I had always thought there was something fascinating about fighter jets. They seemed so sleek but mysterious. They carried on in the direction we had come from, faster than the speed of sound, their rumbles trying in vain to catch up with them. In the distance was London, exactly where the jets were going. In a few moments, the jets had reached London, and that was when the bombs fell.

At first, there was nothing. Then, huge balls of light, heat and fire exploded throughout the city. A depraved firework display. Swirling fiery infernos danced as they engulfed the infrastructure they had hit. Dazzling displays of colours as various pieces of human creation burned. *The New Year's firework display had nothing on it.* It was mesmerising and horrifying all in one. The light reached me first, followed by the crashing roar of the explosion. More and more of those explosions occurred in the distance as they claimed buildings for inferno. The flames engulfed buildings, and the blasts often only left the skeletal remains of the once-strong structures. More jets flew overhead to join the ones above the city. A secondary round of bombs fell, and more destruction unfolded. Huge sections of the city would be nothing but death; the flames that spread would ensure that nothing survived. I watched as more buildings collapsed; their downfall caused other buildings to crumble. I could just see the top of the London Eye in the distance. There was a sudden explosion, and then I couldn't see the London Eye anymore. What was left of the government was destroying London. I didn't understand why they would do it. Maybe they thought that, by destroying the epicentre of the infection, they could solve the problem? That couldn't be it though. The infection had already spread beyond London. It couldn't be contained. It had to be an act of spite.

I imagined some government officials, or possibly military generals, sitting around thinking, "*You kill us, and we destroy you. If we can't have London, no one can.*"

I understood that. I understood *that* logic. Revenge is good, but only when the ones being punished understand it. There is no retribution if the ones it is being directed at can't even acknowledge it. The bombing of London was an empty attack. It would only make people feel superficially better. In that moment, maybe it was the most we could ask for. The future was grim.

I stared at the burning capitol for a while longer before I suddenly became aware of the undead slowly moving towards us.

"James," I said calmly, snapping him out of his thoughts. His eyes pulled away from London and looked at me. His face was slack, and tears brimmed his eyes. I silently nodded behind him. He glanced over his shoulder and nodded back to me. He climbed into the Jeep, as did I. I stared into the rear-view mirror for one last look at London. The city was an inferno. London truly was hell that day. We drove away.

Night approached. There wasn't anywhere safe to go; we were on the motorway. There were a few other cars around, and no undead as far as we could see. There were street lights along the motorway, but they didn't turn on. Darkness was falling and they hadn't even begun to glow. It was going to be a dark night. James and I had agreed that we needed to pull over for the night before it got too dark. If we carried on driving, we would need to turn on the headlights, which would attract unwanted attention for miles. The question was: Where? We discussed the side of the road but decided against it when we saw the edge of the road sloped off into an embankment. The undead could be on us in seconds and we wouldn't even see them before it was too late. We looked at a map we had found in the vehicle for any buildings in the surrounding area. Nothing. The only choice left was the middle of the road. Although it seemed counter-intuitive, it was the safest option. Sure, the undead would see us, but we could also see them. There were also other vehicles on the road, so why would they feel the need to stop at ours? The undead didn't appear to have any supernatural sixth sense to detect the living, so they wouldn't find us. Finally, we also agreed to take shifts when it came to sleeping. James volunteered me to sleep first, since I'd been driving all day. I told him I didn't mind staying up longer but he insisted. I felt uneasy about the idea. Would that be when he would make his move? *Kill him first,* my inner voice said, piping up when I least needed it. I ignored it; it didn't push the subject.

I drove for another hour before the dark was on us entirely. I slowed the car to a stop about midway across lanes in an attempt to look as inconspicuous as possible. I felt more like a beacon with a neon sign which said: "eat here."

"You sure you don't want to sleep first?" I asked one last time as I shut off the engine.

"I'm certain, guy," James reiterated with a smile. "You look exhausted."

I inadvertently yawned after he said that. He was right, I was exhausted. My eyes burned and felt heavy. My muscles ached, and my bones felt like they were made of glass. I felt that if I closed my eyes to blink, I wouldn't reopen them until a few hours later. Sleep was waiting to snatch me into its quiet embrace.

"Fine," I said grudgingly as I clambered out of the driver's seat and into the back compartment of the Jeep. It wouldn't be a comfy sleep on the cramped, cold, metal floor, but sleep would be sleep.

"I'll wake you up in three hours," James explained.

"Yeah," I nodded. I put my head down on my bag and pulled my sleeping bag over myself for warmth. I went to ask one more question but slipped off the edge of the conscious world.

Dreams were always weird to think about; I never

understood the purpose of them. What use was lying down and hallucinating for four to nine hours? Did they keep your mind entertained while you slept? It made sense for survival purposes, hiding away in the nights where we weren't the most feared predator on the planet. Sleeping at night would keep us safe while the night predators prowled; they kept us asleep. Or were dreams simulations-type activities for different scenarios your own brain cooked up? That would also help for survival purposes if you are already prepared for something. Regardless of the cause, I don't know how the dream I had in the Jeep helped as a survival scenario. In the dream, a clown chased me. I hated clowns. Not as a phobia, but they creeped me out. Dream-clown wasn't a normal clown, however. It stood over nine foot tall, with disproportionate limbs. Its arms reached down to the ground and its legs were too short; similar to a gorilla. It chased after me, somehow keeping up even with its stubby legs. He tried to suffocate me but I wriggled away every time. Occasionally, the clown would shout, "Don't you dare run with those scissors!" before trying to decapitate me with an absurdly large pair of scissors. I didn't know where I was running to but I was sure if I found Alice, then everything would be okay. She could deal with the clown. Then the scene changed and I was in Essex. I was on Alice's sofa, where I had slept the one time I visited her family; family values and all that. I heard shuffling and thuds. I stood up and began walking towards the window, the source of the noise. I was in my boxers. I continued my slow and uneasy walk towards the window. The curtains were closed, which my hand reached out to open. I knew what I would find when I opened them, yet I couldn't stop myself. My hand gripped the edge of the curtain. I pulled it aside. Undead pressed against the window. Faces snarling, fleshy sores smeared gore across the glass. A few

131

pounded the glass. Cracks slowly spread across the surface. It would break soon. All I could do was stand there as the glass collapsed and the undead poured over me. I recognised some of the undead. I didn't know where from. The faces blended together after a while. As the undead tumbled in, they pulled me to the ground. Teeth tore my flesh. Cutting. Ripping. I tried to scream but couldn't; my mouth was blocked. Something about the scene felt wrong. As I came apart, I realised what it was with a strange clarity. There was no smell. No stench of the dead. No smell of rotting flesh. It was a dream. I closed my eyes ready to die and, in the same motion, opened my eyes in reality. James' hand was clamped over my mouth, his body pressed down on mine. I couldn't move.

"Shh," James whispered calmly. He pressed his hand tighter against my mouth. I tried to scream, but it was no good. I tried to thrash out but I couldn't. He held me down firmly, using his larger body mass to his advantage. *This is the end for me.* I tried to help someone and he tried to kill me! Suddenly, I'd had enough. I accepted my fate and just relaxed. James eased the pressure on me as I did so, and loosened his grip. Had he thought he'd won and given up prematurely? I felt revitalised in that instant. I pushed forward with my attack, spurred on by his momentary lapse. He pushed me back down: superior strength won again. Once more, he then shushed me and pulled his hands away slowly. He raised his hands to show they were empty and not a threat. I breathed heavily and my heart pounded. I stared at him, confusion on my face. He raised one finger to his lip and made the universal sign for "be quiet." I sat up slowly, still on edge. He pointed out the window. I leaned forward and squinted through the glass and into the dark. Shadowy figures moved around outside. As my eyes adjusted to the limited moonlight, I could tell by their shambling gait that they were undead. They wandered the motorway aimlessly, dragging their feet across the concrete. Their shoulders sagged from the sheer weight of themselves. Suddenly, one walked by the window and scuffed against the vehicle when it got too close. I didn't move and held my breath. The undead woman didn't give us more than a hungry glance. She couldn't see us as we hid in the darkness of the vehicle. I waited for her to move on before I spoke.

"What happened?" I whispered as quietly as I could muster; it still felt like a booming shout. My face felt sore from where James had pressed down on it.

"Undead moved in about an hour ago. Came from the embankments," James whispered in reply. He looked at me rubbing my face and smiled. "It was all well and dandy; they were going to move on but got *distracted*."

"Distracted?" I said, repeating the word he had deliberately emphasised.

"You started to shout out in your sleep. Calling a name," James said. "The undead heard and got a bit excited. Obviously they couldn't tell where it came from; otherwise, this would have been a very different conversation, guy."

"What name?" I asked, slightly groggy, trying desperately to remember. It was all a blur.

"Amongst the screams?" he said with a hushed laugh, and then said with a much more serious tone, "Alice. You called out Alice."

"Alice," I breathed thoughtfully, my dream coming back to me in pieces.

"Alice, huh?" James repeated quietly. He stared into the darkness outside, not really looking at anything. "Is she the reason you're heading to Essex?"

I looked at him. I had a choice to let James, whom I

barely knew, into my life. I'd be telling him something which I hadn't spoken to anyone else about.

I smiled and decided my answer. "Yeah, James; the only reason."

CHAPTER 19

I explained my story to James. I explained almost *everything*. I explained how I had left Bristol. I explained how I had got to where I was. I even explained in detail why I was heading to Essex. In return, James told me his story.

James had never wanted to be a police officer. He had always wanted to be a photographer. He then went on to say he could have as well if he wasn't "bloody poor with a camera." He decided to take a photography course at a local college, something which he failed at so badly that even the teacher was impressed. Apparently, he was the first person to fail the course in the entire time the teacher had run it, which is an achievement all in itself. He then waited a few years and took photography lessons. His logic was "college courses were for kids anyway." He passed the course, barely. When I say barely, I truly mean barely. Although he didn't let on, he made it sound like he had a thing with the teacher, possibly the only reason she passed him. After blaming the school, the course and the "amateur equipment," James decided it was time to do things his way. He went out and bought the most expensive camera his funds could afford, as well as multiple lenses for it. He was determined to be a photographer. He had the best equipment and ambition. He was certain that was all he needed; after all, "the greats didn't take lessons."

On the way home with his newly bought equipment, a man stepped out of an alley. The man was clearly drug-addled, with some possible alcohol abuse in there for good measure. He had been beyond the world of the sober for the previous twenty-four hours and had just come round from a binge. The first thing he saw, when stumbling out of the alley, was James: a young twenty-something, fairly scrawny and waving his carrier bag around. A carrier bag with an electronics shop logo on it, filled to the brim with new purchases. The man licked his bloody and cracked lips. He needed his next fix and flogging the young man's junk would get him that. He approached James.

"Gi-me the bag," he slurred, swaying side to side.

"Huh?" James said, puzzled, turning to look at the source of the voice.

"I said," the man replied loudly, taking time to enunciate his words correctly, "give me the bag!"

James laughed; the sight of the drug addict trying to relieve him of his possessions was hilarious. He didn't stand a chance against James! The reason he stopped laughing was because the man pulled out a knife and pointed it at James. His hand shook wildly as the drugs left his body. A million thoughts and scenarios went through James' head in an instant. Should he tackle the man and wrestle the knife from him? That would probably end badly for himself. So the next option: He could run. Would he be able to make it? Probably. He could easily outrun the man. But was it worth it? Without a doubt, no. His life wasn't worth a bag of goods. He sighed and placed the bag on the ground and took a step back. He raised his hands to show he wasn't a threat. The knife-wielding drug addict smiled, revealing broken and blackened teeth. He walked forward confidently, almost a swagger in his walk.

"Thanks, dick-head," the man laughed as he bent down to pick up the bag. James would have let him walk away with his stuff until he heard the insult, and anger flared inside him. He was angry that his new camera was being taken, but being mocked as well? That wasn't going to happen. The man was fully bent over now; he struggled to keep his balance. Without a word, James ran the few steps between them, pulled his foot back, then swung it forward with all his might, right into the man's face. Facing the ground, the man didn't see the foot coming until it was too late. James' black trainer connected with the man's face. He felt the impact and then the collapse of the thief's nose as it crumpled with the force of the kick. The man screamed and fell back. Blood pumped out of his nose in rivulets. His face was smeared in it, as was James' trainer, the black material glistening with blood. He felt a little sick, not just because it was blood, but because he had no idea what diseases the man carried.

"Yun boke mah nosse!" he cried out in pain. James looked at him in disgust; he was decrepit and disgusting. He walked over to the man, kicked aside the knife and picked up his bag.

James had no idea where it came from, but he announced, "I am performing a citizen's arrest! Try to move, *dick-head*!"

The man looked at James in fear, not understanding what had happened. He knew enough to lay there and not move. James pulled out his mobile phone, a brick of a device, and called the police. James stated over the phone that there had been an attempted mugging. He also reported that the man was injured and required medical attention. James put down the phone and waited for the police to arrive.

"What happened here?" an officer asked as they arrived at the scene.

"He tried to mug me. He had a knife," James reported simply. He pointed towards the knife and held up his bag of camera equipment.

"At it again?" the officer said to the man. He obviously recognised the man from past experience.

"He boke mah nosse!" the man sobbed in reply. He had been sobbing the entire time while James waited for the police to arrive.

"Did you?" the officer asked, looking at James. He frowned, looking at the scrawny kid with more money than sense.

"No," James lied calmly. Blood still glistened on his trainer. The officer saw it.

The officer sighed, pinched the bridge of his nose, and asked, "Well, what happened?"

"He fell over," James replied calmly. The officer carried on staring at James' trainer; he raised his eyebrows, expecting more, which James didn't give.

The officer, with a hint of a smile, pushed on, "What did he fall on?"

"My foot," James replied coldly. He had never liked the law, but the scrutiny he was under was making things worse. He was *not* a criminal!

The officer analysed the situation. He knew James had lied, but it was far more trouble to call him on it. Plus, the officer felt biased as he utterly despised the thief. He had seen the same man get away with more than any one person should; he would take any chance to put him away.

"You aren't under arrest," the officer began, speaking to James. James' anger flared again; he thought the police were trying to screw him over! The officer continued, "But we would like to take an official statement."

"And if I refuse?" James snapped back confidently.

"Then that idiot goes free," the officer whispered quietly so that no one else could hear. He added, "I know you're lying, kid, but I hate this guy enough to turn a blind eye … this time."

James stared intensely at the officer's face. He had always had a knack for telling if a person's intention were true or not. He had a good feeling about the situation, albeit utter confusion at the police officer's attitude about the law. He knew his rights and, if he went willingly, he could leave whenever he liked. He wasn't under arrest after all.

"Let's get going then," James replied, nodding towards the police car. The officer smiled and guided James to the car. He got in, without handcuffs and doors unlocked. The fact James had freedom in the back of the police car made him feel a lot better about it all. He watched the drug addict get manhandled into another police car, a completely different experience to what he had.

The journey was equally as good. James expected tight-lipped, cold officers as he had seen in the movies. That wasn't the case. The officers laughed and had a conversation with him; they didn't refer to the reason he was in the car once. They spoke to him as a human. At first, James was resistant but, after a while, he gave in and managed to have a few laughs. When they arrived at the station, he watched the thief get taken in one direction, while James was taken into another: a waiting room. An officer offered him food and drinks. He also was given plastic gloves and a cloth to clean off his trainers; the officers were so friendly. James felt uneasy to begin with, but realised that the officers were just everyday people doing a job. After a few minutes, James was led into an interview room. On the other side of the table was the officer who had convinced him to come in. He half-expected to see a one-way mirror, but there was none; he actually felt a little disappointed by that. The officer was leaned back on his chair, as most children do in school. When he saw James, he sat forward and smiled. James sat in the chair, and the officer waved the other officers away. When the door shut, the officer made a show of turning off the recording device.

"Happy?" the officer asked with a smile. James nodded, a smile flickering at the corners of his mouth. James loved how sly the officer was acting; he could relate!

There were a few moments of silence before James spoke: "What now?"

"Right. I need you to tell me everything that happened," the officer replied, a little uneasy at what he had just said. James began to protest when the officer cut in, "I really need to know. I want this guy put away. He has caused more trouble than he ever should have been allowed. I need to know what actually happened, to check for inconsistencies."

James stared at him for a moment. The man was genuine. James sighed and opened his mouth and told him everything.

The officer listened intensely to the short tale. He nodded in approval when it came to the kick. He laughed when James told him what he'd said about the citizen's arrest. When James had finished, the officer was silent, deep in thought. After a few moments, he spoke.

"That's interesting," the officer said with a smile. "Now let me tell you what actually happened."

The officer went on to explain how James was *actually* on his way home when the man came at him with a knife without a word of warning. He explained that James panicked and ran. In the chase, the man had fallen flat on his face, breaking his nose. James went back to see if he needed help after kicking the knife away. In the process, James had gotten blood on his trainer. He rang for emergency services, claiming the man needed help. James had explained what happened, and they felt the need to send a police car as opposed to an ambulance. That was the full story.

"And that is what you will write as your statement," the officer finished.

"Won't people get suspicious?" James questioned. He felt uneasy about doing this, but he was still angry at the man.

"Why would they?" The officer laughed. "Who are they going to believe, a known troublemaker and liar? Or a young lad with a police officer to back him up?"

The officer turned on the recorder.

James nodded with a smile. "Should I begin?"

"Yes, yes you should," the officer replied.

When the forms had been completed, and the drug addict had been put in a temporary cell, James was set to leave. On the way out, guided by the officer who had helped him, James looked around. He realised how wrong he had been about the police. These were decent people with a good job. He looked at his bag of camera equipment and wondered if he could take it back for a refund. A smile grew over his face as the officers waved him off.

"Any questions?" the police officer asked before he sent James on his way. James gave one final look round.

"Yeah, I do actually," James replied.

"Oh aye?" the officer asked, surprised.

James took a deep breath and asked with a smile, "What does it take to be a police officer?"

The officer smiled and, eight years later, he was James' senior officer.

CHAPTER 20

Ten years, three months and four days after his life-changing encounter with the police, James was doing a patrol on the streets of London. He had only just been assigned there. There had been a lot of trouble and the London Metropolitan Police Service, as well as the City of London Police, needed extra staff from other departments across the country for assistance. As an up and coming officer with a series of honours, James went for it without a second thought. In London, there had been fighting and violence. It only got worse. People were biting and eating other people! They were crazed. Groups of people, with no prior relationship to each other, displayed the same symptoms. One moment James would tackle a well-suited businessman to handcuff him, who had tried to kill another person for no apparent reason. Next, he would be talking an elderly woman out of attacking him. He had to restrain her, but only after his partner had been bitten by the mad hag. His partner went to the hospital to get checked, and James went to the closest police station with the woman in his back seat. She thrashed like a wild animal the whole time. She threw herself around the compartment and smashed against the metal grill which separated her from him. He had long since stopped telling her to calm down and relax. She was deranged. When James arrived at the station, he didn't bring her in with him. He needed help. He strolled into the police station to find chaos, which was no different from the previous weeks. People ran around or answered phones. Some argued, and others checked paperwork. It was madness. He reported to the desk and asked for assistance for "another one." An officer he didn't recognise went with him. The officer looked tired; everyone had been pulling double shifts and it still wasn't enough. Whatever was happening with the people, it spread fast.

They walked towards to the car, preparing to manhandle the elderly woman. When they got there, they saw there was shattered glass and blood everywhere. There was no sign of the woman. She had smashed through the window and escaped. He had no idea where the little old woman had got all her strength. She was long gone. It wasn't even worth reporting. There would be hundreds of similar cases over the following days. One more wouldn't go amiss. The other officer shrugged at James and went back inside. James sighed and checked his phone. His partner should have checked in over an hour ago. He considered phoning the hospital but knew the lines would be engaged. So many people would be calling as they looked for missing loved ones, or paranoid people checking in with odd symptoms. He had no idea what was the cause. Some thought it was a new drug but no trace had been found by the police, regardless of what the news speculated. James hadn't smoked for over ten years, and he hadn't wanted to since he stopped, but he needed a cigarette right then more than ever. He ran his hands through his hair and headed back into the station.

Three weeks later, James stood in full riot gear with a baton in one hand and riot shield in the other. A line of officers pushed down the street. People, not quite rioters, charged forward. They ran. They snarled. They moaned. They almost frothed at the mouth. Not a white rabid foam, but a red … something. Their movement was awkward and uneasy, and their arms swung as if they had no control over them. A few fell to the ground and were trampled by the others. They weren't fazed by it. James was fairly certain he saw one person get trampled and then get back up and carry on running. He couldn't be sure as the helmet visor made it difficult to see. There were about half the amount of officers as there were people, but they held a firm line and their riot gear made up for the lack of numbers. The police had long since given up trying to arrest the people. The numbers of *rioters* had grown to the point they couldn't try to contain them. They were on riot control. However, unofficial orders told them to crack skulls if it reduced the numbers. The police weren't bothered with the law anymore; rules could be bent where they needed to be. Especially since so many officers had gone missing since it all started. James' original partner never returned from the hospital. That wasn't uncommon either. Officers wouldn't turn up to work, never to be seen again. That was a partial lie; James swore he had seen a few officers amongst the mad rioters. On top of everything, there were rumours of the military moving in. There had been whispers here and there, but the military meant the situation was getting worse, which also meant escalation. Escalation meant they were going to start shooting. Did the higher-ups think martial law was in order? Bringing in armed forces was an extreme move. The rioters got closer, an unnatural rage on their faces. The police shifted and braced themselves in unison. James took a deep breath. The people slammed into the line of tightly packed riot shields. James took a step back from the sheer force of the collision. Pressed up against the transparent high-impact plastic were the contorted faces of the rioters. Although they were all human faces, there was something inhuman about them. Dead eyes, sullen faces, blackened patches of skin. They looked like the corpses James had occasionally seen. James stared into the eyes of the young teenager who was pressed up against his shield. He had a jagged gash on his neck, which seemed odd. Surely no one could survive a wound like that? James closed his eyes and slammed his baton down on the teenager's head.

Two months later, the military operated within the city fulltime. They pretty much moved in overnight; rumour said every city across England experienced the same. The military came in and set up roadblocks everywhere. They checked everyone who came in and out of the city. The tube system was patrolled by armed personnel; there were military in every carriage. They had taken over the police force, and all remaining officers now answered to them. Also, every squad of officers – yes, there were squads – were accompanied with fully armed military. Curfews were enforced throughout the city. The London economy was almost put to a standstill. There were rumours of evacuation. No one truly knew what was going on. It was all hearsay.

It only took another six months for the occasional riots to spread throughout London and occur at an hourly rate. The military disconnected the police phones. There wasn't a need for people to phone in anymore. The riots were happening right outside the station. The military and police were losing. Law and order had broken down. The military and police imposed what law they could, *where* they could. James noted how he wore more gear than he had seen in his entire life. Every police officer had riot gear on, but it was a lot thicker than the regular stuff; it made movement hard. He also had a full helmet on that connected to the body armour. No flesh was exposed. Each helmet had a camera on it to record everything. They looked like something out of a film set in a futuristic dystopia. The police officers were given handguns, as well as a tougher baton. A few officers had made "adjustments" to their batons, which included the odd spike or a metal bolt. The batons looked like medieval weapons made to cause maximum damage on contact and, the truth be told, that was the reason. James never changed his baton; he felt that was too brutal. Besides, the rioters were still human as far as he was concerned. He couldn't help but feel some of his fellow officers took too much enjoyment out of it. He never tried to kill anyone, and only ever defended himself. He had seen other officers openly try to kill others as they worked themselves up into a bloodthirsty frenzy. On one occasion, officers held down a woman while another swung his baton like a golf club into her head. Her skull eventually gave way under the force and they all laughed. James just stood and watched in horror. He had frequent thoughts about escaping London, but getting past the roadblocks would be near impossible. Finally, they received the message that the infection had spread beyond London.

A further two months passed before James realised the infected weren't actually human. He had treated the infected as crazed victims of something unknown. He put them down but didn't cause any deaths intentionally, although that was difficult as the infected rarely stayed down. He saw people clubbed to the ground and receive broken bones, only to force themselves back up and keep going. As time went on, the infected began to look worse and worse. Chunks of flesh hung off faces, bullet wounds were congealed with gore, arms were twisted at horrific angles, and they still kept coming. Yet he still convinced himself they were living, breathing humans. What truly made him realise that they were no longer living was the death of a friend.

One day, during the street wars which were daily life in London, the fighting was especially intense. There was fighting at every second of the day. What made that day different was that there was no break in the combat. Usually, there would be time to retreat to one of the many fortified police stations for a time out and to recover. It was time to grab food or drink, and maybe even a little sleep if they could. Not that day. They had fought nonstop for more than twenty-four hours straight. The men were exhausted. Ammunition ran low, and so did other supplies. When jogging down one street as a group, they got distracted. The men were tired and weren't concentrating. Suddenly, hundreds of infected poured out of an alleyway. They crashed straight into the group. The men were scattered. Several of the officers were knocked to the ground, never to be seen again. The other officers were split into two groups; a wall of the infected separated them. The men fought them, but there was no time for guns. It was up close and personal. It soon became apparent they wouldn't win the little skirmish. James and a couple of men retreated; they could regroup with the rest later. They jogged down a street. They weaved in and out of abandoned cars. They dodged between the infected, knocking them aside until they found temporary safety in an alley. They panted heavily, their masks steamed up.

"I-I can't get me breath," Jim gasped. Jim had been James' best friend over the previous few months. They had been thrown together several times when put on patrol and they had got friendly. His name wasn't actually Jim, it was also James. The only problem was that they both turned up every time someone asked for James. The nickname "Jim" was given to him.

"Just chill for five minutes," James said, also panting.

"I'm taking me helmet off," Jim wheezed. He unclipped his helmet and dropped it to the ground, sucking in huge lungfuls of air.

"Get your helmet back on, guy," James commanded. He was fully aware how much danger they were in.

"Just a few more min—" Jim began but was silenced by a gurgling sound. James looked around and saw an infected man biting into Jim's neck, severing the jugular vein. Blood pumped out and down the front of his armour, pooling on the ground. James smashed his baton against the man's head, and he dropped to the floor dead. He then quickly grabbed Jim, who was close to collapse.

"Cover me!" James ordered the remaining men. He lowered Jim to the ground as his breaths got shallower. "Stay with me, guy."

James tried to stop the bleeding, which he succeeded in doing, but only because Jim's heart had stopped pumping.

"Crap," James shouted angrily. He kicked the wall, his boot bouncing off the brickwork. "We need to get out of here! Now!"

James gave commands on how to proceed. He had to leave Jim's body there; it would only slow them down.

"Sorry," he whispered to his fallen friend. He went to walk away when he saw Jim open his eyes. James' eyes widened and he said confusedly, "Guy?"

Jim stood up uneasily, swaying as he did so. His eyes were unclear and clouded. Jim reached out for James. James put his hand out to support his friend. Jim's eyes focussed on him.

"You okay?" James asked in disbelief. He was sure Jim was gone. He couldn't see how he was moving after such blood loss. Jim opened his mouth for what James thought was a reply, but instead tried to sink his teeth into him. James threw him to one side, unwilling to strike his friend. Jim came back at him again, wild, like the other infected had been. James held him back, striking at Jim's face. The other officers in the group looked on in shock. Jim didn't even register he was being struck. James stared at the fleshy and gory hole in his neck. It was in that moment, when his dead friend tried to kill him, he realised that the infected were no longer human. James pushed him to the ground with one final shove and slammed his baton into Jim's skull. It caved in, bloody grey matter on the end of his baton. Jim's face was unrecognisable. James looked away in shame. His focus was on the rest of the group now; ignoring his dead friend.

"We need to move on," James commanded. They all moved on.

James knew he had to get out of the city if he wanted to live. He didn't know where he would go from there; the infection had spread far beyond London. The last he had heard was that Essex had fallen. How far would it carry on? Things had gone from worse to hellhole in the span of thirty days! The men he fought with were almost non-existent as most had been killed or had taken their own lives. Others had flat out deserted and tried to make it on their own. James thought being on his own was the best way to be. He had seen the men he had become friends with turn into monsters – both the dead and the living kind. Some took pleasure in killing the undead. Others gunned down people who they knew weren't infected. They always said they didn't realise their targets weren't trying to kill them, but the grin always gave them away. If he wasn't killed by the undead, it would probably be by his former friends. James would leave at the first chance he got.

In the middle of a conflict, when his men were deep in gore, he ran. There was nothing special about that conflict; they all played out the same anyway. He deserted his post and ran. He wasn't moving anywhere near the pace he would have liked. He trundled on slowly, weighed down by everything he wore. He stopped for a breather and looked down at his gear. With the armour on, he moved too slowly. He wouldn't be able to get out of London before nightfall at his current pace. Even worse, he might be spotted by his *comrades*. James didn't want to, but he abandoned his armour in a doorway. He held his helmet momentarily, staring into the camera as it still recorded.

"Sorry, London," he muttered quietly. He dumped it with the rest and walked away. A nearby explosion spurred him onwards. He ran. He would get out of the city one way or another. He beat down undead until his baton broke in two, only to pick up a bloody tyre iron and continue in the same way. When he reached a roadblock, he saw it was empty. The chaos in London meant the roadblocks had been lost to the undead. Were they all like it? It didn't matter because he was free to leave. He turned and looked longingly at the city. He couldn't believe it was the end for that monument of human history.

He walked on.

On the outskirts of London, James saw an abandoned military Jeep on the motorway. He hadn't taken any other vehicles due to lack of opportunity, or because they were no longer in a condition to drive. The Jeep seemed almost too good to be true. He approached the Jeep, tyre iron in hand. He knew the former owner of the vehicle could be nearby and ready to take a bite out of him. He tried the handle of the passenger side with no success. He could hear movement. Maybe what was left of the original driver? He walked around the edge of the vehicle, weapon raised. He saw a figure crouched on the floor, gun barrel aimed squarely at his head.

"I suggest you go away, mate," the man said, his face turned into a snarl.

CHAPTER 21

When James had finished his tale, his face was ashen. Silence followed his story for a few minutes. Not because I wanted silence, but because James needed it. He was clearly deep in his own dark thoughts. His head was filled with the horrors he had seen, the death of his friend Jim, and the atrocities he had committed. He was innocent but, in his mind, he was the guilty party. That sort of guilt wouldn't be fixed with words from a stranger; James needed to come to terms with it on his own. I wasn't an expert on human behaviour. I may have taken a Psychology degree, but that was it. I had, however, interacted with a lot of people through my life. I recognised that people would blame themselves when it clearly wasn't their fault. Blame was a funny thing. People always looked for someone to attribute it to; when no one took it, it fell inward. James blamed himself because he couldn't find anyone else. What he should have been blaming was the virus that caused it all. That being said … was it even a virus? I had an above average understanding of how illness was caused, be it mental or physical. Was it a virus? Fungi? Bacteria? A parasite? Did anyone even know for sure? Sure, the media had taken to calling it the Daisy Virus, but that was for the average person who indulged in tabloid news and enjoyed a simple play on words. The scientific journals behind it had a lot more to say about the origin of the illness, but that still didn't amount to much.

Looking at the "sciencey" stuff behind it, it was still undetermined what form the micro-organism causing the dead to rise took. In fact, there was debate whether it even was a micro-organism at all. If it was a virus, that would make the most sense. A virus replicates within living, and only living, cells. In the case of the undead, that meant it would spread and infect each human before causing them to rise as undead. That meant the infection spread while the host was still alive, which didn't explain how it continued to function after the host body died. It shouldn't continue to replicate, yet it did. That begged the question of whether the "undead" were still alive. That didn't bear thinking about. The implications which followed would drive people mad. I doubted they were still alive. The state I had seen so many of the undead in … there was no way that was possible. The next option was bacteria.

Bacteria worked very differently than a virus because, unlike a virus, it could live anywhere. That included door handles, walls, and on food. Bacteria could survive in almost any conditions, even remaining dormant until the necessary conditions to replicate appeared. The Bubonic Plague was an example which was pretty deadly in human history, so why could "Daisy" not be a bacterium? But there are so many other things it could be. What about fungus, for example?

I'm not really sure how a fungus works; my knowledge of micro-organisms didn't stretch very far beyond the common ones. I do remember, however, a very weird fungus I once read about: the Ophiocordyceps Unilateralis. It worked its way into an ant's system and took over. All the ants ended up in a "zombified" state. They would climb to the top of the highest plant they could find and then the fungus would take them over completely. They would develop fungal growths and look generally terrifying. They did that in a continuous cycle to infect even more ants. The fungus completely controlled the ants and could spread it to others, very much like Daisy. Yet I hadn't seen abnormal growths on the undead, so I doubted it was that. Could it be a combination of micro-organisms?

Regardless of the origin of the reanimation sickness, nothing had worked against it. It was amazing what you could find online in the early days of the infection. I used to be amazed at the ability people had for finding films online before the cinema release. The fact you could find governmental and scientific reports of all the things they had tried was unbelievable. There were classified documents and people were posting them in forums. You rarely got chance to read them as they disappeared within minutes of appearing, but I managed to download a few before the inevitable deletion. I didn't re-share the files; they were for me. Besides, I didn't want to mysteriously disappear into a black van in the night, or that was how the rumour went. Many of the reports I read were mainly medical trials of what had been tried. There were several types of antibiotics used in test trials, but nothing restored the recently animated to living, or even to their dead state for that matter. The only cure was a bullet to the brain. Dismemberment did very little. There had been brain scans, body scans, and all sorts of scans and tests used on the undead. They showed very little information other than that those people were clinically dead. There was very little activity in the brain. Coma victims who were close to the end showed more signs of life. Yet there appeared to be some activity in the most primal parts of the brain; just enough to keep the undead moving. In short, the scientists couldn't find anything to suggest where this sickness had come from or how, except for a lead injection, to stop it. I think it was probably about that point the orders to shoot on sight came about. It was very hard to map a timeline with so much conflicting information and propaganda. No one would truly know what had happened unless they were there. That human history would be lost forever.

My internal monologue ended as I finished reflecting on the origin of Daisy. Light was growing outside, and neither of us had actually gotten much sleep. We were both too nervous to sleep, especially with the undead roaming so closely outside. I think we both wanted to get to know each other as well. We didn't entirely trust the other yet, and learning about the other's last few months was the best way to go about this. With daylight flooding through the windows, we were more likely to be noticed by the undead. The protection of darkness was almost non-existent as the sun climbed higher. We moved carefully through the vehicle. We wanted to get moving while it was still dark. I climbed back into the driver's seat. I had become the unofficial driver of our little party. Before I even started up the engine, I saw it wasn't going to be a simple getaway. Throughout the night, the undead had gravitated around the car. Not in a threatening manner, but that just seemed to be where they ended up once they stopped. Normally, that wouldn't be a problem as I would just run them down. However, with the undead so close, I couldn't build up enough speed to be able to turn them into a disgusting red mist. The only other option was to take them out the old-fashioned way: a bullet to the head. I explained that to James, who nodded in agreement. I also asked if he was any good with a handgun. He nodded and explained he was an exceptional shot. I gave my go ahead and he scooped up the handgun from the back of the Jeep. I told him his job was to only shoot if any undead got too close and I hadn't seen them. We needed to conserve ammunition. With that, he passed me the assault rifle and undid the roof hatch on the Jeep. I shouldered the rifle and opened the Jeep door. At the same time, James stood up through the roof hatch, handgun aimed and steady. I had considered using the machine gun on the Jeep, but I hadn't found any ammunition for it. Besides, the attention it would draw would be a hindrance. The door creaked as it opened, drawing the undead's attention. They all seemed to swivel towards me in unison in response to the noise. Upon seeing me leaning against the door, gun aimed head height, they charged. I checked my rifle was still single shot and let off my first shot. It struck the zombie I was aiming at in the head. The undead man crumpled to the ground, spraying a trail of brain and gore across the road where the bullet exited. I saw an undead girl coming from my left in the periphery of my vision. I swivelled to aim at her. I noticed she was pale, even for a dead girl. She was dressed all in black, with black eyeliner and black hair. She would have been classed as a stereotypical "Goth" girl. I stopped focussing on her human aspects and all that she once was, and instead focussed on the missing half of her lower face. Her tongue lolled out; there was no lower jaw to hide the workings of it. It was horrific. I squeezed off another round which dropped her almost headless body instantly. I returned my focus to the front of the Jeep. I needed to clear our escape. I fired a few more rounds. All but one dropped their target.

"Six o'clock!" I heard James shout, panic in his voice. I spun around to see double the amount of the undead that had been there previously.

"Screw this," I protested when I saw the sheer number of

undead running towards us. I ducked back into the Jeep, put the vehicle into reverse, and pushed my foot onto the pedal. I only slammed the door when we had begun speeding backwards. I heard James cry out in surprise, ducking back inside seconds later. He seemed to be breathing heavily from the sudden movement. I kept reversing until I was inches from the undead behind us, but far enough from the undead in front of us. I changed gear and hit my foot down on the pedal again. We sped forward, the Jeep picking up speed quickly.

"Brace yourself!" I said to James, who was sliding around on the metal floor behind me. We were mere seconds from the undead in front. Suddenly, we were mere seconds in front of where the undead had been. All that remained of them was the disgusting paint job they had left over the front of the Jeep. There were bits of gristle and blood all over the windscreen. Without thinking, I turned on the wipers, which made the gory mess so much worse. I felt bile rise in my throat, made worse by the fact I had yet to eat. On the other hand, what was worse? The fact I was thinking about food at a time like that? Or that I was affected to such a small degree by what I had seen that I was more concerned about my appetite? I couldn't help it. I was going down a slippery slope mentally. I gave the window a few squirts from the Jeep's reserves of window wash and then turned on the wipers again. That made things a lot better as the majority of the gore was cleared. However, there was still a reddish tinge to the glass, as the destruction had left a bloody film over the surface. I pretended I didn't see it and carried on driving.

"How're things back there?" I called to James over the roar of the engine.

"Bit bruised but all good," he replied cheerfully. He really was a happy-go-lucky guy. I, on the other hand, didn't want to know how he was doing. I was asking how the situation was going.

"The undead following?" I asked, rewording the question.

"Of course," he replied, looking out the back window. He added, "They're never gonna catch up at this rate."

"Good," I said matter-of-factly. Things had gone surprisingly well that time around. Before I knew it, I would be reunited with my Alice. That brought a smile to my face. Not much did anymore. I started thinking about her face, her lovely smile, and her golden hair which always smelled of coconut. I was slightly worried when my brain didn't recall the image as immediately as I would have liked. It was as if she was fading from my memory, which was impossible. It was like trying to picture someone I hadn't seen for years. I frowned. It had only been days since I had started out on my journey, but the toll it had taken on me was obviously a lot worse. The image of Alice came back to me eventually, and I kept focussing on it. Her little ears. Her brown eyes. No … Blue eyes? What the hell was wrong with me? I slammed my hands against the steering wheel and slapped myself a few times. I decided to think of a specific time. It was the first time I met her family. We travelled to Essex for her grandparent's sixtieth anniversary. We were going for a really fancy meal and it would be the first time I wore a tie. Alice dressed up and looked gorgeous. Her dress was beautiful and she looked so good in it. I focussed on that image. That was an image I needed to remember. I kept thinking about it, reinforcing it in my mind. Eventually, all the images fell into place as clear as day. I smiled again, content for the moment. I looked in the mirror, past my bloodshot eyes, and at James. He had a thousand-yard stare on his face. Every few seconds, his head would drop slightly before he jolted up again, wide-eyed.

"Hey bud," I said gently. James looked at me but he didn't speak. "Get some sleep, I'm good driving for now."

He nodded. He looked slightly confused but laid down on the cold metal of the Jeep and was asleep in seconds. He must have been exhausted. If his story held up then he hadn't slept properly for months. Any sleep he got would have been glimpses here and there. How was he even still functioning?

"How're you even still functioning?" a voice within questioned myself, one I hadn't heard from since it tried to convince me to kill my companion.

"Just leave it," I muttered aloud to myself. I thought I heard a snigger, then realised it was in my head also. I wasn't holding up too well myself, and that was putting it lightly. A combination of mental scarring and exhaustion wasn't going to end well for me or anyone around me. I couldn't break yet though. I *needed* to hold out until I saw my Alice. Blonde hair, blue-eyed, tall Alice. Blonde hair. Blue-eyed. Tall. *Alice*. I repeated the details to myself a few more times. I smiled at myself in the mirror. A wild-eyed lunatic grinned back at me.

I'm slipping.

CHAPTER 22

After sleeping solidly for three hours, James woke with a start. He scrambled for a weapon but didn't find one. The fog of his dreams cleared and he realised where he was. He relaxed, ever so slightly. He sat in silence for a while before finally speaking.

"Can I drive for a bit? Let you get some sleep," he asked, as though he was doing me a favour. However, I suspected he wanted to drive more for himself than to help me. Whatever he had dreamt about, it had shaken him up.

"Sure thing," I said, faked a yawn and laughed. I began to slow. I could pull over nearly anywhere on the miles of open road in front of me. Zero undead. Almost zero cars. I probably didn't even need to pull over, we could have just slowed in the middle of the road and climbed over each other. No one was around. I pulled over anyway. One does not simply forget the rules of the road. James and I both got out and stretched. I didn't realise how cramped my muscles were until I needed to use them. If the situation had been dangerous, it could have been the end for us. We both stretched ourselves. James used stretches he had learned with the police. I, on the other hand, used basic stretches I had previously learned in school over ten years before. I could see James trying not to laugh as he watched from the periphery of his vision. His stretches got more and more elaborate.

"Show off," I muttered as I walked past him. I topped the engine off with one of the jerry cans on the back of the Jeep. I walked away and stood on the edge of the road, staring down the grassy embankment. I waited a few seconds before undoing my zip and began emptying my bladder.

"Dirty git," I heard James say. My bladder immediately seized up when I realised I was on show.

"Aww," James taunted, "a little toilet shy?"

"Shut up," I protested. "I thought I would have time to deal with bladder shyness before it became a problem."

"No time like the present," James replied and strode up next to me, unzipped his jeans and let a torrent of urine flow onto the roadside.

"Dammit," I muttered before moving elsewhere to finish what I had started.

"Ahhh," he called to me, emphasising that he was peeing freely. He laughed and called, "Nothing better than relieving yourself wherever you please! No matter who's around!"

I moved around to the other side of the Jeep to avoid James. I could still hear his chuckles. I unzipped myself again and urinated against the vehicle. I managed to finish without any bladder shyness. James waited for me to finish. I packed myself away, and that's when I heard a low rumble. I looked above for a plane or helicopter. I thought that there could be more jets, but there was nothing. Maybe I imagined it?

"You hear that?" James called to me. Nope, didn't imagine it.

"Yeah," I replied. I didn't have a good feeling about the sound. It was a different rumble to the jets we heard before. It sounded close, and got closer. I turned to look down the motorway from the way we had come. On the horizon were silhouetted figures. They moved down the motorway extremely fast. I grabbed the binoculars out of the Jeep and squinted through them. What I saw were motorbikes. A lot of them. A quick count was anywhere between fifteen and twenty riders.

"What is it?" James asked as he watched me stare intensely into the binoculars.

"Bikers," I responded simply.

"Maybe they're friendly?" James responded hopefully, but it sounded weak. I adjusted the focus of the binoculars and looked at the people on the motorbikes. I couldn't make out much, but what I could see were guns. Each person had a gun either strapped to them, to their motorbike, or held up in the air like a victory stance.

"We need to get going," I commanded, walking back to the Jeep.

James stayed where he was and repeated his question.

"They're not friendly," I replied, tossing him the binoculars so he could look for himself. He did just that and then followed me. I was about to get into the driver's side when James put his hand on my shoulder to stop me. I turned to argue that we didn't have time to mess about but he interrupted me.

"How much experience do you have at evasive driving, guy?" James said, reverting to his nickname for people. Was it a nerves thing?

"None," I replied quickly.

"I do," James said confidently. "You're tired, I'm not. I have experience at this."

I nodded and climbed into the back. He got into the front and started driving.

Initially, he started to build up speed. We had decided that if we could get away from them that would be best. However, we soon realised that, no matter how fast our Jeep could go, it wasn't fast enough to outrun motorbikes. We couldn't keep the distance between us as the bikers crossed the gap in a short time. Before long, they crossed half the distance between us. Soon they would be on us. I had braced myself in the back, worried about being thrown about. I kept risking looks out of the back window to see how far away the bikers were, but every time I looked they were closer than the last time. I was scared to look again in case one of them had their nose pressed up against the glass. Suddenly, there was the loud crack of a gunshot. James swerved. There was then another shot, and then another. James swerved blindly. I risked another look out of the back window. Many of the bikers had their guns pointed into the air and fired shots. They weren't even aiming at us. I watched as they fired a shot, James swerved, and a couple laughed at our panic.

"James," I shouted over the roar of the engine. He glanced over his shoulder to acknowledge he could hear me, "Stop swerving. They're not shooting at us; they're trying to intimidate us."

He stared into the mirror for a few moments, watching the shots being fired. He saw what I saw and a thin smile spread over his face. It made sense for the bikers to do that. For people who may not have ever killed, it would be the perfect way to get supplies. Bikers, in general, looked scary. The ones which followed us had bald heads, leather jackets, and large beards; I wouldn't want to fight a single one of them. So, by adding guns into the mix, they were a menacing group. I hoped they weren't killers and were solely relying on appearance to threaten us. Maybe they thought we had guns, food, or medical supplies. It didn't matter whatever they thought we had, they wanted it anyway. They were going to take it, which *I* couldn't allow. I had a plan. I undid the roof hatch in preparation.

I shouted to James, "Keep us steady for a couple of minutes."

His eyes narrowed at me in the mirror, but I put my thumbs up, to which he did the same in confirmation. The Jeep suddenly steadied and sped along a straight path. I stood up with my top half out of the roof hatch. I stood there, the wind whipping around my face and bellowing my clothes. I couldn't hear a thing. I stared down at the bikers from my heightened perspective. I had a feeling of superiority. The bikers stared at me. Most of them looked confused, unsure of what to do. Others looked bloodthirsty and riled up in the moment. The rest looked scared and not sure of what to do any more. I was about to give them something to be scared about. I lifted my hands for them all to see, like a preacher trying to silence his adoring congregation. They watched my hands raise, and then fall. My hands fell to the two handles on the mounted GPMG: the long, sleek, black metal barrel under my control. I looked at the crowd of bikers, pointed the heavy weapon of death at them, and smiled.

CHAPTER 23

It amazed me to see the same look of fear and panic spread over fifteen or more faces. It was like someone dropped a pebble in a pond and the ripples of fear spread. Some waivered and a few pulled away from the pack and dropped back. Most persisted and pushed forward. It was like a game of poker, each calling the other's bluff; albeit a very deadly game. Each waited for the other to fire the first shot, but neither would give up in the meantime. I didn't know how long I could draw the bluff out, especially since I didn't have any rounds for the gun. I aimed the heavy duty machine gun in front of the bikers and I made a show of the movement. A few more dropped back. Only five remained to pursue us. They didn't know that I didn't have any ammunition, and I didn't want them to realise either. I looked at the bikers' faces, surprised at how many were middle-aged or older. Humanising the enemy. Was it bad? I didn't think so in the world which was quickly evolving. I sighed; I was running out of ways to scare them. I looked at the incoming threat of the bikers. I gave them a look as if to say, "last chance." They persisted. I stared at the front-runner I predicted to be the leader. He stared back. I could see the doubt spread across his face. He was losing confidence in his crusade. Then I did something that insured our survival. I winked at him. I don't know where it came from, but slipping sanity seemed the likely cause.

Nonetheless, I saw something click in the leader's face and he began to drop back. The other four followed. I waved to them as we departed and they looked on.

"What the hell did you do?!" James asked as he watched the bikers stop their chase.

"My charming personality," I replied simply. My mind raced. What would have happened if they didn't drop back?

"Did you … uh. Did you–" James started, unsure of how to proceed.

"You would have heard it if I fired that thing," I replied, running my hand through my hair. I didn't want to discuss our close brush with death. He knew I wasn't telling the full story, but he didn't call me on it. I slumped to the floor in the back of the Jeep and stared out of the back window. I felt a million miles away …

"What's your funniest memory from school?" James asked out of the blue. I had been dozing in the twilight area between the sleeping and waking world.

"What?" I said, disorientated and confused.

"School. Funniest memory," James repeated. He didn't take his eyes off the road. I rubbed my eyes but grogginess lingered.

"Umm," I said thoughtfully, searching my memories for one which would particularly come to mind. There were so many, it was hard to choose. I suddenly remembered one and smiled. "In school, there was a guy who used to pick on everyone. During a sports lesson, I went back into the changing rooms to go to the toilet and saw his stuff just sitting there. I've never been confrontational; I like to mess with someone psychologically."

"Oh right," James said and acknowledged me. I could hear by the way he spoke that he had a smile on his face.

"So, I took just one of his socks and chucked it into the toilet. With that, I flushed it. It was brilliant to watch. The sock spun round and round before just disappearing. The water whipped it away, never to be seen again." I laughed, mirth filling me from good memories.

James chuckled, "That's pretty funny."

"Oh, that isn't even the best part," I continued, leaning forward. I was fully awake at that point. It was amazing what good memories could do for you. "Wanna hear more?"

"Of course," James said, flashing me a smile in the mirror, "One way to pass the time."

I nodded, happy to have an audience. "So, he comes back into the changing room. He gets fully changed back into his normal clothes. Gets down to the last sock and I see him searching around for it. He checked his bag about ten times. Checked his friend's stuff as well. Starts raging, but he let it go. Everyone misplaces stuff every now and again. So I gave it a couple of weeks and struck again."

"Go on," James said. I could see a grin on his face and he wasn't even facing me.

"The next time I went to the toilet, I took his jumper and chucked it across the changing room. He eventually found it. He was angry again but got on with it," I continued. "I was going to leave him alone at that point but, completely unprovoked, he started hitting another kid. I needed revenge for that kid. So I gave it a while, bided my time. Next would be the big one."

James swerved around an abandoned car. I gripped the side of the Jeep to brace myself.

"So, same story again, I went to the toilet and found his belongings. I took his school trousers and wandered into the toilet. I knew they wouldn't flush in one go. It needed some precision accuracy. I dipped one trouser leg into the toilet and pulled the flush. I kept pulling the flush, feeding the trouser leg into it. I watched the leg disappear into the watery depths. I flushed the leg, then the upper thigh, and then got to the crotch area. That was when the problem arose." I paused for suspense. "Whatever I had done, I blocked the toilet. The material stopped disappearing and the water started rising. I tried to pull the trousers out, but it was too late for that. The water just kept rising and overflowed from the toilet bowl. I scampered at that and returned to my lesson."

"Did you get caught?" James asked, enthralled by my story.

"No." I grinned. "We returned from sports to find water everywhere. We investigated the source and found the toilet had *mysteriously* overflowed. This bully was the first to laugh about the fact someone's trousers were in the toilet. Typical idiot that he was. It was only when he started changing that he realised they were *his* trousers. He blew a gasket. Screamed at people and demanded who did it. I spoke up and told him to calm down. He didn't like that and turned his attention to me. He tried to take a swing at me, but he slipped on the wet floor. He was the laughing stock of the entire class."

"Pretty funny." James laughed. "More a story of revenge though, wouldn't you say?"

"Probably why I find it so funny then." I smiled, leaning back. "What about you?"

"I was fairly good in school," James said, but I could already tell he was lying through his teeth. "There were a *few* incidents, however."

"Do tell," I chuckled. It made the journey a lot more bearable.

"This is going to sound really weird, but I used to draw

penises *everywhere*," James said, making eye contact with me.

"I'm not judging you," I said with mock hurt.

"So, every day we would have the same class in the same room. I was sat right at the back of the class. Every day I would draw one on the wall, but not just regular ones," James said, pausing to make me realise he was serious. "There were swirly ones, bendy ones, and Picasso ones. Those things were crazy. Naturally, after five days a week for half a year of me drawing, that wall got pretty full up. Just plastered in my *art*."

"This story is weird," I said, but I couldn't help but laugh.

"So," James continued. "Half-term came and went. We came back to class, and my little corner had been repainted. Just the wall art had been painted over. The rest of the crummy, paint-peeling walls was left, except my corner. I didn't mind … I was running out of space. They had literally presented me with a new canvas to draw on. So I started again with art to make up for."

"Brilliant!" I laughed. I was clutching at my sides at this point. I wasn't just laughing at his story. I was laughing at the fact that, even in the apocalypse, there was still time for penis stories. Perhaps it was madness setting in, but I continued laughing for a good ten minutes after that. James broke down into fits of giggles also, our laughter encouraging the other. The car swerved a few times. Had there been any other cars on the road we would have had an accident for sure, but James managed to get it under control.

"You know what," I laughed, wiping tears from my eyes. "I hated school so much, a lot of idiots, but some random memories like that made it worthwhile."

"Agreed," James laughed, also wiping tears away. He was quickly becoming a friend of mine. Sure, we had been thrown together out of necessity, but I was really growing fond of him.

I would miss him when he left … but he was leaving to go where? I knew very little of where he was going. I needed to ask, my natural curiosity overriding my mirth.

"So, where are you actually heading?" I asked casually, laughter still in my voice.

"Wondered when this would come up." James chuckled quietly. "Long version or short version?"

"I hate clichés, but, do you have anywhere else to be?" I asked with mock sarcasm.

"Very true." James nodded in agreement. "I want to get to Scotland. There are three main reasons behind that. I have family in Scotland. My parents moved up there a few years after I moved out and got my own place. They always wanted to move to the middle of nowhere and live out their remaining years in peace. They bought a cottage on the side of a loch. You can only get there by ferry or an incredibly long car journey. Seems like the best place to be. No one else around for miles, so it's secluded and safe. There's also the chance that the infection hasn't made it that far north yet, which probably means that the armed forces will be making a last stand there. Probably the safest, and most guarded, place as well, it means. That's where they were evacuating a lot of the higher-ups to anyway. Any government left is up there. Probably makes Scotland the safest place in the UK right now."

"Family, seclusion, and safety? Sound reasoning," I said, nodding thoughtfully. Scotland definitely sounded like a fall-back plan if it came to that. There were a few moments of silence. I could sense James wanted to say something.

James sighed and eventually came out with it. "You're welcome to join me, you know."

"Thanks, man," I replied, genuinely happy with his offer. I knew I couldn't take it though. My face dropped, ready for my reply. "I have my own family to look out for."

"I know," James replied simply. "I just want you to know the offer is there. Maybe meet up with me one day."

"Of course," I smiled, although I knew there was little chance of that happening. "Take my number and call me when you make it."

"Will do," he said. He fumbled around his pockets before withdrawing and passing me his phone. "Save it in there for me."

So I did. I typed in my number and saved it as "Sam – The Zombie King," and passed it back to him. I couldn't help but feel we were going through the motions with it. It felt the same as when you see a friend you haven't met for years. You make plans and say you *have* to meet up, but you don't. All the promises of meeting up would come to nothing. I doubted an undead world would make that any more likely.

I chuckled at a thought. James looked at me, so I voiced it. "I nearly gave you my address so you could send me a letter."

"Oh, that would be *so* useful. Hell, I might as well give you my address," James said sarcastically before reciting an address. "How about I literally send you a postcard when I'm there."

"Go for it, one of the Loch Ness Monster if you could," I said approvingly with a smirk. "In all fairness, it will probably arrive faster than the normal postie. Send it by Ze-Mail."

"Ze-mail?" James replied, his eyebrows knitted in confusion.

"Zombie Mail," I laughed. "Jeez, James, get with the times. Was that actually your address, by the way?"

"Of course! Just in case you ever need it." James laughed. I repeated it a few times; I wanted to visit him one day. "By the way, I so will *not* miss you when you're gone."

Our laughter eventually died off when we realised the reality that we were actually going to part ways. We probably would never see each other again. We had become brothers-in-arms out of necessity, but the bond was still there. I sighed, the noise exaggeratedly loud in the silence of the Jeep. No one spoke.

CHAPTER 24

We were miles out of London; away from the epicentre of the Daisy outbreak. The further we got away from London, the busier it seemed to get. I'm not talking about "people" busy, but rather "undead" busy. "We had barely seen anyone alive. We did see one living person speeding towards London on the opposite side of the road. They were going over a hundred miles per hour and didn't show any signs of slowing down. It didn't bode well for what was ahead if someone was trying that desperately to get away from it. They must have heard about how bad London was. How far had Daisy spread? We knew it had passed London and hit Essex, but how much further than that? Wales? Ireland? I didn't want to think about it. The ripples of Daisy spread through Great Britain like a cancer, destroying whatever it got its roots into. I wondered how long it would be before the deaths from Daisy outweighed that of the Black Death, of cholera, of Aids, and eventually of all those combined? There were so many unanswered questions. Had it spread beyond Great Britain? There had been flights in and out of Great Britain when Daisy had first started rearing its ugly head. Maybe Scotland would be the next stop in my journey of survival after all. It would probably be just as safe as anywhere abroad, but easier to get there.

"James," I said, breaking hours of silence. "You say Essex

has fallen, right?"

"Apparently so, why?" James answered dully. He had been focussed on the road for hours and looked as though he hadn't blinked the entire time. Exhaustion was prevalent.

"Instead of dropping you off outside of Essex to make your way to Scotland, how do you feel about sticking with me a little longer?" I began. I had his attention. His entire body language had changed. I continued when I saw his interest. "I pick up Alice and her family before we head to Scotland together. That sound like a plan?"

James nodded approvingly before continuing with, "Sounds like a plan. Safety in numbers."

"It would be awesome to meet your parents," I said with a genuine interest in his family life.

"They'll love guests." He laughed. "My mum makes an awesome coffee cake."

It reminded me of my own family, whom I doubted I would ever see again. I was saddened by it, but then I wasn't. The feelings came and went; I felt *very* cold inside. How long until I stopped caring about everything? *Don't think about it. You're nearly at the end of it all.* It was true. I would come to terms with everything I had seen at my own pace. I would have plenty of time for it later if all went to plan. Not in that moment, not when I needed to think straight. Even if that meant being cold and calculating. I had to match the new world after all. You couldn't get by through being kind and forgiving. In a way, that reflected the *civilised* world we'd soon forget. How long before we became mindless beasts fighting in the dirt and blood for something to eat? How long before humanity, the morality, not the species, would be forgotten? I thought about the death of innocent people at the hands of men who were only following orders. I don't think long at all.

Time together in the Jeep was odd. The atmosphere would be fantastic and full of laughter one moment, and then moody and silent the next. That was the problem with a long journey; there was a lot of nothing. The end of the world was so … boring. There was nothing to distract us except each other. If you spend time with the same person for long enough, they start to annoy you. I started to notice that James made a really annoying noise with his throat, as if he was trying to clear it. It drove me insane. I noticed James gave me an angry look whenever I cracked my knuckles. Whenever we swapped out as the driver, I considered telling James not to get back in; that's how much it got to me. The silence was worse. It was painful. James seemed lost in his own thoughts and rarely spoke. That, in turn, would make my thoughts turn inwards. My thoughts turned to my family. I wondered how they were. As a family, we were far from perfect. We had more skeletons in our closet than most … I realised I couldn't leave them for Scotland. Collectively, we were obsessed with the idea of the zombie apocalypse. We would constantly create "what if" scenarios. We would be at a restaurant, and one of us would ask *"if zombies attacked right now, what would you do?"* We would spend the entirety of the meal discussing it, all giving different and logical answers. Others would then try to poke holes in the plan and be critical, to see if they could justify their decisions. We were pretty good at it too, regardless of the scenario. I, however, was the best at it. I would overthink everything, down to every little detail. I would think about the long-term and short-term survival. I did a lot of survival research too. For example, I learned that even if all freezers stopped working, you could still make and store ice. Dig holes in the winter, line it with some sort of waterproof material, and fill it with water. It will freeze in the low temperatures, and then you can store it wherever you want. Find a deep, cold cave and you can store ice for the summer. Not exactly for survival purposes, but good for a luxury. Anyway, my sister Kelsey was the second best. I considered her my survival prodigy. If anything happened to me, she could keep herself and people around her alive. In an apocalypse scenario, my mum was the brawn and muscle, and my sister would be the brains; not that I would say that in front of them. I thought back to The Tao of Sam. Would my family follow it? Would they follow it like a religious doctrine? I hoped so, because I believed it would help them survive. Did I really have that much faith in myself? The psychologist in me couldn't help but utter the term *messiah complex*. Regardless of what happened, I believed my family could survive in an undead world as long as they stuck together. That is what families do, stick together. The family I had abandoned so easily. I felt myself sink into darker thoughts, which I pushed aside. I had taken care of them in my own way. They would do fine because of me. I knew I was lying to myself, but I started to believe it. If I carried along the path I was on, I would soon be a psychotic and delusional man who indulged in the idea that he could save the world. All I would have to do was become convinced that there was a cure and expend many lives trying to find it; good old movie clichés. The main problem with psychology is that you overanalyse everything about yourself. I would symptom-ise everything. Feeling happy one moment and sad the next? Bipolar disorder! Having a bad day? Depression! I would have every disorder in the DSM if I diagnosed myself. I laughed out loud at that thought; a short bark of laughter. It sounded more like a dog coughing than a display of mirth. I saw my laugh had disturbed James, as I watched him in the mirror flinch at the outburst. His tired eyes focussed on me wearily. He looked confused and a little scared. I considered explaining what my thought process was, but didn't. I didn't need to justify myself and simply carried on driving. James and I stared into each other's eyes through the mirror. Not in a romantic way. Not in a friends way. There almost seemed something sinister in the gaze.

****

James

James stared at Sam in the mirror. He wanted to look away, he truly did, but he couldn't. There was something unnerving about the look in Sam's eyes. While on the road trip, James had seen hundreds of undead monsters pass by on the outside, and he felt safe inside the vehicle. It was only just that second that he became aware that he may actually be travelling with a far worse one. When James first came across Sam, he felt that Sam was just someone trying to survive. He had the vehicle, he had the guns. So, of course it was all about James trying to prove he was sane and honest to Sam. Not for one moment did James think he should try and find out if Sam was sane. Now, he doubted his decision not to do so. James still believed Sam was, or had been, a nice guy. People did crazy things under stress. From his days with the police, he had seen a couple of officers crack, and that was pre-apocalypse. They would be fine one day, see something terrible, and continue to be fine; for the time being. Little things would begin to surface in them though. It would begin with a noticeable decrease in function. Almost depression. Next would be the avoidance. Those officers, the ones who had seen the worst policing had to offer, would suddenly start avoiding simple things. They would ask for a different route to normal, or wouldn't follow their regular routine. On some occasions, those hardened officers wouldn't turn up to work altogether. James recalled one of the officers talking about Post-Traumatic Stress Disorder; something he thought only soldiers got. That wasn't the case, and officers would collapse into themselves after finally having enough. When he fought during London's downfall, he noticed people seemed to go one of three ways when faced with the horrors they saw. The main way was just breaking down. Officers would just sit there, in a catatonic-like state, stress finally getting the best of them. They became lost souls. Those officers were the lucky ones. Next were the most resilient officers who would come out of it stronger; normally classed as a hero. They would face the fear and horror and come out on top, stronger for the experience. The third group came out worst. They faced the horrors. They adapted and defeated them. The difference here was that they enjoyed the madness. In the process, they moved from a normal person to a monster, and there was always a sick and evil look in their eyes. When James looked into Sam's eyes, he saw that same expression. He was fairly certain it wasn't there when they first met, but it had definitely developed, its roots planted long ago. There was hate in his eyes. However, James occasionally saw the thousand-yard stare on Sam's face. The look of those officers who had given up. Sam carefully walked the line between hero, lost soul, and monster. He hoped Sam's choices would lead him away from monster. James liked Sam, but fear for his own safety began to surface.

When staring at Sam in the mirror, James felt as though Sam was looking through him. A smile of unknown origin tugged at the corners of Sam's mouth. He was sure the smile would normally look friendly, but the dark shadows around his eyes made it look anything but. James enjoyed philosophy. He also had a favourite philosopher, a man by the name of Friedrich Nietzsche. One quote which stuck out for James was,

"Battle not with monsters lest ye become a monster; and if you gaze into the abyss the abyss gazes into you."

James had always liked that quote, as there was an air of mystery to it. He also liked it for the meaning behind it. That quote seemed to directly apply to Sam. If he wasn't careful, he would become worse than the monsters he fought … if it wasn't too late already. James knew he would need to leave Sam sooner rather than later. He would come up with an excuse as to why he needed to go his own separate way. He doubted Sam would argue. He didn't want to leave his only friend in the new world. Maybe things would be different after they both slept? There was no doubt that a lack of *real* sleep shadowed the situation unfavourably. There would be plenty of time during the next few days, if not when they reached Essex. Suddenly, the silence was broken.

"What the hell?" Sam exclaimed and slowed to a stop.

CHAPTER 25

Sam

As I drove, James sat quietly behind me. My eyes grew tired and I kept yawing. I stared into the distance for so long that my eyes began to play tricks on me. Black blotches swam in and out of my vision. When I saw a vehicle pull off from the side of the road and start its slow advance towards me, I thought I'd imagined it. As it headed towards me, I noticed it was another military vehicle, very similar to the one I drove. I saw the driver wave at me and try to flag me down.

"What the hell?" I exclaimed aloud, although not intentionally. I began to slow the Jeep and roll to a stop. I reached for my gun.

"What is it?" James asked with unease in his voice. He climbed forward to look out of the window. He saw what I saw and added, "What we gonna do, guy?"

"Defend ourselves … if we have to," I replied vaguely. I put the gun on my lap, ready to pull it up if the approaching man even looked threatening. As suddenly as he started to drive towards us, he slowed and stopped thirty foot away. There were a tense few seconds as we stared at each other through the windscreens. Then he made very slow and deliberate movements as he opened his Jeep door and climbed out. He had both his hands above him to show he was unarmed. He was shorter than me and was on the scrawny side. His military fatigues suggested that he was still better trained than me. He had very short hair, recently shaved. He had a nervous smile on his face but walked towards us with his arms raised anyway. Without consulting James, I placed my gun back on the seat and climbed out. A smile started to break out on the man's face at my peaceful actions and then disappeared when he saw I wasn't a military man. If "oh" had a facial expression, he made it. The man stopped his stride.

"What do you want?" I called to him. I saw James on the periphery of my vision reach for the gun. Smart thinking.

"Sorry," the man began apologetically. He had a croaky voice. "I thought you were military."

"No, we're not," I replied slowly. There was an intense staredown before I asked, "What if we were?"

"Our general is collecting any left-over military forces he can," he replied. "The British Army may be dissolved, but we're still soldiers who spent most of our lives following orders. Why should we stop now?"

He had a fair point, and it was good to see everyone didn't abandon their post. However, it could be a potential problem for James and me.

"We don't want any trouble with you or anyone else. We'll be on our way now," I replied curtly before climbing back into my Jeep. James aimed his gun in the general direction of the man outside.

"We've got a well-defended fortification up the road," the man called to me. "It's safe and you both look like you could use some rest."

I leaned out the window and said, "How do you know *we're* safe?"

He replied without a second's thought, "If you weren't,

I'd already be dead, wouldn't I?"

"Okay then. How do we know *you're* safe?" I asked. I wasn't the most trusting of souls.

"If I wasn't, *you'd* already be dead," the man said. His nervous façade fell away. He clapped his hands above his head, and three men came out of the tree line on the side of the road. They wore leaf-covered netting as camouflage: ghillie suits. Each carried an automatic weapon and a rifle. If they were trained, they could have killed us any time from when we had stopped, and when we were still driving down the road towards them. The scrawny soldier smiled, pleased the deception had worked.

"Now, let's all head back for food and rest, yeah?" he said, phrasing it like a question.

"Do we have a choice?" I asked, eyeing the men suspiciously.

The scrawny man looked around him, confused. Acknowledgement suddenly lit up in his eyes and he laughed. "I'm really sorry. I get what you mean now. Yes, you have all the choice. You can keep heading up this road, you'll see where we are anyway and you can stop by. Or you can just keep going. It really is *your* choice."

"I just need to confer," I replied, turning to James. I looked at him, his dark rings around his eyes evident. He looked close to breaking point. He clutched the gun tightly, like a safety blanket. He was clearly uneasy, and it put me on edge. I looked him in the eye. "What do you think? Keep going, or should we go with them?"

James replied with a very calm determination, "They could have killed us at any point, still could, but they haven't. We have nothing to lose by going with them. Besides, we both need rest."

He had a strange and uneasy smile on his face.

"With them it is," I replied and put my hand on his shoulder. James flinched. I quickly pulled my hand away, unsure of what just happened, and returned to the soldiers with our answer. The soldiers didn't look like they had moved. The scrawny guy barely acknowledged my return.

"We've decided to go back with you guys," I announced.

The scrawny guy smiled. "Excellent!" he said and strode forward. His hand was outstretched, to which I raised mine, almost out of reflex. He clasped my hand and shook it.

"Sergeant Peters," he said. "Former soldier of the British army."

"Sam," I replied and added with a smile, "Former university student."

"What in?" Peters asked, sounding genuinely interested.

"Psychology," I said with a smile.

"Ah, better be careful around you!" He laughed. "You'll be psychoanalysing me the whole time I talk, won't you?"

I laughed too, ignoring the common misconception which *everyone* seemed to have about psychology. I blamed Hollywood.

"The guy in the Jeep is James," I said, introducing James for him. He looked quite firmly stuck in said Jeep.

"Brilliant," Peters announced. "If we're going to head back, we should do it before nightfall."

I nodded and headed back to my Jeep.

"No, no," Peters said, stopping my stride. "I forgot to say, you and James are going to have to ride up in ours. For security reasons. One of the other men will drive yours up for you."

I felt uneasy; surrendering our vehicle seemed like a red flag. However, as he had said, we could have been killed at any time anyway. I nodded in agreement and explained the situation to James. He was also uneasy about the situation but agreed to it. With that, we relinquished control of our vehicle and weapons and climbed into the soldiers' vehicle. Without another word, we started our drive to the mysterious destination. Our *salvation*.

CHAPTER 26

As we drove along in silence, I began to think about what Peters' military group was trying to achieve. Were they just trying to survive in the new world? They would have the training to do so. Were they trying to make a safe haven for others to live in? They would have the equipment to do it. They seemed friendly, which was good for us, yet something still didn't feel right. However, I let that feeling subside. We could reap the rewards of their hard work if they were letting us stay. If society reformed again, I could see it being under a military state. That seemed to be the only way the world could adapt and survive. After all, everyone who was still alive and wanted to stay that way would become a soldier of sorts. It wouldn't be long before the world was at total war. The term "world war" would never be used more appropriately, assuming the infection had spread beyond Great Britain. Looking at the way it had spread, I doubted it would be long before that happened.

The vehicle drove along slowly, but at a consistent pace. We easily dodged the abandoned cars. They looked as though they had travelled that pathway numerous times. The driver barely looked where he was going. Following us from a slight distance was our original Jeep, but it carried other military men. James sat next to me, although stiff as a board. I couldn't tell if it was due to his uneasiness around so many people, or something about me which had set him on edge. It was all a blur. I couldn't remember anything I could have done.

"You okay, bud?" I whispered to him. He nodded, equally as stiffly. Definitely something to do with me; at least a little bit anyway. I would make it up to him after our little diversion. My eyes began to wander to our hosts. Typical military folk. Some on the skinnier side than what I expected from hardened soldiers. I noticed their uniforms were relatively new-looking. There was no battle damage or signs of fighting; not even blood stains. Had they even seen combat? I noticed that where their military insignia normally would be were a few stray threads, as if it had been removed. I asked them about it.

"Well, with no form of organised military around anymore, it seemed a bit silly fighting for Queen and Country. Don't want to give the wrong impression and all that. We're out to protect ourselves," Peters replied and then added as an afterthought, "And the people we come across."

I nodded but remained silent. It didn't make much sense to me. Maybe it was symbolic for them as a unit?

"So who's running the show now then?" I asked casually. I wanted as many details about the men as possible, as well as what they could for me. If things were as good for them as it seemed, they could be a potential ally who I could throw my lot in with if I needed to.

"The same man who has been leading us all this time," Peters replied again, with less enthusiasm for conversation that time. I noticed the others seemed tight-lipped and more likely to be the brawn to whoever was in charge. They seemed to bristle at the mention of their leader; almost like they didn't want to talk about him. I had a sudden wave of uneasiness pass over me. Were we prisoners?

"So, how much further is it?" I asked, adding yet another question to the list.

"We can discuss things when we're back at the base," Peters said with a little annoyance in his voice. He had essentially cut all my questions short; I was *not* to ask anything else. What caught me, however, was the word *base*. I wasn't fantastic at geography, although I was a closet military nut. Not that I kept it very well-hidden. However, I was fairly certain there wasn't a military base in that area outside of London. Did that mean we were just going to another glorified roadblock? My mind raced with doubt and curiosity, my thoughts turning to the "base" in London. I hoped it was better than that one. I reached for my gun, but it wasn't there; I had given it over to our hosts. I felt naked without it. I stewed in my own thoughts. Before those thoughts could develop, the Jeep slowed. I looked up. No base in sight.

"Are we here?" I asked in confusion. There was nothing around.

"Not quite," Peters replied. "We have one stop before we head back. Sorta a patrol stop."

All the car doors opened and the soldiers stepped out. James and I just stayed where we were.

"Not coming?" Peters asked and pulled up his rifle. The soldiers walked out and into the field.

"Why not?" James replied, nervousness in his voice. I could see what he was thinking. They would lead us into the grassy fields and execute us. I didn't see it that way. They could have executed us outside our Jeep if they so desired. Similar thoughts flitted near the surface of my brain when I became aware of the potential scenario. My brain was my own worst enemy. I began walking, followed by James and Peters.

"What're we doing here?" I asked as we waded through

the knee-high grass. There were paths worn into the grass for us to follow. I could see several dark patches of earth dotted around the field, and nearby were two diggers. The patches of ground were about the width of a regular car, albeit longer. I approached them slowly. As we neared, I realised they were actually deep holes in the ground and the diggers were clearly what had been used to make them. An unearthly chorus of snarls and wails grew louder the closer we got.

"Come see," Peters said with a smile as he pressed ahead to stand on the edge of one of the holes. I had an idea of what would be in there, which added to my uneasiness. I didn't want to be that close to it. James and I walked forward slowly until we were on the edge. Once I looked into the pit, I found it hard to tear my eyes away. The pit was about ten feet deep and had very steep sides. There were twelve of the undead in it. They were going berserk. They scrambled over and under each other. The undead attempted to climb the walls, gaining a foot or two before they sank to the bottom again. I couldn't tell if they were actively trying to escape, or our presence had driven them into a frenzy. The contained stench of so many undead was unbearable. James had a green pallor to his face, and I could feel the colour draining from mine.

"Horrific, isn't it?" Peters said with a slight laugh. I was afraid to open my mouth to agree in case my stomach emptied itself. I nodded instead. I looked around at the soldiers; none seemed to have a problem with the foul stench.

"Wanna know how we handle it?" a gruff soldier asked. He towered over the rest and was built like a vending machine. He could have left my face on the back of my skull in one punch if he so desired.

"Sure," I choked out.

"Here you go," the huge soldier replied and tossed me a

small blue pot. I caught it, nearly falling into the death pit as I did so. James steadied me and saved me from the undead hive below.

"Ram it up your nose and take a big whiff," the soldier said and wandered off, taking no notice of my close encounter with the reaper. I watched him walk away before inspecting the small pot, which read "Menthol Vapour Rub."

"Simple yet effective," Peters replied and produced his own pot. He put enough to fill a teaspoon up each nostril. He took a massive intake of breath and smiled. His eyes streamed ever so slightly. I did the same, wincing at its intense burn before passing it to James, who did the same. They weren't lying. It worked brilliantly. The stench of death left my nose and was replaced by the fake menthol freshness of vapour rub. I would remember it for future use. Perhaps the vapour rub industry would thrive? I laughed at my poorly constructed joke, much to the chagrin of others. Someone laughing to themselves rarely meant anything good.

"So, what's with these pits?" I asked coolly, trying to reassert my confidence.

"Our base isn't far from here," Peters answered simply. "Turns out the dead are pretty stupid. They won't go round a hole if it's in their way, so why not make some they can't avoid?"

"Brilliant," James said under his breath as he admired their simple handiwork.

"Isn't it?" Peters said with a smug smile. "Every day we send a patrol past and destroy any dead who find their way into the holes. Been about a hundred these past few days."

"What about the bodies?" I asked in disbelief at the simplicity of the idea; surely there was a downside?

"Another easy solution," Peters said with an even bigger

smile. He then called to his fellow soldiers. "Let's get on with it, gents."

A couple of men produced previously unseen canisters of petrol, unscrewed the caps, and poured an excessive amount of the contents into the holes. The strong fumes, which would make any environmentalist cry, went unnoticed through our nasal defences.

"Hold this a sec," Peters instructed and handed me a piece of the old rag. He lit the end of it using a lighter. When it was ablaze, he took it back and dropped it into the hole. The moment it made contact with the undead, the pit burst into flames, spreading the flame to others upon contact. I watched as the undead continued to try to escape the hole. Not because of the flames which engulfed them, but to try and reach the fresh supply of food which stared at them from just out of their reach. I watched as their rotten flesh fell away from blackening bones and knew that the undead truly felt no pain. I took a step back as the heat intensified; it felt as though it was scorching my face. Black plumes of smoke drifted into the air from all of the pits as each soldier attended to their own. Peters walked up and down to inspect each one and wandered back over when he was happy with what he saw. I, on the other hand, cringed at the waste of fuel.

"Give it a year and it'll be no good anyway," Peters said as he walked by and saw my face. He went back to the Jeeps, his men following as he did so. Peters looked at the sky, saying to himself in disbelief more than anything, "Let's get going. Swear the nights are coming in faster now."

Peters shook his head as he walked away. I noticed a few of the soldiers smiled at me and James. They seemed to be a lot friendlier in general, almost like we had performed an act of initiation. Perhaps we had? We showed we had no qualms about killing the undead, something I am sure they had trouble with at some point. People had such adherence to not killing creatures that had once been human; something I seemed to have no problem with. My slip into the "kill or be killed" attitude happened surprisingly fast. If any of my loved ones saw the rapid change, they would probably be horrified; not me, however. I needed to think about Alice anyway. Everything I did was to rescue her. The only people I had to answer to about my crimes were Alice and whatever non-existent God floated in whatever non-existent afterlife. As far as I was concerned, I was home-free. Not for a moment did my moral conscience come into my thoughts and how those horrors would affect it. I closed my eyes. Exhaustion overtook me. I needed sleep and food. Real sleep and proper food.

TAO OF SAM – HOME: THE BASICS

You should have enough time to prepare your home. It is now your fortress. Build walls and cage yourself in. You want to keep the world out.

I would recommend a ten-foot-high wall made from breezeblocks; two thick. That goes around the entire house. Front and back. Put all your funds into it while you have time. Money will soon be useless. The wall will be too tall for the undead to climb over.

Also invest in a big gate; one big enough to drive a car through. Just make sure it is sturdy and well-made. You can even reinforce it with other things. Make sure the gate is covered so no one can see in. Attach a panel for viewing purposes.

Next, you want some sort of walkway or tower accessible by ladder. Even raising the ground behind the wall will work. It will give you an overview of everything beyond your walls. You will see anything before it sees you. It means you will be completely surrounded and protected.

Renovations inside the house will be pricey but worth it. Try to get big metal shutters over the windows and doors. Having them both inside and outside the house would be best, if you can. The same kind you see on shops. If not, get iron bars installed. Remove the stairs and replace them with a ladder. I'm pretty sure the undead won't be able to climb. All the footage shows how uncoordinated they are, but we shall see.

Move everything you can upstairs. Avoid the downstairs as much as possible. The higher you are the better.

You aren't trying to be comfortable, you are trying to be safe.

Things you will need are:

> • A generator of some kind; it will power everything when the electricity stops.
> • A camping stove; it will come into use instead of the big oven.
> • A water purification system; enough said.

Remember, any security system is only as strong as the weakest point

CHAPTER 27

As I have made clear several times throughout my life, I didn't believe in God. Not in the same way most other people did anyway. Mainstream religion never made any sense to me, especially when the politics of religion appeared more important than the spiritual part of it. It made me reject religion. It didn't mean I was a bad person. I could be a good person even without the "love of God" to guide me. If I was a good person then surely whatever God existed would accept me? I couldn't accept an all-loving God would punish those who simply didn't believe in him. Similarly, there were thousands of people who probably never heard of Christianity or Islam or many other religions. Did that mean they would be punished for simply not being born in the right part of the world at the right time?

As for my lack of belief in religion, I did believe in the soul. Not in the religious sense. I believed that whatever made people tick as their unique selves was their soul. Even if it wasn't a spiritual soul but more a sense of self. Equally so, I believed a soul could be stained by certain acts, like murder. With certain people you meet, you can tell they are evil or have done bad things. I think that is a sort of staining of a soul. An act so bad it scars who you are. I knew certain things I had done over the previous few days had stained me ever so slightly. Perhaps it was like a drop of ink in a glass of water. It was only a little bit, but it would never be the same again. I was certain my soul would be marred a lot more before my journey's end. How it would affect me was yet to be seen fully. It was a bridge I would cross when I needed to. For now, everything would be buried deep and I would pray, and I mean *truly* pray, that my journey finished before I reached the point of no return.

CHAPTER 28

I don't remember falling asleep but I must have drifted off at some point because the next thing I remembered was being nudged awake. I opened my eyes slowly and avoided jerking awake. I wanted to give the impressions that I had been awake the whole time and had just closed my eyes. I looked at James. He was the one who woke me.

"We're almost there," he whispered. I didn't know why he was whispering. We all knew where we were heading, so why the need to be secretive? I didn't ask him. I thought it was best to do that later. I looked at the surrounding area, rubbing the sleep from my eyes as I did so. We moved slowly along the road. There were cars every twenty metres or so, placed horizontally along the road. The Jeep weaved between them. *I had seen that before.* The cars looked as though they had been purposely positioned like it. I was certain that I saw a person sitting in one, gun pointing the way we had come from. It was a smart idea. It was essentially a lookout point to keep an eye on the area. If he saw anything, he could radio back to base to let them know, and then he could hide in the car. Who would question an abandoned car? The positioning of it also meant that any oncoming vehicles would have to slow a sufficient amount. I could only assume why it would be needed, and I thought that could be to question survivors. I didn't want to think of a potentially worst scenario. Sudden realisation hit me when I remembered cars I had seen outside of London earlier. How long had those people known of our approach? Had they planned to cut us off and waited there for that reason? It wouldn't have taken long for the first guy to radio back about an approaching vehicle, and for Peters to drive out and meet us. Very smart indeed ...

I was staring into the distance when the base came into view. It was set off from the road and looked formidable. It was what I imagined a medieval castle to look like had it been built by modern technology. I was one hundred per cent certain it had not been there the previous times I had passed that way. A huge metal wall separated the base from the outside. It looked to be taller than most normal people and was topped with razor wire. Slightly further out from that was a chain-link fence topped with barbed wire. It looked like the initial line of defence before anyone could come into contact with the wall. The fence wouldn't keep people out forever, but it would certainly slow them down enough to be dealt with before they were a real threat. Within the compound, in each of the four corners, stood four tall watchtowers. A man was in each one and they all carried what appeared to be high-powered rifles. The towers were mounted with large spotlights which could probably illuminate the fields around it for miles. There were a few armed men moving dead bodies away from the outside fence and into the back of a flatbed truck. There was no doubt it was the base we were heading for. Almost as if to confirm it, Peters spoke into the radio.

"Come in Zulu-Twelve, this is Foxtrot-Niner," he said with humour in his voice. There were a few moments of static before the reply came back.

"Very funny, Peters, just spam the radio, why don't you," the stern voice came back.

"Don't mind if I do," Peters replied with warmth. "We have two additional mouths with us."

"Roger that. Bed and breakfast?" the voice replied, like they were mocking us. Although it could just be soldier banter for all I knew.

"And all the trimmings," Peters replied. "Just make sure Harrington knows before we get back."

"Which is when?" he replied again.

"ETA one minute," Peters said, clearly teasing the radio operator. They were definitely friends. It reminded me of the way a couple of my friends and I could spend hours just teasing each other up and talking rubbish. I missed them.

"Done and done," the voice came back, interrupting my downwards spiral. "Over and out."

"All the trimmings?" James said after a few moments, repeating what Peters had said. It had been phrased as a question.

"Yeah," Peters replied, "It basically means food, water, and bed. You're not the first survivors we've found, you know."

"We're not?" I asked, surprised, although it did make sense that we weren't the only ones. Some people must have made a similar journey over the previous few weeks.

"Course not," Peters said with a smile. "We've had plenty come and go. Plenty have stayed as well."

"People stay?" James asked, now just as surprised as me.

"Of course." Peters laughed, as if he spoke to small children. "Not everyone wants to leave, you know. People don't like leaving safety once they have it. We have spaces if people are willing to put in the work, but Harrington has the final say on that."

"Harrington?" I repeated, questioning him once more.

"You either are a curious bunch or just like repeating me," he said, resulting in a bark of laughter from the vending machine soldier. He waited for the soldier to stop before adding, "Harrington is the general running this outfit. You'll meet him very soon."

"Brilliant," I said with a smile. I started to feel more relaxed about the whole situation. I still felt naked without any weapons, but the base would probably ease that feeling.

The Jeep took the turning off the road and onto the gravel path leading to the base. The gravel looked out of place and I suspected it was put there when the base was built, to give vehicles traction. The soldier at the chain-link gate checked inside both vehicles and under each with a mirror on a pole before signalling for the gate to be opened. The gate opened and we went in, only to have similar checks by a second man. The same happened again and the two huge metal doors, much more secure than the gate we had just passed through, rolled open sideways. We then drove inside. The Jeeps were driven off to the left and parked up. Men came out of nowhere and took everything out of both vehicles. The vehicles were then driven into a small compound-styled parking lot. There was a metal fence around it which required a key for entry. It was probably to stop any deserters from making a clean getaway.

"Where are they going with our stuff?" James asked, panic in his voice.

"You're not military men, are you?" Peters asked, although he already knew the answer to the question. We shook our heads. He smiled and continued, "Exactly! You don't know how to maintain the equipment you've been using. We do. We'll have your guns cleaned and readjusted in no time and then we can talk about it."

"Cheers," I replied, although he was wrong. I knew how to maintain every weapon in those Jeeps. James didn't say anything but just stared at Peters, who just smiled. For a moment his smile faltered before he waved for us to follow him. I couldn't put my finger on it, but something wasn't quite right. Regardless, we followed him to a washroom.

"Give yourselves a clean, a shave, a crap or whatever else you need to do and then you can meet with Harrington," Peters said, acting like the perfect host. "We will have fresh clothes waiting for you on your return. What sizes do you both need?"

We told him our sizes and he disappeared. He shook hands and spoke to people as he passed.

I examined the showers. It was a very simple design. It was a communal shower, so there was no privacy in the white-tiled room. Several pipes ran overhead with sprinklers set into them. It wasn't the most amazing system but it was the best I had seen in a long time. There was a metal cabinet in the corner, which I looked in. It was filled with soaps, shower gels, shaving creams, razors, and everything you could ever want to feel and smell clean. I grabbed a handful of stuff, feeling very gleeful at the hoard I had found.

"Hey James," I called to him. He turned and I smiled. "Catch!"

I tossed a bottle of shower gel to him, which he caught with lightning quick reflexes. He examined it.

"Pretty and Pink?" he said, reading the name of the bottle aloud. "Isn't this for women?"

"Yeah, and you're going to smell like a princess," I laughed. I heard James chuckle too. The first sign of genuine and open emotion he had shown for a while. James began to undress.

"Whoa!" I said, covering my eyes. "At least let me leave. You can shower first. I can wait!"

"This again?" James laughed, still removing clothes. "We're potentially at the end of days and you're worried about seeing male genitalia? You're one of a kind, you know."

We both laughed. It was a good, and heterosexual, male bonding moment.

"So, I got something to ask," I said, preparing to broach a subject I wasn't too sure of the boundaries of. I turned to face away so James could undress.

"What is it?" James said. I heard him turn the valve, switching the water on above him.

"What's been up?" I said quickly, almost forcing it out. The same way young boys do when asking a girl out for the first time in school. "You've been acting pretty freaking weird to be honest."

"I've been acting weird!" James snorted. "You realise you talk to yourself and looked like you were going to stab anyone you see."

"Wait! I talk to myself?!" I said, shocked. I wasn't aware of it. I turned to face James, seeing full frontal nudity as I did so. I quickly scrunched my eyes shut. I felt ridiculous.

"Yeah, guy!" James replied matter-of-factly. "You mutter under your breath and stuff. You laugh too."

I thought back to the past few days. I couldn't remember anything clearly. It was a massive blur of chaos. How long had passed since I left home? It felt like months. I suspected it was closer to a week.

"I have been pretty tired," I replied uncertainly, still trying to think back. I opened my eyes again, making sure I only made eye contact that time, and said, "You should have said something sooner if I was freaking you out."

"I was sure you'd poison my next meal, or slit my throat while I slept," James said with a smile. I smiled too. He didn't need to know the thought had crossed my mind at one point.

"So we're cool?" I said, trying to see where I now stood with him.

"Of course. I'm just glad we got this sorted now. Cleared the air and such," James said and washed his hair. I started to undress also. With the water travelling over to my feet, I felt it was probably time to wash and then go and meet the mysterious General Harrington. I almost dumped my clothes in the corner before I remembered to check the pockets. It was something I had always been forgetful about and I had lost a fair bit of money that way. I found my phone and a single bullet. I stared at the cold and hard potential piece of death, confused; where had it come from? It was then I recalled David and his advice. *In case you need it.* His suggestion was a mere after-thought at the time, but the reality of needing it was growing ever closer. I placed the bullet on the side, the deadly end pointing into the air. I gave it one more glance before proceeding to wash.

CHAPTER 29

I spent a lot longer in the shower than necessary, and it felt *amazing*. It was poorly constructed and lukewarm, but it felt great. I didn't realise I would miss showering so much. Dirt and dried gore washed off of me. I even picked what appeared to be a bone fragment out of my hair. Not too sure how, or when, it got there. When I was done, I shaved and showered. I considered leaving my hair as it was but remembered my own advice and shaved it off. As I ran the shaver over my head, blonde locks of hair fell to the floor; water carried them away and they disappeared down a drain. Halfway through, a man dropped off two crisp military uniforms for us. The patches of the British Army had been removed from those in the same way Peters and the others' uniforms had. I put on the new uniform and undergarments they had left, finding both a surprisingly good fit. James and I left the shower together, both in better spirits and both a little bit closer from the experience … in a heterosexual way. Peters was waiting for us outside.

"Ready to meet General Harrington?" he asked, clapping his hands together as he did so.

"Ready as I'll ever be," I replied with a shrug. Without anyone noticing, I slipped the single bullet and phone into my pocket. I wasn't letting them go easily.

"Well, let's get going then," Peters said and guided us

away.

While walking through the compound, the one thing I noticed was how much they had squeezed into the limited space. The base was quite big as it was, but every bit of space had a use. They had a reasonably sized area for vehicles where repairs and maintenance also took place, a washroom that I had already seen, and a bunkhouse which was the sleeping quarters for approximately sixty men and women. There was also a munitions shed, where guns were stored and maintained, an exercise yard, and a mess hall. It was almost like a small military-themed holiday resort mixed with a workshop.

With nightfall, unnatural light in the base was kept to a minimum; probably to avoid detection at night from outsiders. Everything was made out of a greenish metal and seemed to follow the same design as snap-together furniture bought from Ikea, but military grade and not cheap wood. It made me wonder how fast they had it set up. It looked as if it could have just appeared overnight, and I had no doubt that it did.

Peters led us to the far side of the base to where Harrington resided. The general had his own small house on-site, separate from the rest of the men and women. He was clearly as important as his rank suggested. It was a simple design, just like everything else, and that is where we were headed. Peters knocked on the door and, without any indication of whether General Harrington had heard, he opened the door and ushered us in.

The interior of the room we first entered surprised me. From the outside, it looked minimalist, but this simple house had been decorated like a fulltime home. There were carpets and rugs, wooden drawer sets and paintings on the walls.

Harrington was a man of luxury.

"Bring them to the office," a gruff voice, of the man whom I assumed to be General Harrington, called from somewhere further in the house. Peters led us to his office. I noticed there wasn't a single door in any of the door frames. The office was as decorated as the rest of the house: carpet, an ornate desk, and walls lined with books. The desk was set to face the entrance of the room, with a large leather swivel chair behind it. The man in the chair faced away from us, looking at something else apparently. Peters snapped off a crisp salute once we were in the room.

"You can leave us now Peters, thank you," the man said.

"Yes sir," Peters said and then left in an equally crisp march. When the front door slammed, announcing Peters' exit, the chair turned around. In the chair sat one of the darkest-skinned men I had ever seen. Perhaps it was because of the contrast of the white walls, but I was genuinely surprised at just how dark he was. He wore what I think was his parade uniform; it was just as ornate as his desk. His uniform was covered in medals and ribbons. He was a highly decorated individual. He was bald, not shaved bald, but bald-bald. He looked to be about forty or fifty years old. His skin clung tightly to his face, pronouncing his cheekbones. All in all, he was a very attractive man. I noticed he had a tumbler of whiskey in one hand; the man noticed me looking and smiled.

"Positions of power have its benefit," he said and drained his glass in one gulp before placing it down on the desk. He stood up. He was very tall, taller than myself. We were very similar in height; taller than most though. He leaned forward, hand outstretched.

"I'm General Harrington," he said, finally introducing himself. I took his hand, much larger than mine, and shook it.

He had black leather gloves on; good quality too. He proceeded to shake James' hand also. I noticed he had a ceremonial sword on his waist, as well as a pistol of some kind. Harrington sat back down and refilled his glass as he did so. He offered us some, which we both rejected, but he filled the glasses he offered us anyway and drank it himself.

"One hundred years old. Rescued from looters," he said, staring through the golden liquid in his glass. "Gone in a matter of seconds, like mankind."

I didn't think he was talking to us, because when he caught us staring at him, he laughed.

"Sorry about that. I probably have had more than my fair share today," he said with the familiar warm smile of a man who had had a few too many whiskeys. The smile never reached his eyes, however; that is one thing which was odd. Then again, he had probably seen a lot of horrible things over the years. I doubt his eyes even remembered how to smile. There were a few awkward moments of silence before James broke it.

"Sorry, sir, I don't want to be rude, but why have you called us in here?" James asked impatiently.

"I wanted to meet you both, to see who I've let into my base. I also have a proposal for you both," Harrington said, stifling a yawn. He slurred his words ever so slightly. He finished his yawn before continuing with, "I think it might have to wait for tomorrow, however."

I didn't say anything and just watched Harrington. I thought he probably was drunk, but nowhere near the degree he had acted. Maybe it was a test of some kind? Harrington saw me staring at him and he returned his own stare, eyes boring into me, making me feel uneasy.

"So, what now?" I asked, looking between James and

Harrington. Harrington yawned again, closing his eyes as he did so. When he opened them again, his focus was on James.

"Just grab some food, there should be some from the day shift left over. When you're done, get some sleep and I'll send for you two tomorrow," Harrington replied simply. He stood up to see us out but stumbled ever so slightly. He gripped the chair for support and laughed. "It may not be tomorrow if this whiskey is as good as they claim. See yourselves out!"

James and I turned to leave when Harrington spoke again, "What are your names?"

"James Morrison, sir," James said, introducing himself. Harrington turned expectantly to me.

"Sam. My name is Sam," I said, being courteous. He didn't need to know my full name.

"Sam, eh?" Harrington said, rolling the words in his mouth, "Not from the West Country, are you?"

"Bristol, actually," I replied, beaming slightly. I had always prided myself on my silly accent. It was good to be recognised.

"I enjoyed Bristol. Interesting history," Harrington said with a nod of approval. "Well, it was a pleasure meeting you both. Goodnight, James and Bristol."

"Sam, from Bristol," I corrected with a smile.

"I don't think so, Bristol," Harrington said with a sly smile. "Nicknames have a way of sticking around here. Yours will fit right in. Goodnight, *Bristol*."

James and I awkwardly made our way out of the house, not sure what to do. Although Harrington had been friendly and a reasonable host, I couldn't help but feel he had insulted me, mocking my birthplace. That didn't sit well with me. I loved Bristol. My fair city had a fantastic history and architecture, and the people were just great; cannot vouch for the bus service however. That being said, I couldn't help but feel unease the entire time I was in his presence.

"Is it just me, or was that really weird?" I asked James in a hushed whisper as we went outside.

"Talk about unprofessional," James said with a laugh, to which I chuckled. It was good to be able to share a laugh with him again, even if it was at our new host's expense. Then again, he had one at mine. Still, James apparently hadn't caught what I had meant. It didn't matter.

"Let's grab some grub, man," I said and wandered towards the mess hall, where Peters waited for us.

CHAPTER 30

James and I walked into the mess hall. There were a few soldiers, and they all turned to look at us like we were infected with the bubonic plague. Or, like we were the walking dead … Peters led us in without hesitation and continued onwards to the makeshift kitchen. I walked among the soldiers, looking at each and every one as I passed. Most were young and innocent-looking. They all had short, or shaved, hair, the women included. Men heavily outnumbered the women, but there were still a fair few of them anyway. Most of the soldiers looked scared, a few looked determined, and the rest looked lost. More than one had the thousand-yard stare on their faces, staring at the wall as though they could see through it and onwards for eternity. It was sad, yet I was relieved to see it. Even the ones trained for it were being affected by the conflict more than me. Turns out I wasn't as far gone as I imagined. It stirred me forward mentally ever so slightly.

We approached the food counter. Peters helped himself to the food that sat under heated lights. It had probably been cooked hours beforehand.

"No five-star chef?" I commented wryly. Both Peters and James smiled at the comment.

"Afraid not, he's on leave," Peters retorted. "You do have the fantastic choice of stew … or stew."

"Umm, what was the first one again?" I asked thoughtfully, imitating the tone of undecided restaurant goers.

"That would be the chef special: the stew," Peters answered, dumping several ladlefuls into the metal bowl he held.

"Excellent! I'll have that," I exclaimed. I turned to James. "And you, Mr Morrison?"

James smiled, clearly not as enthusiastic about our charade as we were, but played along anyway, "I'll take the second option, the stew."

"Excellent choices," Peters said, finally deciding that his two bowls were full enough. "We have a do it yourself policy here in Harrington's Kitchen so, you know, do it yourself."

I scooped up a bowl for James and myself and did exactly as was told of me; I did it myself.

James, Peters, and I all sat together at a table away from everyone else. I don't think Peters chose our table out of disrespect of the other soldiers, but simply because he wanted peace and quiet. We all tucked into our food and ate in silence. A silence we all appreciated after the day's events. When you chose silence, it was so rewarding. When you were forced to be silent due to circumstance, it was one of the worst things. Funny that. I was a few mouthfuls into the stew before I even began tasting it. The food wasn't fantastic. It was too watery for my liking. However, it was warm and nutritious. Something I had missed out on for the past few days. I didn't think I would eat all that much to start with, but once the first spoonful hit the insides of my stomach, my hunger erupted. For days I had mostly avoided food. With it so readily available, I felt as though I had a compulsion and wouldn't be able to stop if I wanted to. So I ate, and ate, and ate. My stomach hurt and I felt bloated, but it was a good feeling. It was a truly full feeling. I knew eating food where and when it was available would be essential to my survival; who knew how sparse supplies would eventually become. I might as well pack myself full of what I could, when I could. James ate with the same intensity and quantity as me, as did Peters. We all finished in silence. We all left in silence. The other soldiers didn't spare us another glance the second time; saw us once, saw us enough. That was fine with me. I never enjoyed too many introductions as I could never keep up with all the names.

Peters led us to the bunkhouse. We would sleep in with the soldiers that night, which I didn't mind, but the fact it was an unknown environment bothered me. He led us through the doors and to our beds. We had a bunk bed at the far end of the room. It was a metal pole frame bed, very similar to what you saw in every military film. The mattresses looked just as uncomfortable as they did in those films also. Most of the soldiers gave us a glance as we passed through the room. A few even gave us a friendly nod. Perhaps they thought we were reinforcements? I doubted that however, as we didn't resemble soldiers in the slightest. We didn't walk and talk with the same rigidness that is drilled into every soldier from day one. Perhaps they were being friendly? Everyone was friendly in the base, a strange but nice comfort. Peters supplied us each with a thin blanket, a sheet, and a pillow. Although I was used to having six or seven pillows at home, I didn't complain. Once you have dozed in the bed of a Jeep, a military bed would be luxury.

"Welcome to Hotel Harrington," I said to James, grinning when Peters left us to sleep. He gave me a weak smile, his eyes half-closed, exhaustion having its way with him. I smiled sympathetically and said, "See you in the morning, bud."

James merely nodded and collapsed into the bottom

bunk. Looks like I *was* having the top bunk. I put my bedding down and heaved my bulk onto the top bunk, wincing as the frame creaked. It held and didn't collapse. If the military knew one thing, it was how to make simple but durable things. I closed my eyes.

TAO OF SAM – FOOD: THE BASICS

This is pretty basic. Eat perishables first. Store cans and tins for later.

Grab what you can in the early days and ration it. Ration it carefully.

With time, you can farm the foods you need. Plant it in an area nearby which you can easily access. You won't need a full-time guard there to protect it. The undead won't be interested in your farmed goods. You can collect food when you need it.

Don't be afraid to loot houses around you. Just make sure the houses are empty of anyone, living or dead, first.

Eat where and when you can.

CHAPTER 31

"Wake up you lazy turd!" a voice demanded. I opened my eyes.

"What the hell?" I grumbled. I felt like I had literally only just closed my eyes and some idiot was shaking me to get up. I was about to shove him away when I noticed daylight flooding through the windows. I groaned, "What time is it?"

"Six in the morning. Time you got up, *newbie!*" the soldier said, yelling the last word. I jumped and rolled out of bed, still fully clothed from the previous day.

"I'm not even a soldier," I growled angrily. I was never a morning person. "You could have at least let me sleep!"

"Pfft, not gonna happen, newbie," the soldier laughed, whipping his clothes off quickly. He changed the bed sheet with precision and pulled himself into the bed I had just vacated, his own pillow and blanket in hand. "You stay here, you pull your own weight. Just be glad you have the day shift. We nighties need our beauty sleep."

With that, he closed his eyes, his breathing relaxed, and he was asleep in seconds! I needed to learn that trick. I grumbled to myself as I watched other soldiers climb into their bunks as the previous occupants vacated their beds and the bunkhouse. James picked up both of our pillows and blankets. He stared at them for a few seconds before shoving them under the bed and shrugging. He rubbed his eyes and walked towards the door. We were the only two left in there; everyone else had left.

"How'd you sleep?" I said to him as we exited. I yawned widely and rubbed sleep from my eyes. I didn't feel like I had slept at all, yet the evidence suggested I had.

"Like a log," he yawned. He looked even more tired than I did.

"Good for you," I said enviously. I saw soldiers milling into the mess hall. I shrugged at James. "Guess that's where we go."

The mess hall was a lot busier than the night before. Soldiers were laughing and shouting, fighting over food, and running for one of the few empty seats. James and I were the last in the queue, last to get food, and last to not be able to sit down. I already hated military life.

When we finished our food, we followed the soldiers back outside. They proceeded to exercise in the open yard. Although we weren't confined to the same rigorous routine as the soldiers, we still joined in. We felt very out of place just watching. So we did stretches, jumping jacks, and a short run around the base. The food didn't sit well with me. My stomach grumbled and felt like it was swaying. The food so desperately wanted to escape me, but I managed to hold it down.

After the exercise routine, the soldiers all disappeared to do whatever activities soldiers do. James and I stood around, unsure of what to do. We didn't remain that way for long.

"What do you two think you're doing?!" a voice demanded from behind. We turned around to see a tall, well-muscled, man. He was older than most of the other soldiers we had seen, even more so than Harrington. He didn't look like he ranked very highly, but he clearly commanded respect. Any soldiers nearby stiffened on his approach.

"No idea. We were hoping someone would tell us," I answered honestly. The man's face went beetroot red. I imagined the words "AWOL" and "insubordination" flashing through his head. I quickly calmed his rage by adding, "We're new."

He relaxed and a smile spread beneath his bushy moustache, which I'm pretty sure wasn't regulation.

"Well, why didn't you say so, boys?" He laughed, flashing tobacco-stained teeth. If there was a British equivalent of the term Jarhead, that fellow was one. "General Harrington told me to give you a message. With all the newbies joining, I wasn't too sure if you were one of the grunts or not."

The word grunt brought forward images of my favourite Xbox game, Halo. The grunts were small and useless enemies which were only good for cannon fodder. I wondered how closely the analogy matched the soldiers he referred to.

"General Harrington," the man said, chewing something as he did so, "said he couldn't see you today, something had come up."

Images of an empty whisky bottle came to mind.

"He did say you could have free roam of the base, as long as you didn't get in the way of anything," the man said, continuing to chew something slowly. "Maybe you could watch some of the men. You might be able to learn a thing or two."

He said it in a mocking way. He thought lowly of us, but not necessarily in a bad way. I got the impression we were in the same boat as civilian women and children to him. I felt a bubble of anger well up inside me. He had no idea what experience we had! I was about to say exactly that when I realised he was onto something. We *could* learn something from the men. We could learn some new skills there.

"What can we get involved with?" I asked, my interest surprising him.

"Uhh, anything, I suppose," he said, surprised at my sudden interest. "Just ask the men."

He did an awkward foot shuffle while he was turning around; it was the walking equivalent of a three-point turn. I waited for him to walk away before turning to James.

"Anything take your fancy?" I asked him.

"Munitions workshop," he said without missing a beat. "I could really do with learning how to clean and assemble a weapon any bigger than the handguns I've been assigned in the past. You?"

I turned to look at the watchtower. The sniper rifle in the man's arms took my interest. James followed my line of sight to the gun and smiled.

"Thought you would like them big," James said with a chuckle and walked away. It was only when I was at the foot of the tower that I realised he was making a dirty joke.

"Sly git," I said under my breath as a smile spread across my lips.

CHAPTER 32

"Knock, knock," I called as I climbed the ladder. It was to alert the soldier of my presence, although I'm sure he heard me thud my way up the ladder. The tower felt as stable as the bed, yet it held.

"Uhh, hello?" the sniper said dumbly, confused by my appearance. "Why you here?"

"I was told to learn something new, so here I am," I said with a smile and shrug.

"What you here to learn?" he said dumbly again. He clearly didn't like his routine being disturbed.

"How to fire that beauty," I said, pointing to the rifle. "Reckon you can teach me?"

The man stared at me for a few moments before simply saying, "Okay."

At first, I thought the man had learning difficulties. I soon learned through conversation that he was anything but. He was a genius in school but suffered because he had no discipline. The words "problem child" were thrown around a lot, but he didn't want to go into it. His family sent him off to a military academy where he showed extreme proficiency as a marksman. With training and a zombie apocalypse, there he was.

"Have you ever fired anything bigger than a pistol before?" he asked, trying to gauge how much experience I'd had.

"An assault rifle. Was fairly decent with it too," I bragged, thinking to my brief stint in London.

"Well, it's nothing like that. The weight and recoil alone is insane," he said quickly. I found that a slight Irish accent came through when he spoke with excitement, which was anything to do with what he was interested in. "First, we need to teach posture."

So he taught me posture. He showed me how to put the butt of the sniper rifle into my shoulder properly. It would prevent the gun kicking too much when it was fired. He showed me how to look down the scope with one eye closed, pace my breaths, and rest my cheek against the butt.

"It's almost like an art," he said with a smile and a dreamy look on his face. He viewed my posture and my breathing and looked pleased. "Fast learner, aren't ya! I'm assuming you know to hold your breath when you shoot?"

I nodded.

"Excellent!" He beamed and, as if on cue, a zombie wandered from the road and into the field. It saw the base and the people within but didn't make an attempt to run for it. The base wasn't going anywhere; it was content to walk. Steve, the sniper, looked at me sternly. "Reckon you can take him out?"

"I can try," I said with a smile. It was one hell of a teaching experience.

I had the gun resting on the rail, and my posture as he had suggested. I controlled my breathing and stared down the scope. I had the zombie's head in my crosshair.

"Remember," Steve whispered. "Aim small and miss small."

I had no idea what he was on about, but I listened anyway. I realigned my shot. Held my breath. I fired. The crack was deafening and I wished I'd had ear defenders on. The rifle jerked in my hands, no matter how tightly I held it. Even without the scope, I could see I had missed the zombie.

"Dammit," I hissed. I realigned and fired. Missed again. I cursed. Instead of realigning my shot again, I got angry and fired repeatedly without aiming. Before I knew it, the clip was empty. I looked down the scope and saw that I had killed the zombie. I beamed. "Got him!"

Steve had his hand on his head and a look of disbelief on his face. He took the sniper rifle back from me. "Yeah, you got him. But you could have done the same up close with a full automatic with the amount of shots you fired."

I felt embarrassed, and then Steve's radio came to life.

"Nice shooting, idiot," a man laughed. I looked around to see who else had seen my outburst. The other three snipers in the other towers all laughed; one even clutched his sides as he did so. Shame burned my face, embarrassment evident. I hoped James was doing better than I was.

****

James

By midday, James was already an expert in stripping and cleaning a variety of guns. The other men were impressed with how fast he had learned. They treated him like an idiot to begin with, acting like it was something newbies couldn't do. After just one demonstration, James could do it. It was simple. Using the demonstration one he had been handed, an AK47 which had been confiscated at some point, he practised. First, he had to unload the gun. Simple enough. Then he had to push, while he pulled up, the top cover of the gun; that revealed a huge spring, and he had to do the same with that as the cover. Next was the bolt carrier mechanism, which he had to pull back to remove. He removed a bolt from the carrier by twisting it. He then removed the gas tube by rotating some sort of lever which caused the tube to slide straight out. The cleaning rod just twisted straight out. Those were the main details. There were other finer details, but the main gist was a lot of twisting and pulling. Then with several tools, he cleaned, wetted, and lubricated many parts of the gun. The AK47 is a sturdy model anyway, but it felt flawless after the cleaning. James grinned at the others, hefting the AK47 smugly.

****

Sam

"God, what a day," I said glumly as I climbed into the top bunk.

"Didn't enjoy it?" James asked with a massive grin on his face. "My day was very informative!"

"Up yours," I grunted before falling into a deep sleep, but even a deep sleep didn't stop the humiliation from finding its way into my dreams.

Goddammit.

CHAPTER 33

Several days went by, and Harrington still hadn't made an appearance. Our days were so full that we barely had time to think. James and I didn't mind so much either. We were actually having fun. We learned something new every day, and I got marginally better at firing the sniper rifle. I felt a little guilty about not seeking out a way to get to Alice, yet I convinced myself I was where I needed to be. I kept telling myself that skills I learned under Harrington's watch would help me survive when I went back outside of the walls, which was true. However, the real reason was much more selfish. I was too scared to leave the gates again. After spending so long in constant terror out on the road, and then living in safety, my body wouldn't physically allow me to leave the base. It was like trying to slap yourself hard enough to cause harm; your body stops, or slows, your hand at the last second. That is your body's way of self-perseveration. That is what happened every time I tried to get near the gate. Peters was right. Once people had safety, they didn't want to give it up. I hated myself for being so scared, but actual safety does a lot to see away your fear. Instead, I just sat there in self-loathing most days. I tried to involve myself with all the different things to learn. I even got friendly with most of the soldiers. That didn't keep me busy enough. Self-hate grew within me as time went on and, before long, I couldn't find ways to distract myself or justify my stay any longer. Next time I saw Harrington, I would tell him I needed to leave. Yet … he was never around.

"James, I really want to leave," I said, confiding in James one day. "I can't stay here any longer. If you want to stay, I completely understand."

"When are we leaving?" James said without a second thought.

"You don't want to stay?" I asked, confusion spreading over my face. James seemed happy there. The fact he was so ready to leave confused me.

"Sure it's great here, we're safe. But our loved ones aren't safe, are they?" James said simply, voicing the fear I had been hiding. He smiled. "Besides, we've already said we're in this together."

He held out his hand and gripped mine firmly in a show of friendship. We had grown a lot closer over the time we had been there; I felt like we had become true friends. We both got up to look for Harrington. He was nowhere in sight. We started for his house when Peters intercepted us.

"How are you lads doing?" Peters asked with a huge smile. He had positioned himself in our way.

"We're going to see Harrington," I replied, ignoring his question and trying to push past him.

"The general is busy, lads," he said, stopping us from advancing.

"We really need to see him," James said firmly.

"Soldiers don't get to demand when to see the general," he said forcefully. He was going to try to stop us. Anger flared throughout me and my vision turned red.

I shoved past him, a lot harder than I initially meant to, and said, "We're not soldiers, idiot."

James followed me closely. I had anger in my belly. I was

full of venom and ready to attack. I felt like we were being played and cheated. I practically threw Harrington's front door open and stormed through to his office. James lagged behind me slightly; I was going a lot faster than he was. Harrington sat in his chair, whiskey tumbler in one hand and pistol in the other. He had a very dark expression on his face and stared contemplatively at the pistol.

"My boys!" he called when he saw us, as if he were a loving father who hadn't seen his children for some time. His dark expression vanished at the mere sight of us. He held the gun loosely, but my eyes were still drawn to it. He continued, "We still need to have our little chat, remember?"

"What chat?" I asked, confused.

"You forgot our conversation from your first night here? It's more of an offer than a chat," he said modestly. "Some of the other lads said how well you fit in and how hard you work. You're perfect here."

"Get on with it, Harrington," I snapped, my venom fuelled by my own self-loathing.

"Well, I thought long and hard about it, and wondered if you wanted to stay and officially be a member of The Harrington Brigade," he said cheerfully. He stood up from his seat, gun held loosely in his hand.

"The what?" James said with a sneer.

"The Harrington Brigade," Harrington repeated calmly. "It's the name of the men under my command. I, someday, hope to have an entire army under that banner. It's the only way we can reclaim the land from the dead. Someone needs to rebuild the world, why not us? The offer, for you, is to join us."

"No dice," I snarled. "We're going on our way, or will you try stopping us?"

I glared at Harrington, who was surprisingly relaxed about the whole situation. He then said words which surprised me to hear.

"You're free to go," he said simply. "We never kept you against your will. You chose to stay as long as you did."

"Only because you didn't come and see us!" I shouted back. My excuse felt weak as I said it.

"You knew where I was all along. You could have visited me at any time. No matter the reason," Harrington said. "We will not halt you on your way out. Just remember, the world is a dangerous one to walk in."

"Good job we're not walking," I quipped back with a sly wink. "We're driving."

"In what?" Harrington said, blinking in genuine surprise.

"Our Jeep. The Jeep we drove here in," I said back through gritted teeth.

"That's not *your* Jeep," Harrington said, a small smile spreading over his lips. "That's property of the British Army. As surviving members of the British Army, it belongs to us."

"I thought you were *The Harrington Brigade*," James interjected mockingly.

"Potato-potahto," Harrington said with a shrug. "The guns were, and are, British Army equipment also. As I said, the world is a dangerous place to walk in. Better get walking."

"I don't give a crap what you say, we are driving out of here with everything we came in with," I snarled, turning to leave.

"You can't without keys to the depot," Harrington said smugly. I heard a jingle behind me. I turned around to see him holding a set of keys in his hands. Anger pulsed through me, James looked even angrier.

"You're scum!" James snarled. He began to walk towards

Harrington, and that's when Harrington raised his gun.

"Take another step and I shall shoot you in the head," he said, remaining unbelievably calm. James smiled at Harrington's threat. Harrington raised his voice as I saw anger from him for the first time, "You think I won't, *boy!* I've killed better men than you for far less! Why would I not kill dirt like you?!"

"You wouldn't dare," James said with a calm smile. He took another step forward, and then there was loud crack. I closed my eyes instinctively. Something warm and wet hit my face. I opened my eyes slowly. The first thing I saw was James' body fall to the floor. He didn't stagger. He didn't drop slowly. He just collapsed into a heap. The back of his skull was no longer there. Blood poured from the wound. I rushed to his side, already knowing it was too late.

"James!" I screamed. I knelt next to him and that was when I realised that I was covered in his blood. The exit wound had sprayed me with brain, skull shards, and blood. It was all James'. I began to scream. My chest tightened. I felt like I was having a panic attack.

"I warned him," Harrington said calmly, holstering his weapon. His statement was justification enough for his action in his eyes.

I continued to scream, tears welling in my eyes, "James! For God sake! James!"

CHAPTER 34

My eyes stung from the tears. My voice was hoarse from my screams. I was covered in blood. My friend's blood. James' blood. I had zoned out after I saw James brutally murdered. All I knew was Harrington had called for men to take me to the gates and leave me outside. I moved on autopilot. We paused at the gate while it opened. The same for the fence. I was guided outside and away from the security of the walls. Harrington had personally come to see me off.

"Good luck out there, Sam," he said sternly. He then said, almost sadly, "Remember, you had every opportunity to live in safety here with James. This is *your* doing. I hope you know that."

I was angry, and his words stung, but mostly because I knew they were true. If we had left earlier, perhaps that wouldn't have happened? Maybe, if we hadn't come to the base to begin with, he would still be alive? I had made those decisions. It was on me.

"I am not a cruel man," Harrington continued, "I am merely doing what I have to do to keep my men safe. You helped me realise that."

I stood there, swaying on the spot, as Harrington's words brushed over me. Nothing felt real. It was as though I watched the events happen to another person.

Harrington then said, "As I have already told you,

227

everything belonging to the British Army now belongs to us. Normally I would not have a problem letting you leave as you are."

I continued to stare into the nothingness.

"However, the little incident back there has dirtied a perfectly good set of military boots," Harrington said with a face like stone. "I am going to have to requisition those back to my base … I'm sure you understand."

With that, I felt hands push me to the ground. I didn't resist. I just wanted the world to swallow me up. I just wanted the numbness to go. I felt my military boots get torn from my feet with the socks still in them, exposing my feet to the coldness of the air. The men returned to the base with the boots, and my body instinctively pushed myself up, almost beyond my control.

The gates closed and Harrington began walking back to his house, boots in hand, almost as if they were a trophy. All the other soldiers had left and returned to whatever they were meant to be doing. The show was over for them. I stared into the base and realised that the sniper, Steve, whom I had spent many days with, was the only one who remained.

"There's a petrol station a few miles up the road," Steve whispered quietly so that he wouldn't be heard. "Get away from here. You should be able to find somewhere safe to go from there … good luck, man."

Then Steve left as well, returning to his post in the guard tower. I stood at the gates for a few more moments, Harrington almost back inside his house. Anger flared within me.

"Harrington!" I shouted at the top of my lungs. He turned to look at me over his shoulder. I stared at him, our eye contact never breaking. "Maybe not today, not even tomorrow, but one day, I will be back. When I am, I will burn this place to the ground and it will be your funeral pyre."

I saw Harrington smile, very briefly, before turning away from me and going back inside.

"I swear to whatever Gods there are," I added, to myself that time. "I will make you *pay*."

I didn't waste my time by lingering for much longer. I needed to move. I headed in the direction Steve had told me. For the first mile, I just walked. My bare feet burned from scuffing the tarmac road. I was sure my feet would be bloody if I looked down. I also had the fear that, at any moment, I would be shot in the back and killed by one of the snipers. I imagined crosshairs trained on me for the entire time I walked. I eventually turned a bend in the road and that was when I finally felt safe; bullets couldn't bend around corners, after all. Evidence of the military presence became less obvious the further away I got. There were no more road traps, no more parked cars, no more snipers; that I could see anyway. When I was well and truly out of sight, and confident there were no undead around, I proceeded to break down. I collapsed to the ground, sobbing and shaking. I clawed at my face and clothes, trying to scrape James' rapidly drying blood off of me. I felt sick and horrified by what I had seen. It was one thing to shoot a zombie and watch its innards spill out, but a completely different thing to watch the same happen to the living. I tried to compare it to one of the many horror films I had watched over the years. It didn't work. In films, you knew it was all makeup and camera trickery. There was something sickening watching it happen for real, and even worse for someone I knew and considered a friend. I continued wailing and crouched down, making myself as small as possible. I felt as though I was literally going to fall apart at any moment. My chest tightened as I sobbed. I knew I was going to need to catch my breath, otherwise I would end up in hysterics. I took huge, racking breaths between sobs to try and calm down. It worked ever so slightly and I began thinking straight. What had happened to James was the worst thing imaginable; at that moment. I could still smell the iron from his spilt blood, which didn't make things any easier. Yet it did make things easier somehow. I focussed on the iron smell and breathed carefully. I needed to move. If I died, then James' death would have all been for nothing. We had got so far together, so I had to continue for the both of us. The plan was to head to the petrol station Steve had told me about and refocus there. I could think and plan there. First things first was getting off the road. I was exposed there, to both the living and the dead. I was weaponless and had approximately four hours left of daylight. Moving in the dark disadvantaged the dead, but put me at one too. I needed to make the journey in the daytime. I had to get off the road and make way through the knee-high grass along the roadside. It would shield me from prying eyes. I patted myself down to see what I had: a single bullet and my phone. I stared at the bullet for a moment before a certain clarity came over me. I spoke aloud.

"This one is yours, Harrington," I whispered solemnly. I picked up a small rock and scratched a crude letter "H" into the side. I would *never* forget …

For the first quarter of the journey, I moved in a crouched position through the grass at a slow and deliberate pace. The slow pace and coolness of the grass made the journey much more bearable on my feet. Sure, I kept out of sight, but I covered barely any ground. Added with the fact I had yet to see a single zombie in the area made me think that walking, or even running, was an option. So that was what I did. I jogged over the uneven ground. My bare feet didn't absorb any of the shock of the impact for me. Most types of footwear would have wrecked my ankles doing that, and barefoot was even worse. Every now and again, my thoughts would stray to James and the brutality of his death. I would sob loudly before quickly regaining control. Tears would flow down my face freely during that time and I let them. The more crying I did then, the less I hoped to do later. I repeated James' address he had half-heartedly told me what felt like a long time ago. It helped to calm me and gave me something to think about. I would visit his parents one day. For James.

About halfway along the journey, I spotted a zombie. It was making its way up the road at a slow and shuffled pace. I dropped to my knees and hid while it passed. A wave of stench washed over me as it did so, and I began to think of how I would get the drop on it and kill it. The zombie got further and further away and I still had no way or plan to end it. Then it struck me as the zombie moved out of sight, I didn't need to kill every zombie I saw. If I was always going into constant battle, I was sure to fall eventually. That epiphany made me realise I *didn't* need to fight every battle I came across. I could simply let them breeze by me. I waited for the shuffling footsteps to be far enough away from me that I couldn't hear them anymore before I continued.

I didn't find another zombie the entire journey. At one point, I discovered an abandoned car on the road, which I thought would be perfect to take. I approached it slowly. If there were no keys, I would have to try and hotwire it. As I got closer, I realised that there was no chance of me driving the thing. One of the tyres looked as though it had been shredded and had continued on its rims; another wheel looked like it had buckled inwards. The front was smashed to pieces and completely inoperable. The finishing touch was the blood-smeared windscreen. The smears were on the inside. The car looked steamed up on all other windows, yet bloody handprints coated the inside of the front windows. Whatever had happened in the car, I didn't need to see. The "Baby on Board" sign furthered that thought. That car was a no-go. I continued onwards to the petrol station.

I found the petrol station eventually. It was in a less than desirable area. It presided just on the inner edge of a small town in the middle of nowhere. I'm sure the town was lovely once upon a time, probably even belonged in a fairy-tale itself. It had old cobblestone streets in some areas, and most of the buildings looked pre-World War Two era. I would have loved to live there … if the world had never changed. Now it looked like a scene out of a horror film. Undead milled about the town as if they owned the place, which I suppose they did. Blood pooled along the lines between the cobblestones, creating a red outline for the old-fashioned brickwork. Cars were smashed up and many had crashed into each other. There were no dead bodies as far as I could see, but that was probably because they were still walking about. That was the problem with a town that small, the military didn't consider it worth defending. As a result, it ended up like the one I was in. That wasn't my concern, however; my concern was finding a useable vehicle to use for the rest of my journey. From my initial look, many cars no longer looked drivable. Plus, there was an issue of keys. I knew I could hotwire a vehicle, but it was something I had never actually done. Just read how to do. My very first stop, however, was the petrol station. That was where I needed to go first of all. I needed supplies. I needed footwear.

I crept along the road, keeping close to the edge of the buildings. I slipped on the uneven and bloody cobblestones. The risk of twisting my ankle was worse without any form of footwear. I tried my best not to think about the congealed, cold blood pushing its way through my toes with every step. I would try to avoid every zombie that I could. An advantage of a small town was having so few residents and, thus, so few zombies. Sure they would be an issue if they all attacked at once, but I doubted they would. I kept skirting around the edges of buildings until I was in viewing range of the petrol station. There were six zombies wandering the area around the pumps. I could also see the doors were wide open and bloody trails led in, or out, of the building. That meant there could be undead in there too. A few zombies shambled along the streets around the petrol station also. I realised I could probably kill two birds with one stone. I needed supplies in the petrol station, but I also needed a vehicle. To my luck, there was a choice of vehicles left at the pumps. There was a large white van which belonged to some landscaping company, a motorbike with a bag attached to it, and a nifty little Ford Fiesta. If I could get the Fiesta, that would be brilliant; the motorbike was my next choice. Unfortunately, there were so many undead nearby. I couldn't fight and kill them all, so I needed a plan. I shrunk back, out of sight, to think. I knew I needed to get the undead away from there, and the idea of getting them to chase me to pull them away came to mind. I quickly dismissed it as I didn't have a plan for losing them once they had picked up the chase, but a distraction of some kind was definitely needed. I thought back over all my experiences, both pre- and post-apocalypse. I was in an urban environment. There was bound to be something I could use. As I crouched there deep in thought, my eyes fell on a mostly ruined car nearby. I smiled as a plan begun to form.

CHAPTER 35

I crept closer to the petrol station with an armful of wheel trims, which I had seized from the destroyed car. I crouched behind another car, which looked as if it had been abandoned where it stood when the occupant ran. I was out of sight from the undead, but I could see the undead clearly from beneath the car. They didn't seem to follow any predetermined path as they wandered. They walked wherever took their fancy, swaying left and right and changing direction on a whim. A little further down a side street sat several cars. They were parked outside a few houses and didn't look like they had been moved at all since the dead began to walk. The fact they hadn't been moved was what my entire plan hinged on. I hefted a wheel trim in my hand. It wasn't heavy but had just enough weight for what I needed it for. When I was confident the undead weren't looking in my general direction, I flung the wheel trim like a Frisbee. It glided majestically through the air and towards the car and … missed. It was okay, I still had a few more to try. I threw another after I readjusted my aim. That one fell ever so slightly short. I threw the third one a lot harder but kept the same angle. It glided through the air faster than my previous attempts. I watched it eagerly as it glided towards the car. I held my breath … it hit home! Within seconds of contact, the car alarm sounded. It was a high-pitched squeal, designed to draw attention, and draw attention it did! The moment the alarm sounded, I dropped to my stomach and looked beneath the car. I watched the undead slowly turned towards the direction of the alarm. They began to shamble towards it, leaving the petrol station completely free of undead. I made my way around the car and moved towards the station whilst crouching. As I passed the pumps, I checked each vehicle for keys. Not a single one had any in, or around, them. The van had a fuel pump sticking out of it still, but that wasn't useful to me. I headed inside the petrol station.

The inside of the petrol station didn't have any lights on, but the dimmed light outside was still enough to see by. There was an intense stench in the store: the smell of death. The store consisted of a till to the immediate left when you walked in and three long aisles that reached to the back of the store. I could see from the door that most of the shelves had been emptied of its goods. There were a few loose tins, which I assumed someone had dropped when they tried to make a quick exit. I also noticed an excessive amount of gore and bloody smears everywhere. It looked as if it had been a killing zone as the undead trapped the living in there. I slowly walked deeper into the store, leaving bloody footprints as I went. I grabbed a plastic carrier bag and proceeded around the aisles; at least I didn't need to pay for the bag! I scooped up a few stray cans which were on the floor. It didn't matter what they were, but it was food. I carried on around the store, finding very little as I did so. A bottle of water here, some bandages there, a tub of vapour rub. Before meeting Peters, I wouldn't have picked it up. It was an odd mix, but I stuffed everything I found into the bag. In the third aisle, I saw a body lying there, back twisted at an unnatural angle, which explained the horrific smell. As I got closer, I could see it was the body of the man who owned the motorbike outside. I don't often go on stereotypes, but the man wore a leather jacket with some sort of insignia stitched on the back. He had a greying beard and looked like he would punch you rather than talk. He was definitely the owner of the motorbike. If he was in the store, and his ride was outside, then that probably meant he had the keys on him! There was a mess of congealed blood around the body, but no sign of a head wound. He could have still been a zombie. I grimaced. I didn't want to do it. I crept closer and could see the keys in his clenched hand. He also had some lovely, heavy-looking, leather boots on. I crouched and undid the laces, tugging the boots loose. I didn't remove his socks for fear that his rotten flesh would coat the lining of them. I slipped the *moist* boots on and shuddered. They were a couple sizes too small but I couldn't complain, considering the situation. Next, I breathed in and pushed my newly booted foot onto his head and nudged him with it. At the moment of contact, the man reacted. He thrashed about wildly and snarled, almost throwing me off instantly. I regained my balance and slammed my other foot down onto the hand with the keys. I heard bones crunch under the impact. His wrist hung limply and he released the keys. His damaged back probably meant that he couldn't feel me touch his legs! I quickly scooped up the keys and made my way to the front.

I ran out of the store and straight to the motorbike; it was the type known as a chopper. It had a stretched, styled frame and a high back on the seat. The handles were high and the seat was low. I enjoyed the thought of riding it. I would look so cool! I looked at my surroundings. There were no undead around, so it was perfect. I climbed onto the motorbike and stuck the key in. A perfect fit. I grinned and turned the key. The engine roared to life. I was about to turn the throttle when I noticed the fuel gauge. It was bordering on empty. I felt so goddamn stupid! Why else would the motorbike be there! I heard an excited snarl nearby; I had alerted the undead with the engine's rumble. I quickly turned it off. I had probably ninety seconds, at most, before the undead were on me. I dived off the motorbike and ran for the pump. I saw the pumps still had life in them. The electronic sign was on at least, and I thanked the Gods. I grabbed one of the hand pumps and pulled the nozzle to the motorbike. I stuck it into the hole for the fuel and pulled the trigger. Fuel poured into the tank. It just didn't seem to come out fast enough! I could hear feet pounding on the street as the undead came around the corner. I had run out of time. I stuck the cap back over the tank and climbed onto the motorbike. I gave a last glance towards the store and saw the undead biker crawl out of the front door. His legs left a gory trail as he did so. Part of me wondered, for the briefest of moments, if any part of him felt insulted about someone else riding his motorbike. The dead look in his eyes suggested not. I restarted the engine and pulled the throttle. The motorbike tore away at an immense speed. It was only then I remembered something very important … I didn't actually know how to ride a motorbike.

TAO OF SAM – MEDICINE: THE BASICS

Medicine is going to be useful for many things. Get your hands on the higher-end stuff, like prescription antibiotic tablets and painkillers. They will be in high demand and in short supply. Keep hold of antibiotics for your own use. Painkillers and other medications will work like currency in the new world; people will trade for it.

Next, get specialist stuff, like diabetes medication. It will be useful for those you know who need it. Make sure you grab inhalers for me also! Remember, those are trade-worthy items also.

Finally, grab as much over the counter medicine as possible. It won't be the best stuff, but it is comforts like throat lozenges and paracetamol which will make the world more bearable.

Bandages and other pieces of first aid equipment will be useful too. Having a decent and fully equipped first aid kit could save your life.

If you can get your hands on medical equipment of other kinds, such as heart monitors or defibrillators, do it. Who knows when it will come in handy? It isn't worth a risk on your life for it though. Don't go searching for it.

CHAPTER 36

I rode along steadily with the wind blowing through my hair. The sunlight was beautiful and I could almost forget that, the previous day, I had narrowly escaped death. I had driven away from the fuel station, albeit, doing a terrible job. I was uncertain of how to ride the motorbike. If I moved slowly, I felt I would fall off, but I found it went just fine the faster I went. I would worry about stopping when it came to it.

When I had gotten far enough from the small town and there were no undead around, I decided to do an inventory of what I had. First things first was stopping. I slowed and carried on slowing. I wobbled erratically before I realised I need to put my foot down to stop and balance. Once I had stopped, I took a deep breath and sighed. I was fairly certain that the motorbike was a death-trap. I started my inventory. I knew what I had from the store, but I didn't know what was in the bag on the motorbike. It was the sort of bag which had parts on either side of the seat: a saddle bag. On one side, it was rammed with different medications. Everything from painkillers, to antibiotics, antibacterial gel to antiseptic bandages. I had found quite the haul. I sifted through it in disbelief. On the other side were tins of food, bottles of water, a torch, and a set of binoculars. I hadn't replaced everything I had lost to the military, but I was almost there! There was also a revolver with a small box of ammo. There were no rounds in the gun, which I quickly rectified. Riding around with an unloaded gun was what would get people killed! I found a small transceiver radio. I also found something else unexpected. I almost left it alone when I first noticed it, but there was a handle sticking out from behind the bag. I thought it was something to do with the motorbike. I pulled at it anyway and it came out with a metal on metal scraping sound. I realised it was, in fact, an extremely sharp and unused machete. I stared at it with some glee; it was definitely what I needed. The owner of the bike was obviously very well-prepared for the apocalypse, but not prepared enough, apparently.

From there, nightfall came fairly quickly. Darkness spread around me, and I had nowhere to go. I needed to sleep, but I was out in the open. I carried on driving until inspiration hit. I found an abandoned car, which I checked the inside of, flashlight in one hand and my new machete in the other. It was empty. No signs of anyone. The car didn't look like it had any reason to be abandoned either. I noticed a fuel can on the passenger's seat and grabbed at it greedily, hoping to take it; it was empty. Lack of fuel probably brought an end to that driver. I was thankful though, as the car would be my bed for the night. I climbed in, shut the doors, and sealed the windows. I brought my saddlebags into the car with me for safekeeping. I laid on the back seat, machete never too far, and fell asleep.

I had a peaceful and uneventful sleep. It was amazing. Another night that I didn't dream, which was strange for me. I got up to a beautiful day. A perfect day for the last stretch of my journey. I was nervous, of course I was, but all previous bad thoughts stayed deep within me. I climbed on my motorbike and drove towards the county of Essex. The road sign claimed it was only five miles away. I had qualms about travelling the world with no helmet. The human body was so fragile, after all. I knew that my chances of a collision were slim. I just had to worry about my own driving ability.

CHAPTER 37

There it was. Essex. I was *technically* already in Essex, but things changed when the dead rose. The outskirts of the county had been abandoned and people in the outer districts moved inwards. It was an attempt to make a more defendable area. An entire county was impossible to defend, but individual districts with established borders were much easier. That was because urban areas have naturally formed defences which the military could take advantage of. The military had set up blockades on all the roads in and out of those areas. They monitored everything. It was, so to say, the "shining example" of how a county should defend itself from an undead threat. In retrospect, it was a shame that Essex didn't have more time; they may have actually pulled it off.

Between the blockades, construction of a giant wall had been started. They had planned for the wall to encompass the districts; the military would man its walls at all hours. They would have an overview of everything and nothing would get through. The idea, I guess, was inspired by medieval castles. I wouldn't have been surprised to hear a moat was being made with a drawbridge for access. The idea of the wall was to cut Essex off from anyone else and for Essex to become fully self-sufficient. The rest of the world could just burn and the United Kingdom would have its own little state protecting itself. I read a lot about the plans of the city in the early days. The rest of the UK heard very little about its other counties; for morale, I suppose. The government and local councils tried to sell the new ideas as exciting to the people. Like the green initiative. Like every initiative, it was met with mixed results. Many people claimed that they would be trapped and that they didn't want to live in a Big Brother state. There were protests because of it.

"I was born in 1984," people exclaimed. "I don't want to die in it."

That became the slogan: "Live today, not 1984." As much as the whole situation was blown out of proportion, the media stayed oddly quiet about it all. Maybe the government's hand was forced to stop mass panic?

The wall initiative happened anyway. They tried to make it a community effort. Every citizen of Essex, every refugee from other cities, had to help erect metal fabrications. I don't know why, though. Even with everyone putting up the wall's pieces, the wall would never be finished in time. Did they seriously underestimate how much work was required? Perhaps they hoped people would get more involved once they started. Unfortunately, people are lazy. The wall was never finished. I knew that because I could see the wall from where I stood with my binoculars. All uncompleted three sheets of it. The most it would stop were the seeing-impaired; the undead would have no problem walking around it.

Something else about the whole situation worried me. Not that the wall wasn't finished, but that the wall wasn't being worked on. What was even more worrying was that I couldn't see any movement at the blockade either. I squinted through my binoculars, trying to see the slightest hint of movement.

Nothing. The place looked dead. Dead as in quiet, not dead as in flesh-eating. I leaned over to the radio transmitter that I had scavenged and turned it on. I then cycled through the radio waves looking for some kind of signal. Nothing but static. No military broadcasts. No regular broadcasts. Just utter silence. I picked up the transmitter and clicked it on so that I could broadcast.

"Hello, this is Sam broadcasting on the military band. I am approaching the county of Essex on the M25. Please do not shoot. I am not infected and am simply seeking asylum," I said calmly and coolly, but it yielded no answer. I clicked off and nothing but static came through. I repeated the message once more just in case, and then again in desperation. Nothing. I chucked the transmitter down and muttered, "Crap."

Moving across the military boundary didn't seem like a smart move. I didn't want to get any closer without a military go-ahead or escort. They could shoot me on sight and probably would be justified in doing so. If not the military, then the undead were likely to have me. I didn't know which one I trusted less in that moment. I felt anger and sadness rise within me. I would have my revenge on Harrington and all his men. It probably wouldn't be for a long, long time, but I swore by the Gods that I would burn his world to the ground. I could wait an eternity for my revenge. My hand automatically caressed the bullet I was saving for Harrington, my fingertip touching the small "H" on it. I had a fire in my belly. The need for action. I hadn't come that far for nothing. I slung the saddle bag back onto the motorbike. I checked that my machete was strapped down onto the motorbike safely, making sure it wouldn't cut me if I fell. I took a deep breath. Nervousness pushed its way through me. It wouldn't be long before I met up with Alice again; for better or for worse. I focussed on the fire and not the fear. All was good to go. I twisted the throttle and was gone, heading into Essex. The ghost county.

CHAPTER 38

I cruised up to the blockade. I moved slowly in the hope that I didn't look like a threat to any potential soldiers. It was also so that I could make a quick turn and retreat should the undead try to swarm me. My stomach writhed with the worms of doubt. Up until that moment, I had been fairly confident with what I was facing. The undead were simple enough to understand, yet I was scared like I had never been scared before. In all previous incidences I had known, more or less, what would happen. What I was moving into this time was a mystery. What would I face? Friend or Foe? Living or Dead? I shook inside, and it wasn't from the vibrations of the motorbike. At any moment, I expected a bullet to hit me from some unseen sharpshooter. I was fifty feet away and nothing. Thirty feet. Nothing. Twenty feet and *still* nothing. I could also see the blockade was *very* empty. There were sandbags where a guard post and mounted gun would have once been, but nothing stood in its place anymore. The guard tower seemed to be devoid of equipment, such as spotlights. It was like the blockade in London, but creepier. It wouldn't be as bad had there been blood or bodies. It would have explained the absence of life, as bad as that sounded. The fact there was nothing at all made chills run down my back. My arms covered themselves in goosebumps and all the hair stood on end. It was like everyone had been abducted.

"I really hope there aren't aliens now as well." I laughed aloud. Although the laugh was a bit extreme, it was more like a madman's nervous chuckle. I expected something to show itself at the sound of my voice, but not even undead reared their rotten heads. I weaved my way through the initial barricade, which wasn't difficult at all. Although the lack of a barricade and men to defend it was a bad thing, it was also promising for me. Abandoned military equipment was a lifesaver. Hell, at the last blockade I'd obtained a vehicle. I couldn't wait to see what this one yielded. I slowed the motorbike to a stop and climbed off. My first stop, machete and binoculars in hand, was the guard tower. I got halfway to the tower before I realised I had left the motorbike running. I turned and considered walking back to turn the engine off.

"Meh," I shrugged, and continued on to the tower. I could be pretty lazy at times; that was one of those times. Besides, it could help in a quick getaway.

The tower was a simple construction with a ladder to get up it. If Ikea made military guard towers, that was what they would look like. I was having a wave of déjà vu … had I thought that before? I shook my head and continued. I had seen that style of build so many times at that point, similar thoughts were bound to repeat themselves.

I climbed to the top, worried that the tower would tilt over in the breeze. Luckily, it held. I didn't need the binoculars to see that the entire blockade had been abandoned, and not rapidly either. There were tents and such still up, but I couldn't see a single gun or vehicle left behind. No blood or bodies to suggest a battle had taken place. I could see a few undead shambling about, but they didn't wear military garb and could very well have just wandered in there, only to become lost in the maze of tents. I could see other guard towers spread throughout the encampment, a tent painted with a red cross to suggest medical supplies which I would make a stop in, and a tent marked "Mess Hall" which would also require a stop. Smoke rose in the distance from several different areas. If I could see it from that far, it was probably a huge fire. That wasn't my problem … yet. I looked at the undead and their positioning. They wouldn't be much of a challenge. They were spread out and few in number. I could probably kill them all without alerting any of the others. I reflected on how my confidence regarding conflict with the undead had grown. When viewing them logically, they were stupid and slow; a winning combination for me. From the watchtower, I had no fear about facing them. I smiled slightly and was amused by how my situation was similar to childbirth. Childbirth is horrifically painful, or so I have heard, but women see no problem doing it again because their bodies trick them into thinking it wasn't that bad. That was how I viewed the undead. However, I knew that once I was up close and personal, the fear would set in. I would see the maggots crawling in their flesh, their skin slack and grey. I would be surrounded by the horrific stench which followed, and the ghastly noises they made. I knew that was when the terror would start. It was the ultimate psychological warfare and they didn't even know they did it, and that was how they became the apex predator. Everything about them struck fear into their prey; their prey being humans. I started to feel uneasy about facing them, but I bottled my fear. After all, I couldn't live in the tower forever.

I sighed and began my downwards climb. I withdrew my machete. It was time to prove myself as the apex predator among the dead.

CHAPTER 39

I crept along slowly, almost crouching as I did so. I had my machete drawn and ready to strike. I went step by step to make sure I made as little noise as possible. I stuck my head in the first tent and saw nothing. No people, no lockers, no anything; it was completely cleared out except for bedframes which stood there eerily. It was the same for every tent I visited. Even though every tent which I came across was empty, I still felt the compulsion to check each one. Not necessarily for anything to take, but for signs of the prior occupants. At least with the encampment outside London, there had been signs of life. In Essex, there was nothing. I could understand if they retreated due to conflict, but there were no signs that there had even been a fight. I couldn't find a single spent shell. The military must have just packed up and left without a fight. Had they received an early warning? I didn't know and doubted I ever would. I knew something really wasn't right about anything though. I was looking around the empty tent when the sound of dragging feet broke my train of thought. I tensed. The sound was just outside the tent. It was a tell-tale sign of the undead. Had I alerted it? I thought I had been careful whilst moving through the maze of tents. I moved to the entrance of the tent and hid behind the flap. I would, at least, get the jump on the zombie. I clutched the machete even tighter and raised it. I held my breath and waited for the zombie to turn into the tent. I waited. And waited. And waited. I heard the shuffle get quieter as the zombie moved further away. I relaxed a little and looked out of the tent flap. The zombie had carried on past the tent; it didn't even know I was there. It continued onwards and up the corridor created by the rows of tents. I considered just letting it go, as I had done after my confrontation with Harrington, but a thought struck me. In most zombie films, a character is normally felled by that *one* which got away. It was normally made obvious to the viewer by marking the zombie in some way so it stood out from the rest. I refused to fall into the same trap as those many hapless movie characters. Added with the idea that I would need to retreat if I hit trouble further up, then I could possibly retreat straight back into that zombie. I sighed. I had to take care of the walking corpse. I stepped out of the tent and crept along slowly. I moved slow enough to be quiet but kept my posture ready to burst into a full sprint should I get noticed. My eyes watered as I breathed in the smell left by the zombie. It was almost as if the dead left a stink trail wherever they went. I wiped my eyes without even breaking stride. Within seconds I was behind the zombie. I raised the machete high and brought it down heavily towards the zombie's skull. The zombie must have realised something wasn't right, because it started to turn as the machete made contact with its head. It hadn't turned fast enough to save itself, though. The machete split the rotten flesh from which its matted hair hung loosely. The skull cracked and split like the shell of an egg. The zombie fell to the ground in a lump; blackened brains poured out of its head in a congealed puddle on the floor. This zombie was clearly in the latter stages of decay. The stench hit me and I began to dry heave. I had barely anything in me to leave on the ground. I almost regretted opening its skull. The way the smell left the body reminded me of the time my mum had once opened some rotten chicken which was in an airtight container. It looked bad through the clear plastic, but we still had to dispose of it appropriately. The moment the seal was broken, everyone in the room was instantly hit with the stink of rotten meat. It was like that. The zombie stunk, but splitting its skull made matters so much worse. I barrelled away from the zombie as fast as I could, retching as I did so. If I hadn't alerted any of the undead, then it would be a miracle. And a miracle it was; not a single zombie appeared. I counted my blessings and moved onwards.

My next goal was the first aid tent. I hoped there would be some medical supplies in there that I could pillage for future use. I knew things like that would be a valuable commodity in the near future, and I wanted to cash in on it. I pretty much pranced between tents, desperately trying to move quickly yet silently. On several occasions, I almost walked straight into a zombie, but I had much quicker reactions than them. I put them down before they even noticed me. They barely let out a moan as my blade crashed through their skulls. I had been prepared for the putrid brain liquid to spill out again and had stuffed tissue soaked in vapour rub up my nose. Sure, it left me without my sense of smell, which was a pretty valuable asset when fighting an enemy which smelled the way the undead did, but I was at even less of an advantage if I nearly vomited after every kill. It worked wonders. Before long I was at the medical tent. The contents were exactly as I had expected, and not as I hoped. There were a few stainless steel desks left behind and medical boxes. They were, however, as empty as the other tents. Not even a used needle to suggest it had ever been used. I restrained myself from kicking the metal table; the racket surely would alert the undead. I bunched my fists tightly instead; the machete handle cut into my hand. I knew there was no point checking the mess hall or any of the other hundreds of tents. The military had well and truly cleared out and left almost no sign of their existence. It was time to move on.

I strolled back between the tents from the way I had come. Anger and frustration overrode my need to be careful. I had cleared out the area previously, so what did it matter? That attitude almost got me killed. I was walking along, not a care in the world, when a zombie stepped out of a tent in front of me. I swore I had cleared out that section previously. Confusion halted my response. Surprise didn't halt the zombie. It lunged for me, moaning as it did so. The rotten flesh tore as the face contorted into a snarl. I plunged the machete up through the bottom of its chin. Its dead eyes went deader, if that was even possible. I panted. It had surprised me, but at least I had managed the situation. I was just catching my breath when I heard more shuffling from behind me. I turned to see undead walking out from between the rows of tents. It was like they were lining up to see a grand attraction. Me. I didn't waste another second. I bolted into a run. The undead chased me. I just needed to make it to my motorbike.

I dodged between more tents, taking lefts and rights. I was trying to throw the undead off my trail. It didn't work. For every zombie I lost, another ten stepped out to take its place. There were just so many of them! They were moving between the tents like a flood. The idea of climbing up the tower to escape came to me, but I quickly dismissed it. The tower was unstable, and that many undead would simply topple it. If not that, the undead could wait at the bottom until I starved to death. I had to reach the motorbike.

I ran and ran. My legs felt as though they were no longer pumping blood but a thick sludge through my arteries. It slowed me down. My chest tightened. I could feel myself on the verge of an asthma attack. I began to panic, which made my situation worse. I hadn't had an asthma attack in years! Why did I have to have one then?! Soon it wouldn't matter that I was faster than the undead. Although they were only ever a hair's breadth behind me, they soon would wear me down through exhaustion. My body started to give up and my windpipe tightened. That was it. I was at my end. I was going to … I saw the sandbag barrier where I had left the motorbike. New energy surged through me. I pounded my feet against the ground harder and propelled myself forward. I managed to get ahead and crossed the extra few crucial feet necessary to get on the motorbike safely. I had never been more thankful that I was too lazy to go back and do something. I kicked up the motorbike stand and raced away, dodging between the undead and tents. I pretty much flew out the other end of the encampment. I was free to explore Essex.

CHAPTER 40

Essex had a statue on a roundabout to commemorate the county's part in the 2012 Olympics. It was of a man riding a bicycle, but all modern art styled; it was odd to look at. It was a proud monument for a proud time, and it was soiled. A body hung limply from it. Some poor soul had decided to "opt out" of the situation. He had somehow managed to tie a length of rope to the statue and hung himself. Now he dangled from it like a wind chime, swaying gently in the breeze. The young man's legs had been stripped of flesh; bare bone and muscle were exposed beneath it. The undead had clearly enjoyed the hanged snack. Was he still alive when he had been eaten? Or had he passed from the world when he became a meal for monsters? I would never know, and that man would probably remain there until the end of days. I continued to stare at him. I couldn't look away for some reason. There was a small chance that I had passed him in the street once upon a time. A few more minutes passed before he started to twitch. Tiny muscle spasms hit his body; in his legs at first, then arms, and eventually all over. I thought he was still alive and tensed myself to help him down. It was only when he opened his lifeless grey eyes that I realised he was still dead.

It stretched its mouth open hungrily. A gaping hole ready to consume everything. Its eyes wandered before they set on me. It then began to thrash around in an attempt to escape its noose so it could eat. I looked away from the swinging corpse and rode away on the motorbike.

I had a good idea which way it was to Alice's house. I had been there before, so I thought I could remember. There was a niggling bit of doubt in my mind though. I could expect a few wrong turns. Human error was always an issue. So I started to ride there. I was surprised by the complete lack of military presence, or people, in general. Essex was always very bustling when I had visited previously, added with the fact there had been an evacuation of London to there. The lack of people was strange, yet it had become commonplace. The further I travelled, the more I saw signs of life, or where there had once been life. Shop windows were smashed, which could be attributed to the undead, but there also appeared to be stuff missing from the shops. It was the work of looters. Why did people resort to looting useless stuff in times of need? The streets were also packed with cars. The cars didn't look like they had been going through an evacuation. Rather, it looked like it had been an average day of shopping and travel when they had been abandoned. Perhaps that was what happened? Essex felt well-defended and continued as normal before the infection spread like wildfire. People panicked. People looted. People died.

I saw an odd corpse or two lying about. Always in groups of one or two; adults and children alike. No one had escaped the undead. I didn't want to wait around for long, as the dead would soon become the undead. I carried on driving and weaved between cars. I found it was easier driving on the pavement than the road. Plumes of smoke rose into the sky in the distance. I thought I could also hear the staccato of gunfire somewhere, but that may have been me being hopeful about the outcome of an entire county of people. I drove along slowly and followed the roads. I remembered many years ago when I made that mistake, I had travelled by coach and was meant to be picked up by Alice's family at a stop. I, however, missed my stop. I ended up in the roughest part of Essex. I stood in the street, suitcase in hand, being eyed up by every person there. I was fairly certain I was going to be shanked there and then. Luckily, Alice's dad knew where I was and picked me up. I survived to see another day.

However, this time I recognised my stop. I knew that I was on the right track. I took a turn down an alley, which I knew led to a car park with a shortcut. It would make it easier to get where I needed to go. The alley was intended to be a footpath, so it was a tight squeeze for the motorbike. The handles bounced softly off the wall and wooden fence on either side of me as they made contact with each surface. I tried to steady myself and kept going. I whizzed around the corner and into the open car park. There were a lot of cars there. There were even more zombies. They turned to look at me as I came into view. I stared at the large crowd of undead, and they stared at me. They charged forward.

The undead climbed over cars, and each other, to get closer to me. They swarmed forward faster and faster. I am certain a few were crushed by the stampede. I pulled the throttle back and rocketed forward. It was going to be a close call. The exit of the car park was dead ahead, but it would mean the undead charged at me from a ninety-degree angle. If I wasn't fast enough then I would be swamped in seconds. I leaned forward, hoping the momentum would carry me forward that little bit more; the same way you see kids lean side to side when playing video games. I sped onwards. I was fully aware of the undead. I was also fully aware that they were only a matter of metres away. I could pretty much feel the undead's clutches around me as I exited the car park. I swerved the motorbike sideways in an effort to stop it. I was thrown off and I tumbled across the ground. I covered my head to protect myself. I came to a stop a few metres from my motorbike, both of us beat up. I quickly picked myself up in an effort to escape from the undead, which were out and onto the street. My leg hurt. An excruciating amount. I looked down and saw there was a lot of blood. My leg felt like it was going to collapse under my own weight. My military fatigues were soaked with my own blood. I didn't have time to worry about my legs. I limped ahead and picked my motorbike back up. My machete was next to it. I scooped it up. I threw my damaged leg over my ride. I could see a large shard of glass sticking out of my leg and through my uniform. I didn't try to remove it. It was probably the only thing stemming the flow of blood. My head spun and I could barely keep my vision straight. How I had survived without a helmet was beyond me. Suddenly, the closest zombie was within grabbing distance. I swung the machete in an arc through its head. I got sprayed with blackened blood and the zombie fell to the ground. I tucked the machete against my side and sped away, desperate to get away from the crowd of undead amassing in the streets.

I kept driving down the road and took a few turns until I was certain the horde I had just escaped from wouldn't find me. I stopped the motorbike. I needed a breather. I winced as I moved my leg. I bent down and tore away a piece of the already torn material that used to be my trousers, using it to mop up the blood. It was no good, it just kept bleeding. I reached for the saddle bag and pulled out some painkillers, downing some quickly. I was sure I took more than the recommended dosage, but I didn't care. The pain was so bad I could barely think. I re-evaluated my leg. The glass looked like it was stuck into my leg in a nasty way. I splashed some sort of antibacterial gel on it which burned a lot, wrapped it in a bandage, and then downed some antibiotics. I didn't have time to be weak. I needed to stop any infection setting in. I had taken care of it to the best of my ability at that moment. I wrapped duct tape around the bandage and glass in an attempt to keep the pressure on it and to keep it clean from any further gore from the undead. It would also stop the glass from moving and causing me pain. I had to sort it out when I had time. If it had cut an artery, I was sure I would have already bled out. I looked around at my surroundings. I recognised it. I was near Alice's street. I kept moving. I started riding towards Alice's. It was the final countdown.

SAM'S LETTER TO HIS FAMILY

Dear Mum and Kelsey,

We all know the world is going bad, and fast. We know enough about zombie films to know that everything will fall eventually. It is only ever a matter of time before the undead win.

I know you will be able to survive without me. Our family probably knows how to deal with it better than most. You can keep our family alive. Play your strengths and guard your weaknesses. Don't let your humanity get the better of you, but don't become monsters either. There will be enough of them out there.

Remember what we've spoken about and treat what I have written as law.

I know I am being selfish, but I need to leave. It's the only way.

Don't forget me. I *will* be back. I promise.

Love, Sam

CHAPTER 41

I turned the corner onto the penultimate road before Alice's. The roar of the motorbike was the only sound around. Even in the days before undead roamed the earth, a motorbike and the noise it came with wouldn't have been a common sight in that particular street. My leg throbbed intensely. I was certain infection would set in soon if I didn't do something about it.

When I had travelled there previously, when the world was alive, everything was always so prim and proper. There was never a hedge out of place, nor did the grass ever grow too long. It was like a perfect and safe world. That, however, was no longer. That was just stories from the past. The once near-perfect street was a shadow of how it once was. Blood streaked the roads and pavements and grass. There were pieces of bone and carrion just lying there, like a child's discarded plaything. There was nothing recognisable as once human. Just carnage, everywhere. I could see smoke rising high into the sky a road or so over; the acrid air it left behind sat uncomfortably in my nostrils. The smell took me back to the New Year's Eve I had spent with Alice. It was my first New Year's Eve away from home and I had spent it with her. It was fantastic. We lit some fireworks in the back garden, one of which didn't sail quite high enough and struck the neighbour's house. I wondered if I would ever see fireworks again. I used to think back to that day, when everything seemed so perfect and right. I snapped out of the thoughts which would lead me down a dark and dangerous path. I continued onwards.

I continued along the road slowly and took in the destruction around me. Most of the front doors of houses were open, blood and gore leading into the house. The trail didn't look like it had left every house. I suppose some of the undead had found some innocent person to sink their teeth into but couldn't figure out how to leave. A few of the undead stood motionless in the front gardens of people's houses. Their heads turned to follow me but they made no attempt to pursue me. Perhaps they'd had their fill of flesh and didn't need more? I didn't know, but I doubted the bottomless pits of hunger could ever be sated. I didn't think I would ever find out why they remained dormant on those front lawns, mingling with their neighbours and killers. I continued onwards.

One thing I noticed was the lack of an attempt to escape. Once again, there were no military personnel, living nor dead. Very few cars had even made it off the driveways; the ones which did just sat in the road, motionless. The whereabouts of their owners were unknown, but the shattered windows and bloody pools of gore around the doors were all the clues I needed as to their fate. One person was still in her car; no longer alive, but not quite dead either. She thrashed about, restrained by her seatbelt. The undead woman snapped her teeth and reached for me with no success. She had half of her face missing, torn away by her attackers. The red-stained bone was exposed, and tendons expanded and contracted with her jaw movements. It was like a living diagram of how the human body worked, "living" being the odd word out. The irony didn't escape me that her seatbelt, which may have saved her life once upon a time, was probably the very thing that got her killed. I was saddened by that. Not enough to slow down, however. I continued onwards.

I weaved in and out of the death smeared across the roads. The carnage was worse in some places, as if the residents had put up more of a fight, but there were no discarded weapons to show that. Still, it looked as if the dead had washed through that particular area with little to no resistance. The military must have pulled out when quarantine broke, unless they realised they would be better off on their own and had just up and left. So why didn't the people fight? Alice had always said it was an area of the elderly, but surely they would have put up some resistance? Did that mean that quarantine had broken so fast and the wave of dead spread too quickly to even form a resistance? Or had the people come to realise there was no hope without military assistance and just given up? I didn't want to think about it. I needed to get to Alice. Surely her street would be better? *I doubt it,* a voice inside me whispered. I didn't even dare to consider this a possibility. I was so close! I hadn't come so far to fail Alice. I refused to believe I was too late. I continued onwards.

CHAPTER 42

I turned into Alice's street, cruising along. I came to a halt just to take in the chaos. The destruction was so much worse there. So much blood. The street was flooded with it. There were patches of exposed concrete, but they were just small islands in the sea of death. You could almost smell the iron in the air from all the spilt blood. Undead, and dead alike, littered the street. Once again, the undead didn't seem interested in me and only gave curious glances as I passed. They stood amid the death, ignorant it was even there. The death and destruction went as far as the street did. It went past Alice's home. An involuntary sob escaped me. The undead stirred slightly, as if the human noise awoke them from their dormant state. I quickly bottled the emotion down. It could get me killed. For better or for worse, there would be time for it later. The undead moved, slowly but determinedly, towards me. I began moving again. I continued onwards.

I avoided the death as best as I could, although that didn't stop the motorbike slipping on the blood occasionally. I didn't look, but I knew the tyres were spraying arcs of gore into the air. I was sure the back of my military uniform would be shades of green and red. There was no way I could avoid getting it on me. I dodged my way between the few cars which had made it onto the road. I wasn't moving fast, just quick enough that the undead couldn't reach me. They moved slowly as it was but, mixed with the obstacles and bloody ground, they weren't going to get me. I moved ahead, the roar of the motorbike slowly grabbing the attention of more of the dormant undead. It was like I was the leader of a very dark marching band, the moaning chorus of the undead almost as loud as my vehicle. I could see the turning into Alice's drive ahead. My chest tightened and my heart rate rapidly increased. It would be the deciding moment. Everything I had done condensed to *that* moment.

This is it. I stepped off my motorbike. I didn't even wait for it to stop. The momentum carried the motorbike forward before it collapsed onto its side. I barely noticed my leg screaming in pain. I almost collapsed under my own weight. I was too transfixed on the house. I stood at the foot of the driveway, machete in one hand and revolver in the other. I walked forward and onto the driveway. My eyes took in everything at once.

Blood covered the driveway. Cars were still in place but no longer resembled their former selves. Blood and shattered glass coated them. I didn't notice any blood inside of them, though. Seeing the cars like that was almost the saddest thing I had seen on my entire journey. Alice, her mum and dad all had the same model of car, albeit different colours. They had named all their cars – Pop, Pep, and Pap – which, as a person who never named their inanimate playthings, I found really odd to begin with. After a while, it became an endearing trait of the Kingsley family. Each car had a little personality. Alice's car, Pop, had the personality of a young girl; an innocent child who is really eager to please. Now, the family of cars sat on the drive, a shell of their former glory. Seeing the cars covered in blood and gore, battered and broken, was heart-breaking.

"Oh, Pop," I said softly and patted her little bonnet. I felt tears well in my eyes but wiped them away. I couldn't let any slip through my defences. I turned away and allowed my eyes to follow the trail of blood. The same trail of blood which headed straight to the door. The same door which was slightly ajar and had a bloody handprint on it.

I walked forward.

Oh no.

My chest tightened.

God.

My breathing became uneven.

Please God.

My legs became unstable.

No.

A lump in my throat.

Oh God.

My eyes blurred.

Not like this. Please.

I placed my hand against the door.

Please let them be okay.

Movement inside.

I'm begging you.

I pushed the door open ...

Oh God.

ABOUT THE AUTHOR

I always enjoyed reading fictional worlds, but creating my own was always my passion. My Year 8 English teacher told me I should pursue writing after a short story I had written for a school project.

Things changed and life moved on, but even while I was graduating from my Bachelors and Masters in Psychology, I still wrote stories and I still loved doing it. Writing is my passion, and everything else I do is a means for me to carry on with that passion.

I'm also prepared to move to a secure location at a zombie's notice …

If you've gotten this far, please leave me a review and message me; I love hearing what people think!

For my website:

www.AmongTheDead.co.uk

For regular updates:

www.facebook.com/AmongTheDeadATD

www.twitter.com/AmongTheDeadATD.

Want to email me?

AmongTheDeadATD@hotmail.com

WILL

Printed in Great Britain
by Amazon

41778132R00155